As ever, for Suzanne & the Two Terrors ...

FEELS LIKE
MAGIC

P.J. JOVANOVIC

CHAPTER 1

(A Thirst for Adventure)

Alfie Trotter was a boy who loved to get out and about. He had never been one for staying in the house, playing video games. He couldn't see the appeal of staring at a screen for hours, tapping away on a controller. His brother Eddie owned an XBOX. Eddie often locked himself in his bedroom for hours, yelling in frustration when he was losing and laughing loudly when he was winning. He liked games such as Roblox and Minecraft. He said that these were great adventure games, but Alfie wasn't interested in them. He wanted to run through fields, climb trees, and make dens. This was *real* adventure, as far as Alfie was concerned. And his best friend Leo Parkes agreed with him.

Alfie's favourite movie was *The Goonies*: a story about seven kids who try to find the lost treasure of a pirate. Alfie had watched it many times. He never tired of the story. This was the type of adventure he wanted to go on. Exploring caves and dodging traps. But there were no caves near the small town of Crompton Meadows: where he and his family lived. The most exciting place within biking distance was the nature reserve.

This was a densely wooded area, which featured a pond. Alfie and Leo often visited the reserve and played games there. They liked to play hide and seek. They loved to jump out and surprise each other: spray one another with foam bullets from their Nerf guns. They also liked to skim stones across the surface of the pond to see who could get theirs to go the farthest. Leo was a stocky boy with muscular arms, so he usually won. But, occasionally, when Alfie concentrated enough, he was able to skim a stone all the way to the other side of the water. This amazed Leo, and scared him a little, too. He didn't know any other kid at school who could do such a thing. Alfie was a skinny boy with hardly any muscles. The most he should have been able to achieve was three or four bounces. Plink ... plink ... plink ... *plop!* Leo said it was like magic. But Alfie would always shrug and tell him it was the way he flicked his wrist.

On rainy days, when Alfie couldn't get out, he often played Lego in his bedroom. And that's what he was doing at this moment. He was kneeling on the floor, building a tower to see how tall he could make it before it fell down. Clipping some more bricks on the top, he moved backwards so he could admire his handiwork. This was easily the biggest tower he'd ever built. And he hadn't even fitted the top section yet. He was searching through his box of bricks when a knock at the door startled him so much that he bumped into the tower and it fell over, breaking to pieces.

'*Oh no!*' he said, stamping his foot in anger.

Then he heard his mother calling up to him: 'Leo's here,' she said. 'He wants to know if you're coming out to play.'

Alfie sighed deeply as he surveyed the damage. The tower had broken in two and a few bits had dropped off. But it looked easily repairable, so he set about putting it back together.

'Did you hear me?' his mother called up again. 'Earth to Alfie! Come in Alfie!'

'Send him up!' Alfie said loudly. 'I'm in my bedroom.'

He heard the *thud-thud-thud* of footfalls on the stairs.

Then Leo stuck his head around the door and said, 'Whatcha up to?'

Alfie gestured towards the busted tower. 'It was going so well,' he replied. 'It was going to be *huggge!*'

Soaked from head to feet and out of breath, Leo looked like he was about to explode with excitement. 'Some workmen have left a skip in the reserve's car park,' he said. 'There's pieces of thick board and bricks, so we can make a whopper of a ramp for our bikes. Are you coming? Tell me you're coming.'

Alfie gestured towards the busted tower again. 'I was hoping to finish this. You can help me, if you like. Or you could build a rival one and we could have a battle with the men. I'm still one nil up from the last time, remember?'

'Forget the Lego,' Leo said. His dark brown hair was plastered to his head and water was dripping down his chubby face. 'It's a Saturday and we should be making the most of it, rain or no rain. And it's nearly stopped, look.' He went to the window and pressed his face against the glass, steaming it up. Then he drew a smiley face with his finger. 'That'll be me next week, when I get my new bike. I *can't wait* to see what other presents I get.'

Alfie felt a tinge of jealousy. His twelfth birthday was two months away and his presents were never as good as Leo's. Alfie's parents weren't as wealthy as Leo's, who ran a printing business. David Trotter, Alfie's dad, was a computer technician. And Rosie Trotter, Alfie's mum, worked in a factory that produced pet food.

'Can I have a go on your new bike when you get it?' Alfie asked Leo.

'Yes. But on one condition.'

'What's that?'

'You have to come to the reserve with me so we can make a ramp. It'll be no fun on my own! Are you in, or what?'

Standing up, Alfie went to the window and looked out. Leo was right; the rain was easing off. The sun was even peeking through the clouds on the horizon. Spears of light were dappling the rooftops of the houses in the distance.

'Okay,' Alfie said, 'I'm in.'

'*Coolio!*' Leo said, punching the air. 'Let's go.'

On the way out, Alfie and Leo put their trainers on by the front door. Alfie grabbed his jacket from the peg. He was easing himself into it when Mrs Trotter came through from the kitchen. She was wearing a white pinny and kneading a ball of dough in her hands.

'Off out, are we?' she asked, looking from one boy to the other.

'Yes,' Alfie replied. 'I won't be too long.'

Mrs Trotter said, 'Just remember dinner is at twelve, so don't be late.' She focused her attention on Leo.

'You really should go home and get changed, you know. You're wet through. You'll catch your death.'

'The rain's stopping now, so I'll dry out soon enough,' Leo replied.

Mrs Trotter waved a cautionary finger at Alfie. 'Don't you come back here covered in mud like last time, traipsing footprints through the house. I know this place isn't a palace, but I do like to keep it clean and tidy, thank you very much.'

'I'll make sure he stays clean,' Leo assured her.

As the boys were going out of the door, Mrs Trotter said, 'Make sure you wear your helmet, Alfie. And your elbow and knee pads, too. I didn't buy those things so they could collect dust in the garage.'

'Ok,' he called back. He had no intention of doing so.

And with that, the boys headed to the garage to get Alfie's bike. This was a silver BMX which he'd covered in Avengers stickers featuring The Hulk (Alfie's favourite), Iron Man, Captain America, Thor, and Hawkeye. The only Avenger missing was Black Widow, because she was a girl and Alfie wasn't interested in girls.

A few minutes later, the boys were on the road, with Leo taking the lead on his BMX. They raced along, dodging puddles. They went up and down curbs, manoeuvring around parked cars. Both boys went faster and faster as they raced down the hill that led to the reserve.

'Whooo-*hooo!*' Leo yelled.

He hunched himself over to try and get more speed. His coat was flapping around his waist, his hair flying back from his temples. Water was spraying up from his rear tyre, splattering Alfie with mud He remembered what his mother had said about not coming home dirty and dropped back a little.

4

When they arrived at the car park, Leo made straight for the skip and Alfie followed. Using a thick piece of board and a dozen or so bricks, they constructed a ramp and took turns riding over it. Then they had a competition to see who could jump the farthest. Just like the stone-skimming on the pond, Leo won most of the time. But Alfie surprised him a few times, jumping farther than seemed possible.

'Can you put some more bricks under?' Leo asked, lining himself up for another run. 'The higher we make it, the further we'll be able to jump.'

Alfie did as he was asked.

And that's when some older boys turned up. Three of them. Each one was riding a mountain bike. Alfie recognised the boys from school. They were a few years older than him and liked to play tricks on younger kids. Alfie had bore the brunt of their mean ways on a few occasions. One time, they pinned him against the wall in the assembly hall and hung him from a peg by his pants. Fortunately, a teacher had seen what was going on and the boys had run away. This time there was no teacher to save Alfie. The only thing standing between him and another bout of humiliation was Leo. And even he wasn't tough enough to take on three at once. They circled around Alfie and his friend, who exchanged concerned looks. Alfie considered getting on his bike and motioning Leo to follow him out of the car park. But Alfie knew that Ryan Salter and his two buddies wouldn't let them get away that easily.

'Well, well, well,' Salter said. 'What are you pair playing at here, then? Making a ramp, are you?'

'Yeah,' Leo said. 'And it's for us to use. Not you.'

Alfie shook his head at him, trying to communicate the message: please don't goad him.

'Hear that, boys,' Salter said. 'It's for *them* to use, not *us!*'

His friends laughed as they continued to circle Alfie and Leo on their bikes.

Salter skidded to a halt in front of Leo and said, 'Think you're tough, do you, little man? Think you're tough enough to cheek a year nine? Come on, say something else, little man. I *dare* you.'

Leo glared at Salter, whose top lip curled up into a snarl.

Then Salter's friends filed in behind him, looking equally as mean. Both were thick-set and muscular.

Salter introduced his friends to Leo. 'This,' he said, pointing at the boy to his left, 'is Mason. He likes to give Chinese burns. He's *very* good at them, aren't you Mason?'

Mason nodded. 'I sure am,' he said proudly. 'Best there is.'

Pointing at the boy to his right, Salter said, 'This is Bradley. He likes to give people dead arms. He's *very* good at it, aren't you Bradley?'

'Nobody does it like me,' Bradley said, showcasing a grin full of crooked teeth.

Alfie didn't like where this conversation was heading, so he tried to come up with a way he could distract them. The only thing he could think of, however, was to issue them with a challenge.

'*Hey!*' Alfie said, drawing their attention. He could feel himself sinking into his jacket as the three boys turned and glared at him. 'I bet me and Leo could jump further than you guys. Whaddaya say? You up for a friendly competition?'

Salter considered this, then said, 'Okay, you're on. But I'm not so sure about the friendly part.'

'Cool,' Alfie said, trying to sound enthusiastic. He cycled around and then lined himself up with the ramp. He motioned for Leo to join him and he did.

'I suggest that you let them win,' Leo whispered.

'That's the plan,' Alfie whispered back.

Salter and his buddies moved out of the way. Still on their bikes, they lined themselves up near the skip. Mason nudged Salter and did some whispering of his own. Alfie didn't catch what he said, but it must have been funny because Salter erupted into bouts of gut-busting laughter.

Calm, Aflie thought. *Keep calm.*

6

'Ignore them,' Leo said, making no attempt to lower his voice.

Mason reached into the skip and pulled out a narrow length of wood. 'I'll use this as a marker,' he said. He positioned himself just beyond the ramp, to the side. Alfie didn't care for the way Mason was looking at him or how tightly he was gripping the wood.

Taking a deep breath, Alfie readied himself. And then he took off towards the ramp, building up speed. A blur of knees and elbows, he pedalled as fast as he could, his hips swaying from side to side.

'Come on, skinny boy,' Bradley shouted, 'you can go quicker than that!'

Alfie was desperate to show him how far he could really jump, but he knew that wouldn't be wise. He didn't fancy being hung from a tree branch by his underwear, or tossed into the pond, or humiliated in some other fashion. And he didn't want to put Leo in danger, either.

Just before Alfie reached the ramp, he slowed down a little. Despite this, he still managed to jump a good distance. He landed with a jolt. Then he skidded to a halt and turned to watch Mason place the stick on the floor.

'*Hey!*' Alfie said. 'I went further than that!' The words were out of his mouth before he could think of the consequences. And he remembered that the game-plan was to lose: 'Actually, I take it back, your measurement is spot on. I couldn't have placed the marker more accurately myself.'

Leo said, 'You were right the first time.'

'I think someone's accusing us of cheating,' Mason said, pretending to look insulted.

'Oh the indignity!' Bradley said, following suit.

'My turn now,' Salter said.

He cycled over to where Leo was and lined himself up with the ramp.

'Now I'm going to show your friend how it's *really* done,' Salter said to Leo.

'Break a leg,' Leo said.

7

Salter looked like he was ready to break something, all right. So Alfie explained what Leo had meant: 'That's what they say in the theatre; it's another way of wishing someone good luck.'

'I know that, dumbo,' Salter said. 'Do I look stupid?'

Not wanting to answer that question, Alfie put his head down and pretended to fiddle with the gears on his BMX.

Salter gave Leo a sly grin, then set off towards the ramp.

'*Woo-hoo!*' Salter yelled as his bike clattered across the board.

He jumped the same distance as Alfie, but Mason repositioned the marker, moving it along a bit.

He declared Salter the winner, then said, 'That'll take some beating.'

'Your go now, tough guy,' Bradley said, motioning Leo to have his turn.

Leo lined himself up. Hunched over his handlebars, he looked focused and ready, like he was determined to beat Salter, no matter what. Alfie shook his head at his friend, trying to convey the message: don't win – *puleeeeze* don't try to win. And then Leo was tearing towards the ramp, pedalling faster than Alfie had ever seen him pedal.

Oh no, Alfie thought. *This is bad, very bad.*

He wasn't surprised to see Leo jump farther than both him and Salter.

As Leo landed, he let out a triumphant '*Woo-hoo!*' of his own. Stopping next to Alfie, he gave his friend an apologetic shrug and said, 'Sorry, I just couldn't resist.'

'Get ready to make a dash for it,' Alfie said, 'because I don't think the meatheads are going to be happy about this.'

Out the corner of his eye, he caught a glimpse of movement to his left. He turned and saw a shadowy figure watching them from the trees. But then he blinked and the figure was gone. Alfie scanned left and right, but there was nobody there, as far as he could see.

'What's wrong?' Leo asked, following his gaze.

'Nothing,' Alfie replied. 'I thought I saw someone, that's all. Think my imagination is playing tricks on me.'

8

Reluctantly, Mason relocated the marker again. He moved it a bit farther along.

'That was impressive,' he conceded. 'But I think we can beat it.'

'I jumped further than that,' Leo said to Alfie.

'I know,' Alfie said, 'but we are meant to be *losing*, remember?'

'Yeah, I know.'

Salter looked ready to explode. His brow furrowed and his bottom lip pooched out.

'I'm next,' he said.

'What about me?' Mason said. 'You've had a go! It's my turn now.'

'You can go next,' Salter assured him.

Then he lined himself up with the ramp and set off with a look of grim determination on his face. He managed to jump farther than his previous effort. But not by much. Half a metre, at the most.

Stopping in front of Alfie and Leo, he said, 'Beat that if you can, losers.' He turned and nodded to Mason, who placed the marker *wayyyy* beyond where even Leo had reached.

'Is it my go now?' Mason asked.

'And let's not forget about me,' Bradley chirped in. 'I want a turn, too.'

Salter focused his attention on Alfie. 'Think you can top that? I bet you can't. Not on that rust bucket. What's up, can't your mum and dad afford to buy you a decent bike? Judging by the clothes you're wearing, I'm guessing not. There's a word for your type at school. D'you know what it is? Ever heard of the word *skank*, skinny boy?'

Alfie felt a surge of anger building up inside him. He could cope with insults being thrown his way. He didn't care what anybody thought of him. But when it came to his parents ...

'You need to shut your hole,' Leo said to Salter. 'Or ...'

'Or what?' Salter said. He glared at Leo, daring him to say something else.

Alfie took off on his bike and lined himself up with the ramp.

9

'*Uh-oh!*' Bradley exclaimed. 'He's going to show us all now, look.' He rested his elbows on his handlebars and began to clap. '*Go, go, go ...*' he chanted.

His friends joined in – clapping and chanting: '*GO, GO, GO, GO, GO ...*'

And then Alfie did. He sped towards the ramp and hit it at an incredible speed. Taking off, he floated in mid-air for what felt like forever. A toothy smile spread across his face as he was about to land. Then his tyres scrunched on the gravelly surface and he squeezed hard on his brakes, bringing his BMX to a dramatic stop.

A stunned silence followed. Nobody seemed to know what to say. Even Salter was lost for words. He looked on with his mouth wide open, not able to believe what he'd just seen. But the look of bewilderment was soon replaced by one of hatred. This reminded Alfie of a cartoon he'd watched the day before where Bugs Bunny had had steam coming out of his ears because he was so angry. Alfie imagined Salter with steam hissing out of his ears and he couldn't suppress another toothy smile.

But then Alfie saw movement in the trees again.

Someone was *definitely* watching them.

'Now *that's* how it's done! *Bravo!*' Leo said, clapping enthusiastically. 'Hey, are you all right?' he asked Alfie, following his gaze. 'You look spooked.'

Throwing his bike aside, Salter said, 'Someone's going to look spooked in a minute.' He strode towards Alfie, his hands balled into fists. 'How did you do that? How did you jump so far?'

'Perhaps I'm not such a weakling after all,' Alfie said.

He was sure Salter was going to hit him. Alfie gulped, waiting for the inevitable.

But then someone said, 'Is there a problem here? Is everything okay?'

Everyone turned to see a tall, skinny boy with dark brown curly hair coming towards them. Alfie recognised him from school and was sure he was in the same year as Salter and his cronies. The boy was wearing a blue duffer jacket and jeans with

10

holes in the knees. He was walking a German Shepherd, which was tugging at its lead and snarling at Salter.

'Keep that thing away from me,' Salter said, backing away. 'My parents will sue you if it so much as breathes on me.'

The boy held up a hand in a calming gesture. 'Relax,' he said, 'he's been fed this morning, so he's not hungry ...' He added the word "yet" with a mischievous glint in his eyes. Then he turned his attention to Alfie and Leo. 'Are these boys bothering you?'

Alfie opened his mouth to respond, but Leo beat him to it.

'Yes,' he said, 'they are.'

'Why don't you mind your own business and get lost,' Mason said to the boy.

'Why don't *you* get lost!' Leo snapped. 'Sore losers!'

Salter strode towards him looking suitably menacing. But he stopped dead in his tracks when the boy blocked his way.

'I'm a firm believer that if you're going to pick on someone,' the boy said, 'then it should at least be someone your own size.' His dog growled, as if in agreement. The hairs on its back were standing erect. Ears pinned to its skull, it bared its teeth and looked ready to pounce.

'That's easy to say when you've got your mutt with you,' Bradley said. 'We'll see how tough you are at school, in the playground, when you're on your own.'

Salter backed away, marking Alfie, Leo and their new friend with a severe look which told them that their business wasn't concluded. Getting on his bike, Salter said to them, 'I'll be seeing you around.' In one last act of defiance, he cycled over to the ramp and kicked the board away. And then he took off out of the car park with his friends close behind him. Alfie didn't begin to relax until the sound of their laughter faded into the distance.

'Well thank God they're gone,' Leo said. 'Those guys have got some serious mental health issues, if you ask me.'

'Thanks for that,' Alfie said to the boy. 'And thank you, too,' he said to the dog, who wagged its tail appreciably.

'Bullies will be bullies,' the boy said.

'Thanks Charles,' Leo said to him. 'You just saved us from a beating.'

'You know each other?' Alfie said, looking from one boy to the other.

'Yeah, we know each other,' the boy named Charles said. 'Our parents go to quiz night at the Ropers pub together on a Sunday night and they usually insist on us being there with them, despite both of us hating quizzes. We usually find something more interesting to do, though, don't we Leo?'

'Pool or darts ... watching paint dry – anything but quizzes,' Leo said.

Charles stroked the dog's head and tickled him under his chin. Then he motioned for Alfie and Leo to do the same. When they looked reluctant, Charles said, 'S'okay, he knows the good 'uns from the bad 'uns; he's smart that way.'

Leo went first, patting Oboe on the head, then tickling him under his chin. Oboe stuck his tongue out and panted heavily. His tail flapped from side to side as he lapped up the fuss.

'Ooh, don't do that,' Charles said, 'you'll never get rid of him; he *loves* having his chin tickled.'

Joining in, Alfie enjoyed stroking Oboe's back.

'I've always wanted a dog,' he said, 'but my mum and dad say we can't afford one.'

'They're not cheap to keep,' Charles said. 'Especially one this size. You wouldn't believe how much food he puts away. If there's treats to be had, he's on it. If there's scraps to be scoffed, he's on it. He's like a walking dustbin, so he is.'

Leo slapped a hand to his forehead. 'I've just remembered!' he exclaimed. 'I'm s'pposed to be going out with my mum and dad today to visit some friends of theirs. My mum'll lynch me if I'm late! What time is it?'

Consulting his watch, Charles said, 'Eleven twenty-five.'

'*Oh poo!*' Leo said. 'I'm s'pposed to be home for eleven-thirty. I've gotta go!'

He thanked Charles and Oboe for their help. He said his goodbyes, then cycled away on his bike.

'Are you out tomorrow?' Alfie shouted after him. But Leo didn't hear.

As he disappeared from view, Charles said, 'Now there's a boy who's in a hurry.'

'You'd be in a hurry too if you had a mother like his.'

'Yeah, she's got some gob on her for such a small woman.'

'She makes Salter look harmless when she's angry. Aren't you worried about his threat? You're bound to bump into him at school.'

'He won't do anything. When was the last time you saw him pick on someone his own size? It's always the little kids he goes for. Gets some sort of power trip from it, I'm sure.'

'He's a twit.'

'I'll second that.'

Silence descended as both boys looked around, not sure what to say next.

Then Alfie nodded towards the bricks and piece of board that'd served as a ramp. 'I better put that lot back in the skip,' he said. He laid his bike on the floor and set to work.

Tethering Oboe to a tree, Charles helped out by picking two or three bricks up at a time. They made metallic clanking sounds as he threw them, one by one, into the skip.

'That was a very impressive jump you did,' he said. 'You went way further than anyone your age should be able to, you know that, don't you?'

Alfie did. But he wasn't sure how to respond, so he just stared at Charles with a blank expression on his face.

Tossing the last few bricks into the skip, Charles said, 'Now I don't know for sure, but I'm guessing that's not the first time you've done something like that, is it? Something *unusual*. Something other people *can't* do. Am I right or am I right?'

Alfie hesitated before replying. Then he nodded and said, 'Yes, you are.'

'So, tell me what you've done?'

Alfie explained how he could skim stones from one side of the pond to the other.

13

'That's cool. What else?'

'I've turned the telly over just by thinking it. I've made things disappear, never to be seen again. Sometimes, lights flicker on and off when I get angry.' Alfie gave it some more thought. 'Oh, and I've made things float in mid-air. If I concentrate hard enough, I can make *anything* float.'

'Anything?' Charles seemed sceptical.

'Within reason,' Alfie said. 'As long as it's not too big.'

'Show me.'

'Okay.'

Looking around for a target object, Alfie's blue eyes fell upon his bike and he began to focus his thoughts. He imagined the BMX rising into the air. A few seconds later, it did. He counted to five, then eased it back down to the ground.

'*Impressive!*' Charles said, clapping his hands.

Alfie looked around to make sure no one else had seen what he'd done.

'S'ok,' Charles said, 'we're the only ones here.'

'When I've done it before, I've had to concentrate a lot longer than that; it doesn't normally happen that quickly.'

'You're getting stronger as you get older. That's how it works.'

'How what works?'

'The things you can do,' Charles said, 'it must seem like magic, yeah?'

Alfie nodded.

'That's because it *is* magic.'

Alfie had always known he was different from other boys and girls, from other people. But he hadn't known exactly *why* he was different. Now, thanks to a boy he barely knew, he had learned that he was a ...

'Wizard,' Charles said, as if reading his mind.

Charles looked at Alfie, waiting for a response. Alfie didn't know what to say, though. He was speechless. He opened his mouth to speak, but no words came out. His knees weakened and his heart began to race.

A wizard, he thought. *I am ... wizard!*

Taking Alfie by the arm to steady him, Charles said, 'Are you all right? You've gone very pale.'

'I'm fine,' Alfie assured him.

"There's a bench by the pond. Sit with me and we can talk, yeah.'

'Okay.'

Oboe whined and raised a paw as if to say: don't forget me.

'Like we could forget you,' Charles said to him. Then he turned his attention back to Alfie. 'Are you okay to walk?'

'Yes,' Alfie said.

As Charles un-tethered Oboe, Alfie got his bike and the three of them made their way along the track which led down to the pond. Charles and Oboe went first. The nearer they got, the more excited the dog became. He began tugging at his lead, eager to get there.

'In the summer, he likes me to throw sticks in the water so he can swim for them,' Charles explained. 'But he's not going in today. You'll catch your death, you crazy mutt!'

Reaching the bench, Charles seated himself and beckoned Alfie to join him.

Alfie rested his bike against a tree and said, 'But the bench is still wet from the rain; I'll get a wet bottom.'

'You can stand if you like. S'up to you.'

Alfie sat next to Charles and looked out across the pond. In the distance, a bird swooped down and skimmed the water's surface, then took off high into the sky.

'I love it here,' Charles said. 'It's so quiet and serene. When I need to think, this is where I come. Sometimes it's nice to get away from it all. Away from the noise, away from life, really. It's beautiful here.'

'It is beautiful,' Alfie agreed.

After a moment's silence, Charles said, 'Hey, want to see something cool?'

'Okay,' Alfie replied, wondering what it could be.

Reaching into his jacket, Charles pulled out what looked like a wand. He winked at Alfie and pointed the wand at a tree on the other side of the pond. Then, with a flick of the wrist, he said, 'Excutite Wincantom!'

Alfie watched in amazement as the branches on the tree began to shake, causing birds to take flight.

'*Wicked!*' Alfie said. 'Can I have a go?'

Charles shook his head. 'You need some lessons before you start waving a wand around,' he said. 'Mutter the wrong words and you could blow something up. Or someone.'

'Oh.'

'Don't look so worried. With the proper training, you'll be fine. You'll be able to do things you never believed possible.'

Charles slid the wand back inside his jacket.

'And how would I get such training?' Alfie asked.

'At the Pendred Academy of Witchcraft and Wizardry. A beginners' class starts in two weeks. It's run in the evenings, every Tuesday, from six-thirty 'till seven-thirty. You'll need permission from your parents if you want to attend, though. No permission equals no admittance.'

Alfie could feel questions boiling up inside him. 'Do I need to bring anything with me?' he asked. 'Do my parents need to attend with me? Do I need to buy a wand and where would I get one? Do I ...'

'Whoa, whoa!' Charles said. 'Hold up! Are you trying to bury me in questions, or what?'

'Sorry. I'm just ... you know, eager.'

'Of course you are. And rightly so. I remember when I first learned about the place, I couldn't wait to get started, either. With regards to your parents, they'll need to attend with you on induction day. Other than them, you don't need to bring anything. Everything else will be explained by Mr Pendred, who runs the school.'

'And what if my mum and dad won't let me go?'

'Like I said, no permission equals no admittance.'

Alfie's shoulders slumped. A feeling of dejection washed over him.

'What's wrong?' Charles asked. 'Don't you think your parents will let you attend?'

Alfie shook his head. 'I doubt it. Probably not.'

'Your family,' Charles said, 'they must know, yeah? They must know what you can do.'

'They know. But they say I mustn't do anything ... abnormal. They think that what I can do is dangerous and that I'll hurt someone, eventually. My mum says that when I was a baby, I made some cutlery hang from the kitchen ceiling. I was sitting in my highchair at the far end of the room when she entered. She screamed her head off, startling me. One of the knives nearly hit her as it fell.'

Alfie watched the water lapping near his feet. He found the rhythmic ebb and flow quite hypnotic.

Snatching up a stick in his jaws, Oboe presented it to him and held up a paw. *Please throw it – puleeeeze!*

'In a minute, I promise,' Alfie said. 'But not in the water.'

Oboe groaned, as if he understood exactly what he'd said.

'Someone else in your family has powers like you,' Charles said. 'Who is it?'

Alfie's brow furrowed as he turned to look at Charles. 'No one can do what I can. Not in my family.'

'You're wrong. The ability to do magic is hereditary.' When Alfie just stared at Charles with a blank expression on his face, Charles explained: 'Heredity is when certain traits are passed on from parents to their children. For instance, you have blonde hair, so I'm guessing someone else in your family either has blonde hair or did have when they were younger. Am I right or am I right?'

'My uncle Jack was blonde when he was younger,' Alfie confirmed. 'I've seen photos of him in an album. Now he's got a bald head, which is always sweaty and shiny. And he has a comb-over, too; it flaps about in the wind. He can never keep it down, no matter how hard he tries.'

'That's too much information,' Charles said, giving a slight cringe. 'Anyway, back to what I was saying. With regards to who could be magical, it could be your mother, your father, your sweaty uncle with the nasty comb-over, your granddad, your great grandmother …'

'If my parents were magical, I think I'd have noticed by now.'

'Not necessarily. Some people hide their power and refuse to accept it.'

'Why?'

'Various reasons. But it's usually because they don't think it's normal.'

'Oh,' Alfie said. He wondered if his abilities made him abnormal; he didn't like the idea of being abnormal. That meant he was different. Kids who were different at school were ridiculed and picked on. One particular boy came to mind: James McNee. He was in Alfie's year and was always being targeted because he was small and puny and had a huge nose. Salter had nicknamed Pinocchio. He liked to sneak up on James, grab his nose and shout, '*HONK!*'

'D'you have any brothers or sisters?' Charles asked Alfie.

'I've got an older brother, but he's not magical; he's just a pain in the backside.'

Charles chuckled. 'That's usually the case with older brothers.'

Biting down on his bottom lip, Alfie thought hard about who could be magical in his family.

Then Charles gave him a reassuring pat on the arm. 'Don't trouble yourself about it. Best thing you can do is ask your parents, because they'll know. If they try to convince you that you're being silly, just remind them about the cutlery you suspended from the kitchen ceiling when you were younger.'

'Oh I will,' Alfie assured him. 'Soon as I get in, I'm going to ask my mum.'

'*Excellent!*'

Charles reached inside his jacket and pulled out what looked like a business card. He gave it to Alfie, who read it:

PENDRED ACADEMY OF WITCHCRAFT & WIZARDRY
(The Midland's Premier Institute)

Mysterium Road – Crompton Meadows **Tel:** 01156 898797
Email: pendredacademy@magic.com

Mysterium Road was about a mile from where Alfie lived. He'd cycled along there many times, on the way to Leo's house, but he had never noticed a witchcraft and wizardry academy. Alfie figured that such a place must be big, so he asked Charles if it was a new set-up.

'No, it's been there a long time. Only those that are magical and are actually looking for it can see it. Well, that's not actually fully true. Non-magical folk can see it if they're touched by a witch or wizard – but the witch or wizard must *want* the non-magical person to be able to see it. The magic rubs off from one person to another. That's kind of how it works. Please try not to be late on your first day. Mr Pendred is a stickler for punctuality. If you're on time, it shows you're serious about wanting to learn.'

'I'll be on time.'

'Good,' Charles said. 'Right, I need to make a move. Places to go, people to see and all that.' He got up and Oboe, who'd been waiting patiently with the stick in his mouth, sprang to life. 'Would you like our new friend to throw it for you?' Charles asked the dog as he unleashed him. 'He did promise, didn't he?'

Alfie got to his feet and prized the stick from Oboe's jaws. He threw it as far as he could, away from the water. Then Oboe took off after it, crashing through the undergrowth, disappearing from sight.

'Sorry,' Alfie apologized, 'that went a bit far.'

'Don't worry, he'll come back; he always does.'

Sure enough, Oboe reappeared and came bounding back towards them with the stick clasped firmly in his jaws. He made straight for Alfie with an expectant glint in his eyes. Alfie took the stick and told the dog that this was the last time. He let go with a second throw and Oboe once again raced off through the trees and bushes.

'He'd do that all day, if he could,' Charles said.

'I bet he would.'

When Oboe returned, Charles grabbed his lead and told him to heel. The dog sat down with its tail wagging furiously.

'Good boy,' Charles said, putting his hand in his pocket and pulling out a bone-shaped doggy treat. Oboe opened his mouth and the stick dropped to the ground, forgotten about. Charles tossed the treat in the air, then Oboe jumped up and caught it in one quick, fluid movement.

'*Bam!* – and it's gone,' Alfie said. 'Almost like magic.'

'Almost,' Charles said, 'but not quite.' He smiled. 'Okay, me and the four-legged fiend really must go. So I'll be seeing you soon, Alfie. In two weeks time, yeah? Six thirty, on the dot.' He backed away with Oboe beside him, heading down the path towards the car park. 'And remember, don't be late!'

'I won't be,' Alfie said. 'I'll most likely see you at school, before then.'

'You most likely will.'

Alfie waved and Charles waved back.

Then Alfie blinked and his two new friends had gone.

For a while he just stood there, looking towards the path and listening to the birds chirping merrily in the trees. And then he grabbed his bike and set off home ...

CHAPTER 2

(The Family Secret)

On the way back, Alfie raced along with a big grin on his face. He could hardly believe he'd met another boy who was like him – another boy who had special powers. Alfie was so busy thinking about what he was going to say to his mother that he didn't see a large rock by the side of the road. He noticed it at the last second. But it was too late.

'*Oh noooooo!*' he yelled as his front wheel hit the rock and he went flying over the handlebars. He landed in the gutter with a bone-crunching *thud*. His hands and elbows took the brunt of the fall. And he went down hard on his knees, as well. But as hurt as he was, he was more concerned about his bike than himself. Looking back, he saw that his front wheel was now buckled. *Great*, he thought, *how am I going to explain* that *to my parents?*

A woman in a red coat who was walking past ran over to see if he was okay.

'Oh my,' she said, looming over Alfie, 'you poor thing – are you all right? Are you hurt badly?'

His pride was hurt more than his body.

Sitting himself on the kerb, he looked at the blood-streaked graze-marks on the palms of his hands. 'It stings,' he said, wincing, 'but I think I'll survive.' He examined his right elbow and groaned loudly because his jacket was ripped. Another thing for his parents to whinge about.

'You need to get some antiseptic cream on your hands when you get in,' the woman said, with a look of genuine concern on her face. 'Have you got far to go, sweetheart? Would you like me to help you home?'

'No thank you, I'll be okay.'

More people were gathering around now, wondering what all the fuss was about. So Alfie got to his feet and brushed himself off. His jeans were scuffed around the knees, threads dangling. Alfie wished Charles was still with him, because he was sure his new friend would be able to repair the bike with a swish of his wand.

Someone else asked Alfie if he was okay and he said yes.

Alfie wondered how he was going to wheel the bike up the steep hill near his house. He considered hiding it somewhere, so his dad could collect it later. But Alfie was worried it might get stolen, which would turn a bad situation into a *very* bad situation. It was one thing for him to have bent the front wheel and another for him to have lost the bike entirely. Alfie was sure he'd be grounded for eternity if *that* happened.

So Alfie thanked everyone for their concern, then picked his bike up and set off home. The small crowd that had gathered began to disperse. As Alfie was trudging away, dragging his BMX along, the woman in the red coat called after him.

'Are you sure you're all right?' she said. 'I can help you with the bike; it's not a problem.'

'You're very kind,' Alfie called back, 'but I haven't got far to go. Thanks for the concern, though. You're a nice lady.'

The woman smiled and raised a hand to say goodbye. Alfie returned the gesture, then continued to drag his bike along the pavement. By the time he reached the end of the road, his arms were beginning to ache. And by the time he was halfway up the hill, his arms felt like they could fall off any second. But he kept going, because he knew he had no choice. Determination and willpower fuelled every step.

When he arrived home, he stashed his bike in the garage and went into the house. He made for the bathroom, hoping to clean himself up before his mother noticed what a state he was in. He made it to the door and was about to enter when a voice spoke up behind him.

'Ahum!' Mrs Trotter said. 'What time do you call this? You were supposed to be home thirty minutes ago for your dinner, young man.'

Rolling his eyes, Alfie turned to face his mother. He looked at the floor, unable to meet her stern gaze.

'What's happened to your jeans?' she said, kneeling in front of him. 'You've fallen off your bike, haven't you?'

With his shoulders slumped and his chin down, Alfie nodded.

'And would I be right in thinking that you weren't wearing your helmet and pads?'

Alfie nodded again.

He could hear his brother Eddie playing on his XBOX upstairs.

'Well that was daft, wasn't it?' Mrs Trotter said. 'How many times have I told you about being properly protected?' When Alfie just stood there, looking sorry for himself, Mrs Trotter took hold of his hands and turned them over. 'Oh, Alfie,' she said with a pained look on her face, 'they must *really* hurt.'

'They did at first, but it's not too bad now.'

He explained how he'd hit a rock and gone flying over the bike's handlebars.

'At least you're still in one piece; I suppose we should be thankful your injuries aren't worse. You could have been badly hurt, you know. Come on.' Mrs Trotter led him into the kitchen. 'Let's get you cleaned up and sorted.'

She made Alfie wash his hands. Then she got a medical kit from one of the cupboards and pulled out a tube of cream.

'This will sting a bit,' she warned.

And it did. Alfie winced as she rubbed the cream in.

'What about your bike?' Mrs Trotter asked. 'Is it damaged?'

'The front wheel's buckled and I think it'll need a new tyre.'

'Who's going to pay for that?'

'I ... erm, me,' Alfie said, knowing that he didn't have much money. He had some in his piggybank, but he was hoping that would go towards buying a new pack of Lego. 'I'll do chores if I have to. Anything you want me to do, I'll do it. I'll mow the lawn, wash the dishes, run errands ...'

Mrs Trotter held a finger up. 'Shush now, please. Don't worry about that at the moment. I'll discuss it with your father when he gets in and see what he has to say. For now, what I want you to do is get changed and eat your dinner.'

Alfie got a waft of something that smelled delicious and remembered that his mum had been baking cookies. He saw them on the sideboard and his eyes widened.

'You don't really deserve them,' Mrs Trotter said, 'but you can have some if you gulp all of your dinner down.'

'I'll soon make those disappear.'

'I'm sure you will. And now it's time for you to disappear – go on – upstairs – now, mister – go!'

Alfie ran upstairs and found Eddie blocking his way on the landing. With his arms folded across his chest, he was sporting a huge grin on his face.

'Can I get past, please?' Alfie said.

'I heard the conversation between you and Mum. You're in the doghouse, bro.'

'Tell me something I don't know.'

'And when Dad gets in, you're going to be in even *deeper* trouble.'

'Please move out the way; I've got enough problems without you bugging me.'

Stepping aside, Eddie motioned for Alfie to pass. As he did, Eddie grabbed hold of him and ruffled his hair.

'Ger off!' Alfie said, trying to break free. 'Ger off me!'

Eddie began tickling Alfie.

'*Ger off!*' Alfie said. 'Ger off me or I'll ... *I'll* ...'

'You'll what? Tell Mum?'

As if on cue, Mrs Trotter called up to them: 'What's going on up there?'

'It's Eddie,' Alfie said through fits of laughter. 'He's ... tickling me!'

'Let your brother go, Eddie,' Mrs Trotter said. 'I've warned you about bothering him before.'

But Eddie continued to tickle. And Alfie continued to struggle.

'*GER OFFFF!*' he yelled.

'Don't make me have to come up there, you two.'

Finally letting go of Alfie, Eddie said, 'In the doghouse, bro – dawg house!'

'Whatever,' Alfie replied, disappearing into his bedroom.

He changed into some clean clothes: a pair of jeans and a Spiderman jumper.

Then he went downstairs to eat his dinner: mashed potato, mixed vegetables, chicken pie in short-crust pastry, all drenched in rich, thick gravy. Whilst he was tucking into his food at the kitchen table, Mrs Trotter was busying herself washing some pots. With Eddie back in his bedroom on the XBOX and Mr Trotter not home yet, Alfie thought that this was a good time to quiz his mother.

'Mum ...' he said, not sure how to start.

She threw a sideways glance his way, eyebrows raised. When he just stared at her with an open mouth, she said, 'What's wrong? You look like you're about to tell me you've done something else wrong.'

He shook his head. 'No,' he replied, spooning carrots into his mouth. 'I haven't done anything else wrong.'

'Don't talk with your mouth full; you know that's one of my pet hates.'

Mrs Trotter was still looking at him with her eyebrows raised: go on, spit it out, then.

'Well,' he said, 'the thing is ...' He paused, still not sure what to say.

'You know what, Alfie, sometimes, when you're struggling for the right words, it's just best to blurt it out. So please blurt it out and then I can get on with my chores.'

'Okey-dokey,' Alfie said. 'I'll blurt it out.' Speaking quickly, hardly pausing for breath, he explained how he and Leo had gone to the reserve and been challenged to a contest by some bullies. He explained how he'd jumped farther on his bike than any of the other boys. Much farther than seemed possible. Then he explained how he'd met Charles and how his new friend had told him that he was a wizard.

'Whoa, whoa!' Mrs Trotter said. Soapsuds dripped from her hands as she held them up and made a time-out gesture. 'He told you you're a ... *what?*'

'A wizard!' Alfie blurted. He thought he would feel daft saying it again, but he didn't; he felt proud. The word rolled off his tongue with no hesitation – *Wizard!* 'Charles is one, too. That's how he recognized me for what I am. He's got a wand and he made a tree shake with it – it was really cool.'

Alfie couldn't tell whether his mother was angry or just stunned. She was looking at him with a blank expression on her face. Soapsuds were still dripping from her hands. And they were going all over the floor now, because she had turned to face him. Alfie was sure she was about to tell him that he was being silly: that his new friend was just playing games with him. Charles' words came back to him: if they try to convince you that you're being silly, remind them about the cutlery you suspended from the kitchen ceiling when you were younger. Alfie was about to remind her ...

But then Mrs Trotter nodded and said, 'We'll talk about this when your father gets in. He's gone to the gym, so he won't be long.'

'There's a school of witchcraft and wizardry not far from here. A beginner's course starts in two weeks and I'd really, *really* like to go.'

'Enough, Alfie!' Mrs Trotter said. 'I told you that we'd talk about it when your father gets home, so just ... please, for now just concentrate on eating your dinner and nothing else.'

Alfie felt too excited to eat. He did as he was told, though.

He wanted to ask his mother who else in the family had magical powers, but thought it best to keep quiet. For now, at least.

Half an hour later, when Alfie had finished his dinner and was watching TV in the living room, Mr Trotter returned. He came through the front door and dumped his bag in the hallway. Then he stretched dramatically, as he always did after a good workout. He was a tall man, so his fingers almost touched the ceiling. In the living room doorway, he greeted Alfie with a warm smile and a nod of his head.

'Where's your mum?' he asked.

'In the kitchen. She wants to talk to you. She wants to talk to both of us.'

Mrs Trotter blustered past her husband and stood in the centre of the room, arms folded across her chest. She looked at Alfie, then her husband.

'What's up?' Mr Trotter asked.

'Tell your father what you told me,' Mrs Trotter said to Alfie.

He composed himself, then he began. As before, when he had explained everything to his mum, Alfie spoke quickly, hardly pausing for breath. By the time he'd finished, Mr Trotter was staring at him with an open mouth. A short silence followed. Nobody knew what to say.

It was Mr Trotter who broke the silence. 'I thought we agreed not to discuss this,' he said, looking at his wife. Then he focused his attention on Alfie. 'And you promised us that you wouldn't do anything strange again. You gave me your word, remember?'

Alfie remembered. 'I know, Dad. But those boys were picking on me and Leo; I just wanted to show them that they're not all that. You should have seen their faces when they saw how far I'd jumped. I wish I could have taken a picture of them – especially Salter. I'd frame it and hang it on the wall in my bedroom.'

'You do that again – or anything like that – and people will start to talk,' Mrs Trotter said. 'I understand why you did what you did and I'm sure you could have bounced that boy up and down the street on his head, but ...'

'Now that's an idea,' Alfie said.

Mrs Trotter held a finger up. '*But*,' she said, continuing, 'you need to think before you act. Your father is right. You keep doing things like that and people will start to talk. And we don't want that, now, do we?'

'No,' Alfie said. He couldn't suppress a smile, because he was still thinking about bouncing Salter up and down the street on his head.

'What's so funny?' Mrs Trotter asked.

Alfie replied, 'Nothing.'

'And what about this boy you've met?' Mr Trotter said. 'What's his name?'

'Charles,' Alfie said. 'He's like me; he can do things other people can't.' He relayed the same story that he'd told his mum: about how Charles had made a tree shake with his wand.

'Our son wants to go to a school for wizards and witches,' Mrs Trotter said to Mr Trotter.

'Well, we knew this day would come,' he said.

'Really?' Alfie said. 'You did?'

Someone coughed. Everyone turned to see where the noise had come from.

'Looks I'm being excluded from an important conversation here,' Eddie said, standing in the doorway.

'Go back to your bedroom,' Mrs Trotter said. 'This doesn't concern you.'

'If my brother is going to a school for weirdos and whackos, then it does concern me.'

'He isn't going,' Mr Trotter said.

'I'm not!' Alfie said. '*Why?*'

'Because what you can do isn't normal,' Eddie said.

'You wish you could do what I can,' Alfie said.

'No I don't,' Eddie replied.

'Yes you do!' Alfie screamed.

'Maybe I can do what you can,' Eddie said. 'Maybe I can and you just don't know about it.'

Before Alfie could reply, Mrs Trotter stamped her foot on the floor so hard that the ornaments above the fireplace shuddered on the shelf and some nearly fell off. '*Enough!*' she cried. 'I don't want to hear anymore arguing.' When Alfie opened his mouth to speak, she said, 'Eh, what did I just say?'

'I wasn't going to argue,' Alfie said. 'I just want to know why I can't go. Is it the cost? There are no fees. I'm guessing I'll need a wand and a few other bits, but I wouldn't imagine they'll be too expensive. How much do Eddie's football lessons cost?'

'What's my football lessons got to do with anything?' Eddie asked.

'It's not the cost,' Mr Trotter said to Alfie.

'So what is it?' he said. 'Why can't I go?'

'Because ...' Mr Trotter said, shaking his head. 'Because I'm your father and I'm telling you that you can't.'

Alfie felt like crying. Tears were welling in his eyes. But he held them back because he didn't want to turn into a blubbering mess in front of Eddie. Alfie was desperate to attend the beginners' class and had never been so determined to do something in his life. He was sure that this would be his best chance to harness his powers and improve them. *If you don't give me permission to go, I'll go anyway*, he thought. *Somehow, someway, I'm attending that first class. Nobody is going to stop me – NOBODY! – and that's that.*

Appealing to his mother, Alfie said, 'Please tell me you don't agree with Dad. Surely you can see that it's best for me to go?'

'He said no,' Eddie chirped in. 'And no always means no in this house.'

'Go to your bedroom,' Mrs Trotter said to him. 'I don't want to have to tell you again.'

Eddie didn't budge; he just hovered in the doorway, looking sullen and grouchy.

Mrs Trotter said to Alfie, 'I'm sorry, sweetheart, your father's decision is final. If he says you can't go, then you can't go.'

Without another word, Alfie got up and went to storm out of the room. But then he stopped and said, 'Charles told me that I can't be the only person with magical powers in this family. He told me that it's heredistry – or something like that – which means someone else in this family can do what I can. I want to know who it is!'

This question was directed at everyone in the room, but more so at Eddie, whose mean and grouchy look had been replaced by one of blankness.

'It's heredity,' he said, 'not heredistry – *dumbo.*'

'If you can do magic,' Alfie said to him, 'then show me. '

The look of blankness on Eddie's face was now slowly changing to one of anger.

'This discussion is over!' Mr Trotter declared. 'Both of you go to your rooms – *now!*'

'Make something hover,' Alfie said to Eddie. 'Go on, if you can. Turn a light on without touching a switch. Make the hoover come on by itself and have it clean the floor. Make something disappear, *if you CAN* ...'

'I'll make you disappear in a minute,' Eddie said through gritted teeth.

'*THAT'S IT!*' Mr Trotter yelled, his face flushing as red as a beetroot. '*I DON'T WANT TO HEAR ANOTHER WORD!*'

A vase near the window shattered, spraying everyone with bits of porcelain. Mrs Trotter let out a shrill cry as she ducked. Eddie backed into the hallway, narrowly avoiding a large chunk of pot which whizzed past his head like an angry insect. Alfie's legs splayed apart as he sat down on the settee with a *THUMP*. The only person who didn't move or seem surprised at all was Mr Trotter. He stood rooted to the spot, his eyes flicking from left to right.

And then he said, 'Oops, that wasn't supposed to happen.'

'That was my best vase!' Mrs Trotter exclaimed.

Alfie looked at his father and said, 'It's you – you're the one!'

Mr Trotter was still standing motionless, as if he'd been frozen in time.

Then Mrs Trotter said, 'Oh well, I guess they were going to find out sooner or later.'

Standing up again, Alfie said, 'How come you didn't tell me, Dad? You knew how I've always felt different – like I was the only one – but you didn't tell me. *Why?*'

'It's not exactly something you drop into casual conversation,' Mrs Trotter said.

'We were going to talk to you about it when the time was right,' Mr Trotter added.

Alfie noticed that Eddie had disappeared. He heard footsteps going up the stairs – *bang, bang, bang ...* – and then a door slamming shut.

Mrs Trotter said, 'I'll talk to him.'

She went upstairs, leaving Alfie alone with his father.

'I didn't want you to find out like this,' Mr Trotter said. 'I wanted to be the one to tell you. You're only twelve years old, son. You're just getting to an age where you can comprehend what you're capable of. You get that, yes? You understand?'

He nodded, because he did.

He was torn between feeling elated that his father was a wizard and being dumbfounded as to why he wasn't allowed to attend the school for magic.

Brushing bits of vase off the settee, Mr Trotter sat down and said, 'Your mother will give me the silent treatment for weeks now, you know. Not only have I broken her best vase, I've managed to upset both you *and* your brother.'

Alfie said, 'I think it was me who up upset Eddie.'

Then he seated himself next to his father.

'I was about seven when I noticed I could do things other boys and girls couldn't,' Mr Trotter explained. 'I can't remember much about it, but apparently I scared your grandmother – my mum – half to death. She was in the kitchen one day, cooking dinner. She had her back to me, so she didn't see me enter the room. When she turned around I was walking up the wall with a big smile on my face. Like something out of a Michael Jackson music video.'

Alfie laughed.

'It's not funny. Poor grandma was so scared that she fainted. She hit her head on the floor and had to be taken to hospital. For a while she thought she'd imagined it, until I started to do other things. You saw how that pot exploded when I got angry. Well, that happened a few times – when I was throwing tantrums.'

'So that's where Eddie gets it from,' Alfie said.

'Yes. And from your mother, too; she's been known to throw some tantrums in her time.' Mr Trotter glanced towards the hallway, to make sure Mrs Trotter hadn't overheard. 'Anyway, back to what I was saying. I made things explode. I made things hover. I made things disappear. All of which scared the pants out of my parents. They were going to take me to a priest, because they thought I was possessed by Satan. Can you believe that?'

Alfie found this especially funny. He erupted into fits of gut-busting laughter.

'It might seem hilarious now,' Mr Trotter said, having a chuckle to himself, 'but it wasn't at the time, I can tell you. Not for my parents; they were genuinely scared and worried about me. When I was old enough to fully understand, they banned me from doing anything ... abnormal (their choice of word, not mine). But I still did things on the sly, when they weren't around.' Mr Trotter waved a cautionary finger at Alfie. 'And don't think that means you can go doing things on the sly. I didn't know how dangerous magic could be, until I was older ...'

'Dangerous?' Alfie asked, intrigued. 'How come? In what way?'

'It wasn't until I was thirteen that I found out I was a wizard,' Mr Trotter said, skirting the issue. 'It happened when I was at school. I was in the boys' toilet, washing my hands at one of the basins. The floor was wet and slippery and the caretaker hadn't put a sign down to warn anyone. So muggins here turns around and falls over, doesn't he. My right foot slid out from underneath me and I went down, doing the splits.'

In his whole life, Alfie could not remember laughing so much as he was now. Tears were streaming down his face as he struggled to contain himself.

Mr Trotter waited until Alfie had got himself under some sort of control, then resumed his story. 'When I went down, with my legs spread like a gymnast's, I let out a cry of surprise, which shattered every light in the room. Glass showered down on me and a piece hit me on the head, cutting my cheek. I thought I was alone, but I wasn't. As I was standing up, my feet scrunching on glass, a cubicle door opened behind me. A boy came out and said, "That was a heck of a scream, matey!". He was new at the school, but I'd seen him around a few times. His name was Ronald Spriggins and he knew a wizard when he saw one, because he was one himself.'

They heard footsteps coming down the stairs. Then Mrs Trotter came into the room, looking concerned. 'He's in bits up there,' she said. '*Very* upset.'

'Why?' Alfie asked.

'Because,' Mrs Trotter said, 'he's just found out that both you *and* your father have magical powers, so he's feeling like the odd one out at the moment.'

'But you don't have magical powers,' Alfie said to her. 'Do you?'

'No,' Mrs Trotter said. 'I most definitely do not.'

'So he's not the only one, then,' Alfie said.

'No, he's not,' Mr Trotter confirmed. 'But he is the only boy. Which is why we need to be careful about what we say and do around him. We don't want him to feel excluded, now, do we?'

Alfie shook his head. 'Of course not.'

'I need to talk to your father alone,' Mrs Trotter said to him, 'so go to your bedroom for ten minutes, please. I'll call up to you when we're done.'

'Okay,' Alfie replied. Before he did, however, he had one last question. 'Other than me and Dad, who else is magical in this family? I was told that it's passed down from one generation to the next, so we can't be the only ones.'

'There's been no one else that I'm aware of,' Mr Trotter explained. 'But it can skip generations, so it could have been my great, great, *great* grandfather, for all I know.' He shrugged his boney shoulders. 'Who knows.'

Mrs Trotter clapped her hands together. 'Right,' she said, 'up to your bedroom now, mister. Be gone!'

Without a word of protest, Alfie did as he was told. He went upstairs, but he didn't go into his bedroom. He opened the door and shut it, so his parents would think he was out of earshot. Sitting down on the landing, he crossed his legs. Then he pressed his face against the wooden stair rails, looking through them like a prisoner through metal bars. There was no noise from Eddie's bedroom. Just silence. Alfie considered knocking on his door to see if he was okay, but thought better of it. He didn't fancy being punched in the eye for his troubles. Better to wait until he'd calmed down, then try and chat with him.

Alfie listened as his parents began their discussion:

'I heard him laughing,' Mrs Trotter said. 'What did you talk to him about?'

'I told Alfie the story about me doing the splits and busting all those lights at school,' Mr Trotter replied. 'I wanted him to know how I found out that I'm a wizard.'

'Did you tell him why you stopped using your powers?'

'No, we didn't get that far.'

There was a short pause, then Mrs Trotter said, 'Are you adamant about not letting him go to Pendred's?'

They know about the school, Alfie thought. *They know all about Pendred's!*

Mr Trotter said, 'I think it would be better for all concerned if he didn't.' There was another pause, then Mr Trotter spoke in a surprised voice: 'Why are you looking at me like that? I take it you don't agree.'

'I'm not sure it's going to be as simple as telling him he can't go. You saw how crushed he was and you know how determined he can be. When he sets his mind on doing something, he does it. He's like me: he's got a stubborn streak. If he wants to use his powers, then he'll use them, no matter what we say.'

34

'He won't be able to attend the school without our permission.'

'No, he won't. But that won't stop him using his powers.'

Alfie felt a spark of hope ignite inside him. His mum had obviously come to the conclusion that he *should* be able to attend, which only left his dad to convince. Easier said than done.

'I just don't want what happened to me to happen to him. I don't want him to lose control like I did. I nearly killed that boy, Rosie. If that car had been travelling a little faster or I'd forced him into the road a split second earlier ...'

'That's all ifs and buts. The simple fact is that you *didn't*. Yes he got badly hurt, but if he hadn't have been picking on you, then you wouldn't have had to use your powers to push him away. And you were only fifteen years old. That was a long time ago. What's in the past should stay in the past. You haven't hurt anybody since then, have you?'

'No,' Mr Trotter conceded. 'But that's because I haven't used my powers (apart from the odd time where I've lost my rag and blown something up, that is).' He chuckled.

'The school will help Alfie harness and control his abilities.'

'What, like they helped me harness and control mine.'

'Don't blame the school for what happened with that boy. You have to be responsible for your own actions and you can't punish Alfie for *your* mistakes.'

Alfie still had his face pressed against the stair rails. He was listening intently, hanging on every word. *You tell him, Mum*, he thought. *Make him see sense.*

'Why are you so adamant he should go?' Mr Trotter asked Mrs Trotter.

With no hesitation at all, she replied, 'Because it's what he wants to do and I know it'll make him happy.'

There was a long silence, as if Mr Trotter was giving careful consideration to what Mrs Trotter was saying. Then, finally, he said, 'Fine ... okay ... okay, then ... we'll let him go and see how he gets on. You'll have to attend the first class with him, because

I'm not going. And if it all goes wrong, on your head be it. Don't say I didn't warn you.'

Clenching his fist, Alfie punched the air in jubilation.

Then he noticed that Eddie's door was open and that his brother was watching him.

'Looks like you've got what you wanted,' Eddie whispered. 'Looks like you're going to wizards' school, bro.'

'Only because of Mum,' Alfie whispered. 'Dad was dead-set against it.'

'I'm sorry,' Eddie said. 'I should ... be happy for you. I hope you enjoy it as much as you think you will.'

'Oh I will,' Alfie assured him. 'It's going to be *great!*'

Realizing he was speaking too loud, he cupped a hand over his mouth and snatched a glance down the stairs. He hoped his parents hadn't heard him.

Then Mrs Trotter called up to him, asking him to come into the living room.

Alfie looked back to see if Eddie was coming too. But he'd already disappeared into his bedroom and shut the door behind him.

Descending the stairs two at a time, Alfie went to talk to his parents.

His heart was thumping with excitement and he was sporting a wide, toothy grin.

CHAPTER 3

(An unexpected trip & an unexpected ambush)

In the days that followed, Alfie spent most of his time at school trying to avoid Salter and his friends. If he saw them in a corridor, he ducked into a classroom to get out of their way. At playtime, he mingled with crowds so he wouldn't get noticed. And at home time, he didn't hang around, either. Soon as the bell went, he was gone: across the field at a rate of knots, checking over his shoulder to make sure no one was coming after him. Alfie knew he couldn't avoid Salter forever, but he was going to give it a good go.

On the Tuesday, when Alfie bumped into Charles in the playground, he told him that he would definitely be attending Pendred's. Charles was elated and gave him a high five. He reminded Alfie not to be late and Alfie assured him that he wouldn't. He felt safe when he was with Charles, because he knew there was less chance that Salter and his thugs would try anything.

With regards to Alfie's busted bike, he agreed with his parents that he would do chores so he could earn money to pay for a new wheel. His first chore would be washing his dad's car. Not a task he relished. But it was a step towards getting him out of trouble, so he would have to grin and bear it.

On several occasions, Alfie was tempted to walk along Mysterium Road to see if he could locate the academy. Curiosity was gnawing at him. Charles had said that only those who were magical and actually looking for the academy would be able to find it. Alfie wanted to see if this was true, but he resisted temptation.

But then, a few days before Alfie's first lesson, curiosity finally got the better of him. It was a Sunday and he was stuck at home, bored. Leo had gone somewhere with his parents for the day and none of Alfie's other friends wanted to come out to play. Alfie couldn't stand the idea of staying in all day, so he told his parents that he was going for a walk. It took him twenty minutes to reach his destination.

Standing at the end of Mysterium Road, Alfie put a hand up to shield his eyes from the sunlight. He looked at the houses on both sides. All of them were big and old. They had steeply-pitched roofs, topped by tall chimneys. Large bay windows fronted each property, the glass in them glinting darkly. Neatly trimmed hedges and bushes rustled in the breeze as Alfie began walking along the pavement. He looked left and right as he went. About halfway down the road, he noticed a huge and imposing iron gate. There was a sign above it that read: **PENDRED'S ACADAMY OF WITCHCRAFT & WIZARDRY**. Beyond this, snaking off into the distance, was a long, tree-lined, cobble-stoned driveway.

Part of him wanted to leave and another part – the curious, mischievous part – wanted to explore. Because the trees were obscuring his view, the school wasn't visible from the road. Alfie wanted to take a look at the place – just a peek – and then he would leave. What harm could it do? The only problem was the gate. How was he going to get past it? It was too tall to climb over. He concentrated hard on the lock, his gaze unblinking. At first, he didn't think anything would happen. Then there was a clicking sound and one side of the gate opened slightly. Looking around to make sure no one was watching him, Alfie slipped inside and began walking.

'Just a peek,' he kept saying to himself in a low voice. 'Just a little peek.'

Slowing his pace a little, Alfie wondered what he should say if someone asked him why he was trespassing. An honest answer seemed the best course of action. He would explain that he was checking the place out so he'd know where he was going for his first lesson. With regards to how he had gained access to the grounds, a bare-faced lie would have to suffice. He would say that the gate was open, so he'd just wandered in. The only thing that worried Alfie was that he was a terrible liar. His mother could easily spot if he was fibbing. It was like she had an in-built radar for lies (or porky pies, as she called them).

Reaching the end of the driveway, the first thing that came into view was a car park to the right. Then Alfie looked to his left and saw a huge ivy-covered building, complete with raised corner turrets. A huge, wooden front door was set into an arched entry, which had stone gargoyles either side of it, up high. Like the houses on Mysterium Road, the school had a steeply-pitched roof. But instead of just one chimney, four lined its length, all evenly spaced. From the farthest one, black smoke was billowing, spiralling into the sky. This, Alfie realized, was not a good thing. It meant somebody was probably home. Time to leave.

He backed down the driveway, heading for the gate. But then he heard a rustling noise. Looking around, he couldn't see anything. Sure it must be his imagination, he once more went to leave. Then he heard the noise again. Walking towards the academy, Alfie focused on a bed of plants in the front garden. He had never seen anything like them before. They had long stems, which were topped with bulbous purple heads. Intrigued, Alfie moved in for a closer look. He was almost certain that this was where the noise had come from. He went to prod one of the plants with his finger, then changed his mind.

'Erghh!' he said, noticing a slug in the soil.

Alfie hated them. If there was one thing guaranteed to give him the creeps, it was a slimy, wriggly slug.

Overcome by a feeling that someone was watching him, Alfie turned his attention to the academy. For a brief moment, he was sure he saw a face at one of the diamond-shaped turret windows. But Alfie blinked and nobody was there. *Just my imagination again*, he thought. Or it could have been a shadow. Yes, that's it, he tried to convince himself – just a shadow. Doubt still niggled at the back of his mind, though.

Alfie heard the rustling sound again. He saw one of the plants moving. The stem was bending, the bulbous head getting closer to the ground, closer to the slug. Kneeling down, Alfie leaned in to get a closer look. He reached out with his finger to give the plant a prod ...

Then someone said, 'I wouldn't do that if I were you.'

Springing up like a jack in a box, Alfie snatched worried glances here and there. But he couldn't see anyone.

A snapping sound turned Alfie's attention back to the plant. It'd bent itself right over and its bulbous head had opened up like a Venus Flytrap, revealing long, sharp teeth. Lashing out at the slug, the plant scooped it up in its jaws. Alfie watched in horror as it began chomping on the slug.

He had seen enough. Turning deftly on his heels, he went to leave. But before he did, he cast one last glance towards the turret. No doubt about it this time: there was a face at one of the windows. Someone was *definitely* watching him.

Alfie sprinted for the gate. And then he ran all the way home, as fast as his legs could take him.

####

At school, on Monday, Alfie couldn't concentrate. He was worrying too much about who had seen him trespassing on academy grounds. Had it been Mr Pendred? Or someone else: another member of staff, perhaps? Alfie didn't know what Mr Pendred looked like – or anyone else associated with the academy, for that matter – so he had no way of knowing. The person had long, grey hair. Because he had been in such a hurry to get away, this was the only identifiable feature he'd registered. In-between lessons and at playtime, he kept an eye out for Charles, hoping to quiz him about who the person could be. But Alfie never saw him. At the end of the day, as he walked across the field, heading home, Alfie was still busy looking for Charles. He was so busy that he didn't notice someone creeping up behind him.

'Well, well, well,' a voice said. 'Look what we've got here.'

Alfie recognized the voice straight away: Salter.

Not turning around, or even casting a backwards glance, Alfie broke into a sprint. He didn't get far, however, as strong hands shoved him in the back. He went down face-first, sprawling in the muddy grass. Then Salter appeared in front of him. Alfie had an excellent view of his black boots from his position on the floor.

'You're where you belong,' Salter said, looming over him. 'In the dirt.'

Alfie heard laughter, so he knew Salter wasn't alone. At least one of his cronies was with him. Alfie looked back and saw Mason, who was grinning like a fool.

Alfie went to stand up, but Salter pushed him back down.

'Did I give you permission to rise?' Salter said to him.

Manoeuvring himself into a sitting position, Alfie said, 'Where's your other buddy Having his nails done, is he?' Soon as the words were out of his mouth, he regretted it. He began to backtrack. 'Not that he needs them done, of course; I'm sure his nails are perfectly fine as they are.'

'I'll tell him what you said,' Mason snarled.

Other kids were gathering around now. A circle of curious on-lookers was forming around the three boys. Alfie looked at them each in turn, hoping to see a friendly face. Leo had left early for a dentist appointment and Alfie couldn't see any of his other buddies.

'My shoes need shining,' Salter said to Alfie, 'so get busy.'

'I'm not shining your shoes,' he responded.

He tried to get up again and Salter shoved him back down. More forcefully this time.

Mason said, 'You can stand when we tell you to stand. Now get shining – or else!'

'No chance!' Alfie replied.

He cursed himself for being so careless.

He wondered how he could get out of this situation and keep his dignity intact. He also wondered how he could get out of this situation without getting beaten up. Running away wasn't an option. The circle of onlookers was blocking any escape route. Alfie considered trying to reason with Salter, then changed his mind. Salter had a look of blind hatred in his eyes: the look of someone who was hell-bent on revenge.

'Get shining, loser!' Mason yelled. 'I won't warn you again!'

The on-lookers began to chant, 'Shine ... shine ... shine ... shine ... shine ...'

Salter grinned at Alfie and gestured for him to get working.

A surge of rage welled up inside Alfie. He focused his attention on Salter, with the intention of using magic to dangle him upside down, then yank his pants around his ankles. And he would have done too, if a teacher hadn't intervened:

'What's going on here! Let me through! Let me through, you lot!'

A gap appeared in the circle and Mr Langford, the year 7 maths teacher, came blustering through the crowd. He was a short man with a pot belly. Sunlight glinted off the sweaty bald patches on his head as he took in the situation. He looked at Alfie, who was still on the ground, and then at Salter, who was backing away, fixing to make a hasty getaway.

'Not so fast, you,' Mr Langford said, hooking a stubby finger over, beckoning Salter to him.

'He'd fallen over,' Salter said. 'I was just trying to help him up.'

'Of course you were,' Mr Langford said. He noticed that Mason was walking away, so he called him back, too: 'Both of you – come here now!' When neither of them did as instructed, Mr Langford deepened his voice to show he meant business. 'When I say now, I mean NOW!'

Alfie got up. He watched as Salter and Mason stood in front of the teacher, with their heads bowed.

'The rest of you can go home,' Mr Langford said, addressing the crowd. He clapped his hands together. 'Anyone loitering will get detention – *so get GONE – NOW – SHIFT IT!*'

A mention of the d-word got the crowd dispersing.

'We were just playing with him,' Mason said to Mr Langford.

'What a load of hogwash,' he replied. 'I know perfectly well what you were doing.' He glared down at the boys. 'Detention – tomorrow – after school – in classroom 3C. Got that, you pair?'

'But sir!' Salter blurted.

'No buts,' Mr Langford said. 'I'm looking for a yes or nod of the head. Either will do.'

The boys nodded.

'Good,' Mr Langford said. 'Now disappear.'

As the boys were walking away, they fixed Alfie with a stare that conveyed one simple message: we aren't done yet.

'Are you okay?' Mr Langford asked Alfie.

'I'm fine,' Alfie replied. 'No bruises or cuts, so I should think myself lucky, I guess.' He brushed himself off. 'My mum's going to give me a roasting when she sees the state of me.'

'Tell her what happened; I'm sure she'll understand.'

'I'd rather not. I know what she's like; she'll come to the school and create a big fuss. It'd be embarrassing.'

'As embarrassing as having those pair trying to humiliate you? It's a good job I was looking out the classroom window when I was, otherwise heaven only knows what they'd have done to you. They're nasty, those boys. Best avoided.'

'I've been avoiding them all week. I'm going to need eyes in the back of my head, at this rate.'

'I think you could be right. Maybe the detention will make them think twice before they terrorize somebody smaller than them.'

Alfie wasn't optimistic. He was sure it would take more than that deter Salter.

Alfie thanked Mr Langford for helping him.

Then, as Alfie was walking away, Mr Langford said, 'That crowd was only siding with those boys because they were scared of them. Not because they hate you. You know that, right?'

'I know,' Alfie said. But it didn't stop him from feeling like an outcast.

When Alfie got home, his mother did indeed give him a roasting. She waved her finger at him, then told him that he was *very* inconsiderate. Alfie tried to tell her that he'd tripped and fallen over. But she didn't believe him. Mrs Trotter's in-built lie detector was sounding and nothing Alfie said could silence it. She sent him to his room, where he changed into clean clothes.

Lying on his bed, lost in his thoughts, he wondered what Salter might try next. His attempt to humiliate Alfie had been partially successful, but that would not be enough. The icy stare Salter had given him as he was walking away had conveyed that message. Loud and clear. *Maybe I should just let him beat me up*, Alfie thought. *Perhaps that would end it*. Somehow, Alfie didn't think so.

Cue Eddie ...

'In trouble again,' he said as he came sauntering into the room. 'Taken up mud wrestling after school, have we? Is this a new hobby alongside with your magic classes? Or is there something you want to tell me?'

'I tripped. Fell over. It was embarrassing.'

'Well, I believe the last bit,' Eddie said, sitting himself on the edge of bed. 'Some friends of mine saw what happened. If you're being picked on, you need to let me know. I can help you.'

'You don't need to; I can deal with it.'

'Not according to my friends you can't. Ryan Salter and his sidekicks, yeah?'

Propping himself up on his elbows, Alfie said, 'You've heard of him?'

'I think most people at school have. He's a year nine. Likes pushing around kids who are smaller than him. I'm a year eleven. I'm bigger than him. My friends are bigger than his. I can have a word, if you want? Or I can just punch him in the eye, which is what I'd like to do.'

Alfie was always amazed at how sometimes he could hate his brother so much that he wanted to strangle him and sometimes he could love him so much that he wanted to hug him. This was one of the latter occasions.

'Do you really think it'd help?' Alfie asked. 'It might make things worse.'

'I'll make sure he doesn't bother you again, don't worry about that. How long has this been going on? Why haven't you told me about it?'

Alfie shrugged. 'You're based at the Upper Block, so I don't hardly ever see you during the school day. I know I could have told you at home, but, to be honest, I didn't want to drag you into my troubles. I was hoping he'd get bored of terrorizing me then move onto someone else. And I've only just started having real problems with him.' He explained about what'd happened at the reserve. 'I'd had run-ins with him before that, but no more than any other kid. He just couldn't bear being beaten by a seventh year.'

Eddie smiled. 'I bet he couldn't. And did you use magic to win?'

'I might have.'

Eddie's smile widened. 'Nice one. When he was bullying you, why didn't you just magic him away to another dimension? Make him disappear in a puff of smoke. That would have been cool.'

'Now *that* would have been cool, but it'd have also got me into a lot of trouble. Plus, everyone at school would think I was a devil or something, which would not be a good thing.'

Leaning a little closer to Alfie, Eddie said, 'Do you think you could have done it? Do you think you could have made him disappear?'

'Maybe ... Probably,' Alfie replied, giving careful consideration to this question. 'But it's not as easy as clicking my fingers. I can only do these things when I'm angry or I concentrate *really* hard. It scares me to think about what I could do to someone if I lost my temper in a big way.'

'I'm sure the magic school will help you with that.' Eddie said, tapping Alfie on the knee, then making for the door. 'And as for Ryan Salter, he won't bother you again. I've got your back on that one, bro.'

Another warm rush of affection towards his brother washed over Alfie. He went to thank Eddie, but he'd already gone. Alfie listened as the sound of his brother's thumping footfalls diminished on the stairs. Then he relaxed back on his bed, putting his hands behind his head.

A knowing smile spread across Alfie's face.

####

At five-thirty, Mrs Trotter called him down for dinner: jacket potato with lashings of butter and cheese on top. Alfie wolfed it down like he hadn't eaten in a week. This was followed by desert: chocolate sponge pudding with custard. Alfie made the pudding disappear so fast that it was as if wasn't even there in the first place.

CHAPTER 4
(The First Lesson)

On Tuesday, when Alfie's alarm clock sounded at 7:30am, he
sprang out of bed like it was Christmas. Normally, Mrs Trotter
would have to call up to him at least three times before he even
considered venturing out from beneath the warmth of his covers.
Not today. Never in his life had he been this excited. Later, in the
evening, he would be attending his first lesson at Pendred's
Academy. He couldn't wait to get started.

At school, during lessons, Alfie couldn't concentrate on his
work. During science class, whilst heating a magnesium strip, he
was so lost in his thoughts that he reached across the table and
nearly set light to his sleeve. If it hadn't been for another boy
warning him, Alfie would have gone home with a char-grilled
shirt. This would have got him another roasting from Mrs
Trotter, whose patience only stretched so far.

During lunch break, Alfie passed Ryan Salter in the corridor
and not a word was exchanged. Not even a look. Salter walked
past Alfie with his head down, looking at his feet. *Eddie*, Alfie
thought, grinning: *that was because of Eddie*. Alfie wondered what
his brother had said or done to Salter to prompt this reaction.

'Maybe he didn't see you,' Leo said as he and Alfie walked
home after school.

'Oh I think he did. The way he scurried past me, anyone
would have thought that his boots were on fire.'

'That's great, if that's the case. I wish I had a brother like
Eddie. In fact, I wish I had a brother, full stop. I love Poppy to

bits, but she isn't going to protect me from the school bully. Although I'm sure she'd try to.'

Poppy was Leo's five year old sister.

'Eddie's great when it comes to being protective, but you should try living with him; he can be a *real* pain at times.'

'So can my sister.'

'Yes, but at least she won't get you in a headlock if you annoy her.'

'That's true. She does nip my ankles, though. And she's got sharp teeth.'

Leo gnashed his together for emphasis, which Alfie found funny.

'Hey, do you want to come over this afternoon?' Leo said. 'We could play football in the garden.' He shrugged. 'Or we could do something else. We could have a blast out on our bikes, if you're up for it?'

'I haven't got around to fixing my bike. I'm supposed to be earning the money to pay for it, but I haven't done any chores yet. No chores equals no money. That's what my mum likes to say.'

'We can play football, then, yeah?'

'I, erm ... I'm going out with my parents to ... visit their friends – sorry,' Alfie said, doing some quick thinking.

Alfie wasn't sure if Leo had an in-built lie detector like Mrs Trotter, but the look on his face suggested he was detecting porky pies. Leo slowed his pace a little as he eyed Alfie with a sideways glance. Alfie wasn't keen on lying to his friend. It felt like he was betraying him. Telling him the truth wasn't an option, though. Alfie had promised his parents he would never tell anyone about what he could do.

'Maybe tomorrow, then?' Leo asked.

'Yeah,' Alfie said enthusiastically. 'Tomorrow – definitely.'

Reaching the edge of the field, the boys made their way along the dirt track that led to the main road. They walked in silence until they got to the road, then they said goodbye to each other and went their separate ways.

As Alfie walked away, he turned and said, 'Definitely tomorrow, yeah?'

'Yeah, yeah,' Leo replied, without so much as a backwards glance. 'Whatever.'

Making his way home, not only was Alfie worried about having upset his best friend, he was also concerned about not seeing Charles at school again today. He assumed that Charles must be ill or something. What other explanation could there be? Charles had said that he would be there for the first magic lesson, so Alfie was keen to see if he would be good to his word.

####

Normally, when Alfie was going somewhere with his parents, they would have to harass him to finish his dinner and get changed. Not today. When dinner was served – bangers and mash with baked beans – he was at the dining room table, waiting. He wolfed the lot down, hardly pausing for breath. And then he had to sit there for ten minutes, because he wasn't able to leave the table until everyone had finished.

When Mr and Mrs Trotter were out of earshot, Alfie quizzed Eddie about Ryan Salter.

'Did you threaten him?' Alfie asked. 'Or did you *hit* him?'

'Never you mind,' Eddie replied, tapping the side of his nose. 'All you need to know is that your big bro has done a little magic of his own and he won't be bothering you again.'

At 6:10, Alfie was pestering his mother, telling her it was time to leave.

'It's only a mile or so away,' she said, 'so it'll only take us five minutes to get there.'

'But what if we hit traffic!'

'It's after rush hour and we won't hit any traffic as we won't be going along any busy roads.'

'We might break down.'

'We won't break down. My car's never failed me.'

'Don't tempt fate,' Mr Trotter said, chirping in.

Mrs Trotter gave him a sharp look, then said in an equally sharp voice, 'Maybe you should take him. After all, you're the other magical one in this family.'

'There's no need to adopt that tone,' Mr Trotter muttered, looking like he wished he hadn't opened his mouth. 'And you know why I'm not going. Honestly, Rosie, I can't believe you just said that.'

Alfie wished his father was taking him. As Mrs Trotter had pointed out, Mr Trotter was the only other magical person in the family, so it seemed fitting and right that it should be him. Of course, Alfie knew why his father wasn't going with him, but he couldn't engage him in a discussion about it, because his parents would know he'd been ear-wigging.

'I was warned not to be late for the first lesson!' Alfie exclaimed.

'All right, okay, let's go,' Mrs Trotter said, getting her car keys from the kitchen, 'Anything to stop your whinging.'

Eddie wished Alfie good luck and told him not to blow anyone up.

At the front door, Mr Trotter knelt before Alfie and put his hands on his shoulders.

'You're going to learn how to do some weird and wonderful things,' Mr Trotter said. 'Some of it will be easy and some of it won't. Just make sure you enjoy yourself, yeah. That's the main thing.'

'I will,' Alfie assured him.

'Good boy,' Mr Trotter said. He ruffled Alfie's hair.

Twenty seconds later, Alfie and Mrs Trotter were on the road, chugging along in her battered old VW Beetle. She had been right about not hitting any traffic and a few minutes later they were nearly there. As they were driving down Mysterium Road – with the light bleeding out of the day as the sun began edging below the horizon – something occurred to Alfie:

'Hey,' he said, turning in the passenger seat to look at Mrs Trotter, 'how did you know where to come? I didn't tell you where the school was.'

Mrs Trotter cast Alfie a sideways glance. 'You, erm ...' she said, clearly hesitating. 'You must have ... mentioned it.'

Alfie thought back to the conversation he'd had with his parents about the academy and he was *certain* the address hadn't been mentioned by anyone. So how could she know? The only possible answer was that Mr Trotter must have told her – or that she'd been here before with him.

Mrs Trotter drove down Mysterium Road, looking left and right.

Alfie gestured towards the gate, which was to the right, up ahead. 'Slow down or you'll miss the entrance.'

Squinting through the windscreen, Mrs Trotter was clearly unable to see it. She stopped the car and shifted forwards in her seat, still squinting.

'It's between number thirty-two and number thirty-four,' Alfie said. He remembered what Charles had said about people only being able to see the academy if they were looking for it. Well, Mrs Trotter was looking for it and still not able to see it – because she wasn't magical.

Alfie touched her arm and pointed. 'Over there, look.'

Following the direction of his finger, she continued to squint. And then a look of recognition slowly spread across her face.

'It's there!' she exclaimed, pointing. 'I can see it!'

'Hooray!' Alfie said, clapping his hands. 'Now can we go in?'

'One second there was nothing there, just a hedge on one side and some bushes on the other and then ...'

A blue jeep came towards them and turned through the entrance. It disappeared up the driveway. Putting her Beetle in first gear, Mrs Trotter whizzed after it as if she was afraid the gate would vanish any second if she didn't get through it quick enough.

The jeep pulled into the car park and Mrs Trotter reversed into the space next to it. In the jeep, a small, round face peered through the passenger side window and smiled at Alfie, who smiled back, then looked away.

'It looks quite busy,' Mrs Trotter said.

'It does,' Alfie replied.

Including the jeep and Mrs Trotter's Beetle, he counted eight other parked cars.

People were queuing by the door: children and the adults who were accompanying them.

'What time is it?' Alfie asked.

Checking the digital clock on the dashboard, Mrs Trotter said, 'Twenty-five past six. Got you here on time, like I promised. Now aren't I just the best mum in the world?'

'The best *ever*,' Alfie agreed. After a short silence, while he and Mrs Trotter watched another car pull into the car park, Alfie said, 'You didn't tell me how come you knew where the school was?'

'As I said before, you must have mentioned it.'

'I *didn't*. And you know I didn't.'

'Don't you take that tone with me, young man,' Mrs Trotter said.

'But I didn't, though!'

Mrs Trotter sighed. For a moment she just sat there, staring through the windscreen. Then she leaned forwards and looked up at the school.

'It's a beautiful building, isn't it?' she said. 'Very Gothic and kind of spooky. I wouldn't like to guess how old it is. Must have been here hundreds of years, I'd imagine.' She paused, as if not sure what to say next. And then she told Alfie what he wanted to know. 'I have been here: a long time ago, with your father. He wanted to show me this place, because this is where he studied magic when he was a boy ...'

'Dad came here? To Pendred's?'

'Yes,' Mrs Trotter confirmed. 'He said that he wanted me to see the school, but I think it was *him* that wanted to see it, really. This was back before you or Eddie were even born. In the winter of '99, if I remember right. That's eighteen years ago. Crikey, how time flies. It only seems like yesterday. Well, not exactly yesterday, but you know what I mean. Now I come to think about it, I recall having the same problem when we pulled up outside. I was driving along and couldn't see the gate. Then your father tapped my arm and I did. Perhaps a little of his magic rubbed off on me when he touched me and I bet that's what happened when you did the same. It makes sense now. I can't believe I forgot.' Mrs Trotter paused and shook her head. 'Oh dear, I really shouldn't be telling you this and your father will be upset if he finds out.'

'Why?'

'He just ... would. For reasons I can't discuss.'

'Is it because of the boy he pushed into the road with his magic? The one he nearly killed?'

The words were out of Alfie's mouth before he'd had a chance to engage his brain.

Mrs Trotter gave him a harsh sideways glance.

Then her expression softened and she said, 'Been ear-wigging, have we? I've warned you about that before, haven't I? When I say go to your room, it means go to your room – not loiter on the landing with your lug-holes flapping. Honestly, Alfie, I expect better from you – but I never know why.'

'Sorry,' he replied, lowering his head a little. 'But that's the reason why, isn't it?'

'Yes – where his power was concerned, he just didn't trust himself after that. He convinced himself that magic was dangerous. Something to be avoided at all costs. He stopped attending classes and snapped his wand in two, vowing he would *never* do magic again. His parents, your grandma and granddad, tried to persuade him to stay on at Pendred's, but he was having none of it. Even Mr Pendred himself couldn't convince your father to resume his studies.'

'How old was he when this happened?'

'About fifteen, I think. This was a good few years before I first met him, so I can only tell you what he's told me.'

'He snapped his wand,' Alfie said dreamily, talking more to himself than his mother. 'But I haven't needed a wand to do magic and neither would he, if he's powerful enough. I bet he didn't pull it out and wave it at the boy to push him away; I bet he did it without one.'

Mrs Trotter shrugged. 'I have no idea. But you're probably right. With regards to the wand, I think it helps focus and channel your powers; it makes things ... easier. You've only made extraordinary things happen when you've been angry or emotional or concentrated really hard and it's the same for your father.'

More people were coming up the driveway now: a black woman and two boys, who were so alike that they could only be twins. They were even dressed in the same clothes: wearing matching black jackets, blue jeans and red trainers. Alfie was amazed at how they walked in step, like soldiers on parade. He wondered how anyone could tell them apart.

Another car parked near the far side of the building. An old man and a girl got out. They held hands as they made their way towards the entrance. Alfie sat forwards so he could get a better look.

'Who's the pretty little thing with the blonde curls?' Mrs Trotter asked.

'She's in my form at school. Her name's Melissa.'

'You could sit with her,' Mrs Trotter said, giving Alfie a nudge.

Alfie could feel himself blushing, so he looked at the dashboard clock, noting the time. 'It's six twenty-eight,' he said. 'Let's join the queue, because someone will be opening up in a minute.'

Come on Charles, he thought, *where are you? You said you'd be here ...*

Alfie and Mrs Trotter got out of the Beetle. Melissa looked in his direction as she and the old man were walking past. A flash of recognition sparked in her green eyes. She smiled and waved as she bobbed along with the old man (her granddad?) at her side, struggling to keep up. Then Alfie returned the gesture.

Along with the others who'd been waiting in their cars, he and Mrs Trotter joined the ever-growing queue. Alfie listened as people chatted away:

'Look at those gargoyles,' one boy said, pointing. 'They're really *scarrrry!*'

'My wand's made from the purest Willow,' one girl said, pulling it out of her bag to show everyone.

'Oooh!' another girl said, moving towards the bed of strange plants in the front garden. 'Look at these, Mum – aren't they weird-looking.'

'I wouldn't touch those,' Alfie said. 'One of them nearly ...' *bit my finger off*, he thought, but didn't say. 'They're dangerous; I'd keep well away, if I were you.'

The girl looked at Alfie, then back at the plants, with an expression that suggested she didn't know if he was joking or not.

'He's right,' the girl with the wand said. 'They are Limus Carnivorous – slug eating plants. I know someone who nearly lost a finger to one of those.'

'So did I,' Alfie whispered.

'What's that?' Mrs Trotter said. 'What did you say?'

'Nothing,' Alfie said.

He looked up at one of the turrets, towards the diamond-shaped window where he had seen the face, almost expecting to see someone watching him again. But no one was there.

At six-thirty, on the dot, the door slowly opened, creaking on its hinges. A tall, slim shadowy figure, dressed in black robes, gestured everyone to come inside.

As they began filing into the hallway, Alfie said, 'Here we go, then.'

Mrs Trotter said, 'Yes, here we go.'

Entering through the door, Alfie's eyes took a few seconds to adjust to the gloom of the spacious, wood-panelled hallway. Then the tall, slim figure greeted him and Alfie realised it was Charles.

'Where have you been?' Alfie said, elated to see him. 'You haven't been at school for days.'

'I've had a touch of gut rot,' Charles said, rubbing his belly. 'Been back and forth to the toilet more times than you'd believe.

Sorry, that's a bit too much information. Feel a lot better now. though. Is this your mum you've brought with you?'

'It is,' Alfie confirmed.

'Pleased to meet you,' Charles said, offering his hand to Mrs Trotter.

'Likewise,' she said, shaking hands. 'So you're the one who's got my son into all this magical goings on.'

'Guilty as charged,' Charles said, checking his watch. 'I'm sorry to be rude, but I just need to check if Mr Pendred is ready for everyone.' He slipped through a door to the left and shut it behind him.

The hallway buzzed with chatter as everyone stood around, talking.

'Hey, look at this,' one of the twins said, standing in front of a painting that was displayed on the wall. 'That's the coolest dragon I've *ever* seen!'

'That's not a dragon,' the other twin said. 'It's the Teenage Mutant Ninja Turtles.'

'No it isn't,' another boy disagreed. 'It's the Millennium Falcon from Star Wars.'

'Huh!' Alfie said, looking perplexed. 'Mum, what do you see in the painting?'

'A beach with golden sand and a glistening blue ocean,' she replied longingly. 'And you?'

Alfie took a step closer, then said, 'I see ... I see me wearing black robes, holding a wand ... with Dad standing behind me. He's got a hand on my shoulder and he looks proud. What does it mean? Why does it show different things for different people?'

All the kids crowded around the painting, eager for their turn.

'I think it's showing us what we most want it to,' the girl with the Willow wand said, looking proud of herself for figuring it out.

'She's right,' someone said. 'That's exactly what it does.'

Everyone turned to see Charles standing in the doorway he'd disappeared through.

'Okay,' he said, motioning the new students to come through, 'we're all set.'

Alfie and Mrs Trotter followed everyone as they filed into a classroom. The first thing that caught Alfie's eye was the chandelier hanging from the ceiling. Decorated with glistening crystals, candles flickered on every curling arm, filling the place with a warm glow. A huge cast-iron fireplace, stacked with wooden logs, dominated the wall to Alfie's right. The room was filled with wooden desks, all evenly spaced. But it was the big desk at the end of the room that was now receiving Alfie's full attention. And the man with long, grey hair who was sitting behind it, facing him. Alfie couldn't be one hundred percent certain, but he was quite sure this was the man who'd been watching him from the turret when he'd been trespassing.

Uh-oh, Alfie thought, *this is not a good start.*

'Youngsters, please seat yourselves at the desks,' Charles said. 'And adults, there are benches at the back of the room, along the wall, if you'd like to use them.'

During his time at school, Alfie had noticed that the kids who sat nearest the front of the class were always the ones who were keenest to learn. With that in mind, he gave his mother a smile, then scurried to the front row and seated himself at a desk near the window. The scraping sound of chairs being pulled backwards and forwards across the hardwood floor filled the room.

When everybody was seated, the man behind the big desk stood up and Alfie saw that he was wearing black robes, like Charles'. 'Good evening,' the man said, introducing himself. 'My name is Ulthar Pendred and I'm going to be your teacher here at the academy. In the coming weeks and months, you will learn some weird and wonderful things. You will learn how to do *magic*. Some things you'll find easy to master and some you won't. With time and perseverance, working together as a team, we shall find out what your strengths are. And your weaknesses. All I ask is that you try your hardest. If there's something you're not sure about, just ask; I'm here to help, so don't be shy.' Mr

Pendred leaned forwards, placing his elbows on the desk. His bright blue eyes swept the room, taking in every new student. 'My, you look a keen bunch. And such a good turnout, too. This is the most we've had for the beginners' class in years. Right, Charles, I think it's time to get some details, don't you?'

Charles nodded and pulled a pen from his pocket. Then he clipped the pen and a piece of paper onto a slate board.

'All we need is your full name, your child's name, date of birth, address, and a telephone number,' he explained to the adults. 'Just in case we need to contact someone in an emergency, heaven forbid.'

Mrs Trotter was first to write down some details. As she scribbled away, with the slate board on her lap, the woman next to her said, 'Well this isn't very magical, is it? I was expecting something a little more quirky than a biro and a sheet of A4.' She chuckled to herself, like she'd cracked a funny joke. No one else was amused, however.

'We have a telepathic typewriter called Doris,' Mr Pendred said. 'Would that be magical enough for you? You can use her, if you like?'

The woman, who obviously wasn't keen on the idea of her thoughts being read, shook her head. Alfie recognized her as the adult that was accompanying the girl with the wand. *A telepathic typewriter*, he thought, wondering if Mr Pendred was pulling the woman's leg.

'Has it been enchanted?' one of the twins asked.

'Yes,' Mr Pendred said. 'By yours truly.' He turned his attention back to the students, 'Okay, let's have some names, please, so I know what to call you. We'll start at the front and work our way to the back.' His unflinching gaze fell upon Alfie, who suddenly realised he was first. 'Just a name: that's all we need. First and last. Nothing more, young man.'

Alfie could feel himself sinking into his seat as everyone looked at him. He had never been comfortable being the centre of attention. In class, at school, whenever he was asked a question by a teacher, he would always blurt out the answer.

This was so the focus of attention would shift away from him as quickly as possible.

'Alfie Trotter!' he blurted.

The boy seated next to him said, 'Troy Tempest.'

But his voice was barely a whisper, so Mr Pendred asked him to speak up. 'I'm old and, alas, my hearing is not what it used to be,' he said, pushing his long, grey hair away from his temples. 'So let's try that again, shall we. And this time with a little more gusto.'

'Troy!' the boy said, blurting his name like Alfie had.

'*Excellent*,' Mr Pendred said. 'That's more like it.'

Next was one of the twins. 'Marlon Reid,' he said, without hesitation.

And then the other twin: 'Murray Reid.' He glanced around nervously.

'Melissa Tate.'

Alfie turned and was pleased to see she'd seated herself behind him. She smiled, dimples forming in her rosy cheeks, and Alfie smiled back. Then he looked away, unable to hold her gaze.

On it went, until it was the girl with the wand's turn. 'Amelia Loveday,' she said, puffing her chest out proudly. She held the wand up, twirling it around, as if she was about to cast a spell.

'Please put that away,' Mr Pendred said. 'You'll be using it soon enough, but now is not the time. And a wand is not something to be waved about like a toy. Utter the wrong words and you could blow something up. Or someone.'

Alfie could remember Charles saying the same thing.

Lifting her desk lid, Amelia placed her wand inside and then folded her arms across her chest. She did not look happy about being told off in front of the rest of the class.

When all the boys and girls had given their names, Mr Pendred said, 'Now we know who's who, we can press on. During your first lesson you'll use wands supplied by the school. After that, if you're going to continue your studies, you'll need to buy your own. It's best you use the same one all the time as you will get to know it and it will get to know you. There are other items you'll need, as well. I'll give your parents a list.' He turned his attention to the adults. 'Don't be too concerned about the cost as the shop you'll be going to is very reasonable. Have any of you been in The Enchanted Cove on Thurland Street?'

Some nodded and said yes, whilst others shook their heads. Alfie noted that Mrs Trotter was in the latter category. He knew where the shop was and had cycled past it a few times. The mural painted on the outside had always caught his eye. It depicted a purple dragon swooping down to attack a castle. Other than that, however, he had never taken much notice of the place. Apart from a wand, Alfie wondered what other items he would have to purchase? A broomstick? In films and cartoons, witches usually rode broomsticks, so Alfie figured not. A cauldron? Again, he pictured a witch owning one of those.

'The Enchanted Cove is a great place,' Mr Pendred said, pacing back and forth at the front of the class with slow, measured steps. 'Full of weird and wonderful things. And they'll have everything on your list. I always like new students to have attended at least one lesson before they go out and buy everything. The last thing you want is to get all those bits and bobs only to find out that magic isn't for you. This is highly unlikely, but I think it's better to adopt this approach. Just in case.' He stopped pacing, clapped his hands together, then faced the class. 'Right-o, that's the preliminaries out of the way, so I think it's time we got on with things.'

Taking this as his cue, Charles slipped through a side door and returned with a wooden box. From inside, he pulled out a wand and said, 'Please don't touch these until instructed. Safety is our number one priority and always should be.' Then he began handing them out, placing them on desks, in front of the children.

When he got to Amelia, she said, 'I don't need one, because I have my own.' She opened her desk and took it out. 'Mine is better than any of those.'

I'm soooo glad she's not my sister, Alfie thought.

'It's not about the wand,' Melissa said to Amelia, 'it's about who's using it. Some wizards and witches are more powerful than others.'

Amelia glared at her, but said nothing.

When Charles had finished handing out the wands, Mr Pendred said, 'Just one more thing before we start. I've planted some slug-eating Limus at the front, so if you could take care around those as they may mistake your fingers for slugs.' His gaze fell upon Alfie for a second and Alfie had to look away. 'I've put a sign up warning people to keep away,' Mr Pendred continued to explain, 'so if you can just ...'

'There's no sign,' one of the adults said.

'But I placed one down myself, this morning,' Mr Pendred said.

'She's right,' Charles confirmed, 'there isn't one.'

'Ah,' Mr Pendred said. 'I think one of our resident ghosts has been playing tricks again. We have a few mischievous spirits here, so don't be alarmed if you come across one. They'll try and scare you, but they're all perfectly harmless.'

The boys and girls exchanged worried looks.

'*G-g-g-ghosts!*' a chubby boy on the other side of the classroom said. He was visibly shaking and snatching nervous glances around. Alfie was sure that he'd introduced himself as John.

'As I said,' Mr Pendred assured the class, 'they're all harmless. If you come across one, just say *boo!* That'll usually get rid of them.'

A clanking sound from above made the chandelier rattle. Everyone looked towards the ceiling.

'Ah-hah, right on cue,' Mr Pendred said. 'That'll be one of them now. As for the sign, I'll replace that tonight. And I'll put a spell it, so it *can't* be removed. Not even by a ghost.' He pulled his robes around him and shivered. 'It's getting a bit nippy in here, so we're going to start things off with a relatively easy spell. One that'll warm us up. You're going to learn how to start a fire and, more importantly, how to put one out. I shall demonstrate and then you'll each have your turn.'

Rounding his desk, Mr Pendred stood before the fireplace, then raised his wand and said in a slow and measured tone, 'Lucidum Elevare.'

Flames erupted inside the hearth, filling the room with warmth. Chairs scraped across the floor as everyone stood up to get a better look. Alfie couldn't see very well, so he moved closer. Then Mr Pendred, who still had his wand raised, said, 'Extinctus Elevare.' The flames snuffed out, leaving nothing but a puff of smoke and smouldering embers.

'So,' Charles said, looking in Alfie's direction, 'who'd like to go first?'

Before he could reply, however, Amelia beat him to it. 'This looks easy,' she said, stepping forwards.

Mr Pendred moved to the side and motioned for her to have a go. With her chin held high, she looked around to make sure everyone was watching. Then she raised her wand and said very dramatically, 'Luc-id-um El-e-*vare*.'

A small flame lit on one of the logs and died away in less than a second. Amelia stamped her foot on the floor, then tried again. But her every effort was a failure. As she grew more and more frustrated, Alfie noticed that Mr Pendred was struggling to suppress a smile.

'You have to say the words very clearly and with no pauses,' Mr Pendred said.

Amelia had one last try and finally managed to get a small fire going. 'Look Mum!' she said to the woman that'd come with her. 'I did it – I did it!'

'That's fabulous,' her mother said, clapping. 'I *knew* you could.'

'Well done,' Charles said to Amelia. 'Now you need to extinguish it.'

After several failed attempts and a lot of foot-stamping, she said the words correctly and made the flames gutter out.

'Okay,' Mr Pendred said. 'Let's form a line and then you can each have a turn.'

Filing in behind everyone else, Alfie found himself standing next to the twins.

'I bet she hasn't got many mates,' one of them said, nodding towards Amelia, who was now watching from the other side of the classroom.

'I bet she hasn't got *any*,' the other replied.

Next to have a go was Melissa. She pronounced the words clearly and with no pauses, as Mr Pendred had advised. She made a fire and put it out with ease, much to Amelia's dismay.

As each child took their turn, with varying degrees of success, Alfie began to feel nervous. Everyone had managed it so far, so what if he wasn't able to do it? Would they laugh at him? The more Alfie thought about it, the more worried he became. And then it was his turn …

He went to step forwards, but Charles stopped him.

'Just a second,' he said, grabbing more logs and placing them in the hearth. 'Okay, you're good to go.'

Standing in front of the fireplace, Alfie raised his wand and noticed his hand was shaking. He opened his mouth, but no words came out. Realising he'd forgotten them, he looked towards Charles, who said in a low voice, 'Lucidum Elevare.' He winked.

Focusing as hard as he could, Alfie said the words and flames roared inside the hearth. The fire caught so fast – with a *whoosh!* – that it forced everyone to take a step backwards.

Mr Pendred wasted no time. With one quick flick of his wand the fire was extinguished. He wafted smoke away from his face.

'That was quite a blast,' he said to Alfie. 'Very impressive.'

Alfie could feel himself blushing as he turned to see Mrs Trotter give him a thumbs up. Then he went and sat at his desk. He watched as the remaining boys and girls took their turns.

'Mr Pendred was right,' a voice to his left said. 'That was very impressive.'

Alfie turned to see Melissa perched on the desk next to him.

'You must have done that many times,' she said, 'to be able to do it that well.'

'No, I've never done magic before. Well, not with a wand.'

'Wow,' Melissa said, twirling her blonde curls with her finger. 'Some wizards and witches are more powerful than others. Looks like you're one of the big hitters.'

'I probably just got lucky.'

'That's not something you could get lucky with; you've either got it or you haven't.'

Alfie shrugged and smiled. 'Maybe I've just got it, then.'

'Extinctus Elevare!'

They watched as a boy snuffed out the flames he'd struggled to create.

'Is that your mum you've come with?' Melissa enquired.

'Yeah,' Alfie replied. 'It should have been my dad who brought me, 'cause he's the magical one.'

'Why didn't he?'

Alfie told Melissa that something had happened to Mr Trotter when he was younger, something that'd made him turn his back on magic forever. He didn't mention any specifics though, because he was sure his father wouldn't want him to.

'That's a shame,' Melissa said. 'My dad wanted to bring me, but he's not a wizard; it's my grandparents who're the magical ones. My granddad was *so* proud to bring me.' She waved at him and he waved back from where was seated. 'How long have you known that you were, you know, different?'

'Since I was about five or six, I think. And you?'

'I was around that age, too. It's funny to think that we've been at school together all this time and neither of us knew what the other could do. Makes you wonder who else might be magical at our school.'

'There'll be others, I'd imagine. I bet Charles will know. He can tell a wizard or witch when he sees one. He spotted me jumping way further on my bike than should have been possible.'

'Lucidum Elevare!'

BANG!

Alfie and Melissa turned to see a huge puff of black smoke erupting from the fireplace. The boy named Troy was having his go and had said the words incorrectly. He turned around. His face was covered in soot. Laughter erupted throughout the classroom and he looked like he was about to burst into tears. Then the laughter turned to coughing as the smoke spread through the room like a blanket of smog.

Holding his wand up, Mr Pendred said, 'Fumi Et Abiit!' And all the smoke began to disappear into the wand.

'He's using it like a hoover,' Alfie said to Melissa.

'I'll have to remember that spell,' she said. 'I'm sure it'll come in handy at some point.'

When Mr Pendred had finished, he noticed that some students were still laughing at Troy.

'*Silence!*' Mr Pendred said. 'One thing I will *not* tolerate is students mocking other students. You will all mess up at some point, believe me. All of you – without a doubt. So how would you feel if everyone laughed at you?' His eyes swept the room, marking every boy and girl with a hard stare. 'I do not want a repeat performance of this behaviour, do you all understand?'

A few boys and girls nodded. Some said yes.

'Do you *all* understand?' Mr Pendred repeated with a harsh edge to his voice.

'YES!' all the new students said in unison.

The man that'd came with Troy scurried over and knelt before him. 'Oh, son,' he said, putting a reassuring hand on his arm. 'Don't worry about it; I ended up in a worse state than this on a few occasions when I was learning, so there's nothing to be ashamed of.'

'Charles,' Mr Pendred said, 'could you please take Troy to the bathroom so he can clean himself up.'

'C'mon,' Charles said, taking Troy by the hand, 'let's get you looking right again.'

Troy's dad followed them out of the room.

'Just in case you were wondering,' Mr Pendred said, addressing the class, 'the toilets are off the hallway. Please leave them as you would expect to find them. Right, how many of you haven't had a go yet? It's ten past seven and time is pressing.'

Two students raised their hands. The first one, a heavy-set boy named James, who kept blowing his nose, lit a fire and put it out with no problems. Last, but certainly not least, was a mousy little girl called Leila. She created a fire that was nearly as big and ferocious as Alfie's. Everyone *oohed* as the flames roared high and *ahhed* as she extinguished them.

Stowing his wand beneath his robes, Mr Pendred said, 'Well done, all of you. I can see that we've got a fine batch of new wizards and witches here. I look forward to seeing what else you can do. For now, however, because time is pressing, I'd like to show you the library.' He led everyone out of the room and then through one of the many doors that led off the hallway. Up some stairs they all went and through another door.

'This,' he said as everyone was filing in, 'is the library.'

Alfie pursed his lips together, then sucked in air dramatically as he beheld the rows and rows of age-old tall bookcases that stretched into the distance.

'If you want to look up a spell,' Mr Pendred said, 'then this is where you should come. You'll find every book that's been written about magic in here. And when I say every book, I mean *every* book. You can borrow any that you like, but make sure you keep them no longer than a week, just in case someone else wants it. The maximum you can take out is four at a time. The only ones that you cannot read are those in the Off-limits Section. Some of them are very old and prone to fall apart, which is why I keep them locked away. Permission to access that area will need to be granted from me and is not often given, for obvious reasons.'

Alfie led Mrs Trotter past some tables at the front of the room, then down an aisle to a section marked: **POTIONS**. The twins were hunched over a book, whispering and giggling to each other. Alfie wondered what they had found that was so funny. Positioning himself next to them, he tried to snatch a sneaky look.

'Here's one for turning someone into a toad,' the one on the left said. 'I think I might add a drop to your coffee in the morning.'

'You better not,' the one on the right replied. 'If you do I'll … I'll find a potion that'll change you into a cockroach.'

'And how will you be able to do that if I don't change you back?' the one on the left said.

'*You'd better not!*' the one on the right said.

He closed the book with a snap and placed it back on the shelf. Then he stormed off with his brother following behind him.

'Brotherly love,' Mrs Trotter said, rolling her eyes.

Alfie checked out the book, reading the title on the spine: *A Practical Guide to Potions.*

'Can I take this one, too?' he said.

'Yes. But remember that you're only allowed to borrow four at a time.'

Showcasing an even wider smile this time, Alfie tucked the book under his arm.

'If Eddie gets out of line,' he said, 'I'm going to change *him* into a toad.'

'Don't you dare, young man!'

'Just kidding,' Alfie said, walking away, sporting a sly grin.

Reaching the end of the room, Alfie noticed a door. He tried the handle, but the door was locked.

'Where's the Off-limits Section?' Alfie asked. 'Do you think it's in here?'

'It's locked for a reason, so that may well be the case.'

Alfie put his ear to the door, sure that he'd heard a tapping sound.

'What are you doing?' Mrs Trotter said.

'I heard something.'

Alfie kept listening. But he heard no more noises.

'Maybe it was one of the ghosts,' Mrs Trotter said.

'Really?' Alfie said, giving her a wide-eyed, worried look. 'Do you think it could be?'

'Possibly. Don't fret too much, though. Remember what Mr Pendred said: they're all harmless.'

'That won't stop me being scared if I see one.'

He put his ear to the door again, continuing to listen.

'Come on, we haven't got long left. Mr Pendred will be calling time soon, so if you want more books you better get a move on.'

Maybe it's just my imagination playing tricks on me, Alfie thought. But he was *sure* he'd heard something.

They continued to explore the library, walking up and down the aisles. They came across Melissa and James in the Astronomy Section. Melissa was holding a book, thumbing through the pages, and James was quizzing her about it.

'I don't see what astronomy has to do with magic,' he said. 'That's more to do with science, isn't it?'

'It is a scientific subject, yes,' Melissa agreed, 'but some magical practices centre around the positions of planets and stars in the sky, so it's important for our reading.'

'What sort of practises?' James asked. He made a trumpeting sound as he blew his nose.

'Telling the future,' Melissa said.

'It's important to know the position of Uranus,' Alfie couldn't resist saying.

'Oh, please,' Mrs Trotter said, shaking her head. 'That's not even funny.'

Melissa managed a giggle, though. Then she continued thumbing through the pages.

Determined to borrow the maximum of four books, Alfie kept walking up and down aisles until he found two more that caught his eye. One was about wands and the other, which got him excited, was about the different makes and models of broomsticks.

'Will I be getting a broomstick?' Alfie asked his mother as they worked their way back to the top end of the room. 'Is that something we'll be studying?'

'I have no idea,' she said. 'But nothing would surprise me.'

Charles and Troy had returned from the bathroom. Troy had cleaned himself up and already snagged himself something to read.

'*Magical Creatures of Myth and Lure*,' Alfie said, reading the title. The picture of a strange two-headed bird-like creature on the front caught his eye and got him wondering. 'Care to do a trade?' he asked Troy, offering up his astronomy book for a swap.

'No thanks,' Troy said. 'I'll stick with what I've got.'

'Where did you get it?' Alfie asked him.

'From over there,' Charles said, pointed towards the section marked: **MYTHICAL CREATURES**.

'How did I miss that,' Alfie said, speaking more to himself than anyone else. 'Have we got time to look, Mum?'

Mrs Trotter opened her mouth to reply, but Mr Pendred answered the question for her.

'Okay,' he said, clapping his hands together and summoning everybody back to the front of the room, 'it's nearly time to leave, so if you're going to grab something, do it quick. And remember, you can borrow a maximum of four.'

All the students and parents began making their way towards Mr Pendred, carrying books of various types.

'I'm reading this one about potions tonight,' Amelia said to her mother as they walked past Alfie, 'because it pays to be ahead of the game.'

'Absolutely,' her mother agreed. 'Couldn't have said it better myself, darling.'

'That's the first sensible thing that girl's said,' Mrs Trotter whispered to Alfie when they were out of earshot.

'Can I just take a quick peek at the Mythical Creatures Section?' he asked her. 'I promise I'll be no more than a minute.' She shook her head, so he revised it to less than a minute. 'Thirty seconds at the most. I *promise*. I've only got three, so I'm allowed one more.'

'Next time,' she said. 'I'm sure you'll be allowed in here next time.'

Mr Pendred confirmed this. 'You can come after lessons, or before, if you turn up early. The academy will be open from five-thirty onwards on study nights: Tuesday, Wednesday and Thursday. I trust my students, so there's no need to log out your borrows. Just make sure you *do* bring them back on time, otherwise I'll have to send one of the ghosts to your house to get them.'

Silence descended as everyone looked at each other, wondering if Mr Pendred was joking. Then he smiled and said, 'Don't worry, I'm just having you on. On a more serious note, while I can remember to mention it, please do not use magic outside of the academy. You're only just starting out with your studies, so you could easily harm someone without meaning to. If you wa –'

'What's the point of learning magic if we can't use it?' one boy said.

'If you'll just allow me to explain,' Mr Pendred said. 'As I was about to say, if you want to practice what you've learned at home, then that's fine (under the supervision of an experienced magical adult, of course). But don't go getting any ideas about hexing other kids at school, or trying to impress your non-magical friends with what you can do. Other people, other children, will not understand your abilities, so all you will do is scare them. People always fear what they cannot comprehend. You'd do well to remember that. This academy is hidden from the eyes of non-magical folk for a reason. You'd do well to remember *that*, too. As tempted as you might be, do not tell your friends - even your best, most trusted friends – what you can do. That's a dangerous path to slide down. You'll risk everything. Not only for yourself, but for everyone else in the magical community. Don't do it! Are we all clear on this? Do you all understand?'

A low chorus of yeses echoed throughout the room.

'Not loud enough!' Mr Pendred said. 'Stick your chests out and give it some gusto, by gab!'

'*YES!*' all the boys and girls said in unison.

'That's more like it,' Mr Pendred said. 'Now, I mentioned earlier that you'll need to buy some things that are essential for your studies to progress. Charles will hand out lists as you leave. If you have any questions about any of the items, then Mrs Tippings at the The Enchanted Cove will be able to answer and assist you. She's a lovely lady – very, *very* helpful. As I said before, she's always delighted to see new students. And if you can't get everything by next week, do not worry. We have spares, so it won't be an issue. Thank you, all of you, for coming.' He bowed. 'Did you enjoy your first lesson?'

A resounding '*YES!*' rang out through the library.

'Excellent!' Mr Pendred said. He bowed again, then gestured everyone towards the doorway. 'I will see you all next week, then. At six-thirty – on the dot – do not be late.' Pulling his robes around him, he swept from the room, nodding and acknowledging the adults as he left.

Charles positioned himself by the door and began handing out lists as everyone was leaving.

Snatching hers eagerly, Amelia said, 'I've already got half this stuff. And my wand is better than any of those in The Enchanted Cove.'

'Better than any of those in the The Enchanted Cove,' one of the twins said, mimicking her in a low voice.

Alfie put his books on a table so he could read his list:

Two sets of robes (black)
One Wand (Willow, Oak, or Hazel)
One Cauldron (Medium)
Amethyst Runes
Potions for Beginners by Charlie Pepwick
Entry Level Spells by Miranda Clutterbuck
One Broomstick (Grade 1 or 2)

'A broomstick!' Alfie gasped. 'So we really *are* going to be learning how to fly?'

'Yep,' Charles confirmed, 'you really are.'

'Wicked,' Alfie said as he showed the list to his mother.

'Is that lot going to cost as much as I think it is?' Mrs Trotter asked Charles.

'Less than two hundred pounds,' he said.

'Oh,' Mrs Trotter said, looking relieved and surprised in equal measure. 'That's excellent value.'

'I'll probably see you at school, Alfie,' Charles said. 'If not, I'll see you here next week, yeah?'

'Definitely,' Alfie said, glowing with excitement. 'Nobody will be able to keep me away.'

On the way out, Alfie stood in front of the painting and saw the same thing as before: him wearing black robes, wand in hand, with his father behind him, looking proud.

'Do you think dad will ever come with me?' Alfie said.

Mrs Trotter put a hand on his shoulder. She gave it a hard squeeze.

'I think … maybe in time he will. When he realizes how serious you are about all this, I'm sure he'll have no option but to come with you. Don't worry about it too much, Alfie; things have a way of working out in the end and it will in this instance. Trust me – I'm your mother; I know what I'm talking about.'

As they were walking away, Alfie asked her if she'd seen the beach again.

'Ahuh,' she replied. 'Time to break out the holiday brochures and show them to your father, me thinks. He'll moan that we can't afford it – and he'll probably be right – but there's no harm in asking. The worst he can do is say no, isn't it?'

'Which he most likely will.'

'It's been three years since we went away and the last time was only a few days in Blackpool. Hardly living it up. We can manage something better than that this time, even if it means we have to sell stuff to do it.'

'None of my stuff, I hope?' Alfie said.

'No,' Mrs Trotter assured him. 'Nothing of yours.'

With both of them back in the Beetle, Mrs Trotter placed her keys in the ignition and gunned the engine to life. She switched her headlights on. The cone-shaped beams cut through the darkness, illuminating those who were leaving on foot. Candle-lit lanterns had been lit on the exterior of the building. This gave the place a strange orange glow, which Alfie found comforting.

'I was very proud of you when you made that fireplace roar with flames,' Mrs Trotter said.

'I felt proud, too, Mum,' Alfie said. Then he realised he was missing something. 'My books!' He'd been so excited about reading his list and finding out about the broomstick that he'd forgotten the books. 'I left them on the table.'

'Can't you just leave them there until next time?'

'What, a whole week? No way; I'm going to get them now.'

'Okay, but be quick. Don't mess around. Straight in and out, yes?'

'Yesss!' Alfie said as he got out and headed for the door.

In the hallway he encountered Melissa and her grandad as they were leaving. Melissa smiled at Alfie and he smiled back. He said goodbye to her and told her that he would see her the following day at school. When they were gone, Alfie went to go through the door that led to the library, but then he stopped. Hearing voices in the classroom, he put his ear to the door and listened.

'He knows it's here,' he heard Mr Pendred say.

'How?' he heard Charles reply. 'Not many people are aware it's being kept at the academy. And I most *definitely* haven't told anyone.'

'Neither have I.'

'Well I think you can rule Graham out. He wouldn't betray you like that. He's a friend of yours, sir. He teaches here at the academy sometimes, so I really can't see him betraying your trust. As for Ullin, he gave you it to look after, so I'd say that pretty much rules him out ...'

'I'm not ruling anything or anyone out at this stage.'

'Not even me?' Charles said.

Mr Pendred did not reply.

'Who told you?'

'Ullin. He's heard whispers from those on the inside.'

There was a long pause, then Charles said, 'It'll have to be moved. You can't keep it here; it's not safe now, even with it locked away. And you may have to cancel the classes. For now, at least – until it's away from here.'

'The safety of the students is of prime importance, of course. But it will not be necessary to cancel Tuesday and Wednesday's classes as Ullin has assured me there will be no immediate danger. "You Know Who" is busy visiting the Marsh Ghouls, trying to get their support. It's their two day Festival of Light. During this time, they worship their god: Mordrigan. It would be seen as an insult if one were to leave before proceedings have ended. As far as moving the Stormbringer is concerned, things are already in hand. Ullin and some others will be here on Friday evening: between six and seven. Hopefully, after it's been once again re-located, "You Know Who" will not be able to find it for some time.'

'Just because he's dealing with the Marsh ghouls, doesn't mean he can't send others to get the Stormbringer.'

'Those on the inside have assured Ullin that there are no plans for such an attack. Not in the next two days, at least. "You Know Who" will want to be a part of any attack, because he will want to make sure nothing goes wrong.'

'What about next week's classes, will they be running as normal?'

I hope so! Alfie thought, bewildered. *I've only had one lesson, so they better not get cancelled!*

'Let's get Friday night out of the way and then we'll take things from there. You know, Charles, if you weren't aware that the Stormbringer is being kept here, I wouldn't be involving you an any way. You know that, don't you? You're still only fourteen years old and I have a duty to your parents to keep you safe. You need to give me your word that you won't come to the academy if I tell you it's not safe? Can you given me your word?'

Alfie he shifted his weight from one foot to the other, the floorboard he was standing on creaked. He grimaced. Then he considered what he should do next. Mr Pendred and Charles had stopped speaking to each other, so Alfie was torn between going to the library or fleeing back to the car, where his mother would no doubt be wondering what'd happened to him.

'Who's out there?' Mr Pendred said.

When Alfie didn't reply, Charles said, 'We can see your shadow in the gap at the bottom of the door.'

Oh no, Alfie thought. For a second he considered leaving, getting out of the academy as fast as he could. Then he changed his mind and entered the classroom.

Mr Pendred was sitting at his desk and Charles was standing beside him.

'I ... erm, forgot my books in the library,' Alfie said sheepishly.

'How long were you standing out there?' Mr Pendred asked, his grey eyes fixed on Alfie. Unblinking, unflinching.

'I wasn't ear-wigging,' Alfie assured them. 'I heard voices in here, so I stopped outside the door.'

Mr Pendred looked at Charles and Charles shrugged back at him.

'Well,' Mr Pendred said, gesturing for Alfie to get a move-on, 'go and get your books, then. Chop-chop!'

Alfie left the classroom in a hurry.

He got his books and went back to the car, where Mrs Trotter quizzed him about what had taken him so long.

'I was just talking to Charles,' Alfie said as Mrs Trotter drove her Beetle towards the gate.

On the way home, Alfie's thoughts turned to the conversation he'd overheard. What were Charles and Mr Pendred talking about? What was at the academy that would have to be moved? And who was trying to steal it? Alfie thought: *I'm going to have a lot of questions for you tomorrow, Charles, if I see you at school.*

CHAPTER 5
(Detention & the Telepathic Typewriter)

When Alfie got home, Eddie darted into the hallway and began quizzing him about his first lesson. He asked him what he'd been taught and whether he would be able to give a demonstration.

'I learned how to make fire,' Alfie said. 'I don't think a demonstration would be a good idea, for obvious reasons. Plus, I haven't got a wand yet.'

'I'll second that about a demonstration not being a good idea,' Mrs Trotter chirped in. 'Remember what Mr Pendred said about doing magic outside the academy? Only under …'

'… the supervision of an experienced magical adult,' Alfie said, completing her sentence.

'That's right,' Mrs Trotter said. 'It's good to know that you were listening in class. Maybe now you'll start listening to me when I tell you to do something.'

'I doubt it,' Eddie said, smiling at Alfie.

Alfie told him that he'd be getting a broomstick.

'Whoa!' Eddie said. 'Have you ridden one yet? Can you take me for a ride when you get it?'

'*Nooooo!*' Mrs Trotter said. 'Alfie isn't allowed to ride that thing outside of class, never mind giving you a piggyback on it. Can you imagine what the neighbours would say if they saw you flying up and down the street. Mrs Draper would think she'd finally gone senile. She keeps telling me she's losing her mind as it is, the poor old dear.' Mrs Trotter disappeared into the kitchen. 'Don't even think about it, you pair.'

'Where's Dad?' Alfie asked Eddie.

'Upstairs, I think. Reading a book in his bedroom.'

'I'm here,' Mr Trotter said, coming down the stairs. Dressed in blue pyjamas, he appeared in the hallway, clutching his book. He regarded Alfie with an inquisitive look.

'I want you to come with me next time,' Alfie said.

'I don't think that would be a good idea,' Mr Trotter said. He raised a hand in a warding off gesture. 'Alfie, don't look at me like that. And please don't press me on this issue, because I don't want to discuss it any further. You're happy going to your classes and I'm happy for you to go to your classes, but I won't be there with you. I'm not saying another word on the subject, and neither are you.'

'If I was in Alfie's position,' Eddie said, 'I'd want you with me.'

'Oh don't you start as well!' Mr Trotter said.

Mrs Trotter came through from the kitchen. 'I've heard enough,' she said to her sons. 'Leave your father alone. If he doesn't want to go, then he doesn't want to go. You have to respect that. Now go and clean your bedrooms, both of you. It's like a tip up there.'

Alfie opened his mouth to say something else, but a stern look from Mrs Trotter got him moving. He stamped his feet as he followed Eddie upstairs.

'And you can quit that, as well!' Mrs Trotter called up. 'Five-year-olds do that sort of thing, Alfie Trotter!'

Eddie rolled his eyes at Alfie, then disappeared into his bedroom.

After clearing up the Lego in his room, Alfie crashed out on his bed, lost in his thoughts. Part of him felt happy and part felt sad. And part of him felt intrigued. He was happy because he'd attended his first lesson at Pendred's Academy and enjoyed himself . He was sad because his father wouldn't come to classes with him. And he was intrigued by the conversation he'd overheard between Charles and Mr Pendred.

'I will find out what's going on,' Alfie whispered to himself. 'I *will* find out.'

####

Later that evening, when Alfie was bored of watching TV, he decided to get an early night. In bed, cosy under his covers, he skimmed through the potions book he'd borrowed from the academy library. He marvelled at the weird and wonderful concoctions he could brew: one that would make someone fall in love with him (perish the thought!); one that was used for treating acne (*Eddie would be interested in that*, Alfie thought); one for improving a person's memory (hmm, that could be useful) ...

Alfie kept turning the pages until he came across a potion that caught his eye. Springing up out of bed, he got a pen and sheet of paper from his drawer. Then he copied down the list of ingredients he would need. He tucked the list away in his drawer, over the back where no one would find it.

When he was back under his covers, he reached out and turned off his bedside lamp. Darkness sucked in around him. Alfie had always been afraid of the dark, but not tonight. He was too preoccupied thinking about other things: thinking about the potion he was going to brew and what he was going to do when it took effect.

####

The following day, when Alfie saw Charles on the way to school, he sneaked up behind him, then tapped him on his left shoulder. As Charles was turning, Alfie moved to the right and began walking with him.

'Ah-hah! Gotcha!' Alfie said. 'And I didn't even need magic to do it.'

'Oh well who needs magic,' Charles said, making an effort to look startled. 'Real school is going to seem pretty boring for you today compared to being at Pendred's Academy, wouldn't you say?'

'Mind-numbingly. I can't wait for my second lesson. Any idea what we'll be learning?'

'Not sure. Mr Pendred never has any set timetable; he just takes things as they come, but he'll teach you everything you need to know, make no mistake about that.'

'There will be a second lesson, won't there? Please tell me that the lessons aren't being cancelled.'

With one eyebrow raised, Charles stopped and gave Alfie a curious sideways look.

'So you *were* listening at the door, then,' Charles said.

'I was,' Alfie admitted. 'And now I'm more than a little curious. What's being kept at the academy and who's after it?'

Charles resumed walking and Alfie hurried along after him.

'I can't say,' Charles said. 'I gave my word to Mr Pendred that I wouldn't tell anyone.'

'Who's Ullin? And who's Graham? And what are the Marsh Ghouls!'

'Can't say. Sorry.'

'All those beginners who enrolled last night are about to go out and buy the things on their list. Are they wasting their money? Should I even bother? I need to know because my parents will do their nuts if I get everything and then the course gets cancelled.'

'Buy what's on the list. Beginners' class should be running as normal next week. If there's any change, I'll let you know. I'll let everybody know.'

'Will you be there for the second class?'

'I might be. I don't go every week, just every now and again because I enjoy helping out.'

Charles had quickened his pace, so Alfie was struggling to keep up with him.

'So what's being kept at the academy?' Alfie asked again. 'And who's after it?'

'I can't tell you that, so please don't ask again or I'll ignore you.'

'Whatever it is, it must be *very* important for Mr Pendred to be so concerned. He doesn't seem like the sort of man who worries easily.'

Charles didn't reply. He kept walking.

'I'll find out one way or another, you know; so you may as well just spill the beans now.'

Charles didn't reply. He kept walking. And he quickened his pace even more.

'Okay, okay,' Alfie said, falling behind. 'Whatever! Don't tell me then!'

'You're going to be late,' Charles called back, 'so you better get a move on.'

Nearing school, Alfie stopped and watched Charles disappear across the playground with the other kids. Alfie noticed a huge boy that he'd never seen before and assumed he must be new. *Wouldn't want to mess with him*, he thought.

Then Alfie heard footsteps behind him and turned to see Leo passing. Alfie opened his mouth to say hello, but Leo looked away and kept walking.

'Great,' Alfie muttered. 'Does anyone want to talk to me?'

'I do,' Melissa said, appearing at his side. 'Everything all right, Alfie?'

'Oh, eh, yeah,' he said, not sure how to respond.

'Come on,' she said, hurrying along, 'the bell will go in a minute.'

Alfie hurried along, as well. 'Hey, if I tell you something, will you promise not to blab to anyone?'

Pinching her index finger and thumb together, Melissa ran them across her lips in a zipping gesture. 'Your secret is safe with me,' she replied. Then, when Alfie didn't say anything more, she said. 'Well go on then, spit it out.'

'I'm not sure I should. I might get in trouble if a certain someone finds out that I told you.'

'How will they find out? You have my word that I won't tell anyone and you've got to tell me now. You can't say "if I promise not to blab, will you promise not to tell anyone", then leave me hanging. You have to spill the beans. And if you don't, I'll harass you until you do.'

Alfie didn't like the idea of being harassed, so he explained about the conversation he'd heard between Mr Pendred and Charles.

'What do you think it could be?' Melissa said. 'And who do you think is after it?'

'That's what I was going to ask you. Charles is keeping quiet; he won't give anything away. But if Mr Pendred is so worried that he's thinking of cancelling some classes, then it must be something really powerful or really valuable.'

'And the person that's after it could be dangerous,' Melissa said.

'Probably *is* dangerous,' Alfie put in grimly.

As they neared the school, the bell sounded. Kids rushed past either side of them, eager not to be late for the calling of the registers.

'So is the beginners' class running next week or not?' Melissa asked Alfie. 'I haven't even got the stuff on my list yet. Should I bother?'

'That's exactly what I said to Charles,' Alfie said, 'and he told me that I should. He said that the beginners' class should be running as normal, but he'd let everyone know if that wasn't the case. If whatever it is that's causing all this fuss is being moved on Friday evening, you'd think that it wouldn't affect any classes after that. With the object away from the academy, surely there'll be no threat towards the students. Mr Pendred is just being very cautious, I suppose.'

'I don't blame him.'

'Hey!' a deep, gruff voice said. 'The bell has rang – get to class!'

Alfie turned to see Mr Foster, the P.E. teacher, bearing down on them.

'Uh-oh,' Melissa said. 'Time to move.'

She headed for the entrance, sunlight glinting off her blonde curls as she gave Mr Foster a wide birth. Alfie skittered after her, not daring to look in his direction.

He caught up to her as she was about to go into class.

As she put her hand on the door handle, Alfie said, 'I'm going to the academy library later to swap some books, do you want to come?'

'But it's the intermediate class tonight,' Melissa said.

'I know,' Alfie said, 'but Mr Pendred told us we could use it on *any* study night. I'll be there at five-thirty.'

Melissa regarded Alfie with a curious look. 'Why do I get the impression that this isn't about books.'

Alfie didn't respond. He just looked at her with a smile playing at the corners of his mouth.

'You'll get yourself into trouble,' Melissa said. 'If you get caught snooping around, you could be expelled from the academy. Is it worth the risk?'

'I won't get caught,' he assured her.

'How can you be so sure?'

Alfie's eyes widened as he said, 'Because I'll be *invisible.*'

'Invisible? Really? And how are you going to manage that? You're a beginner. You've had one lesson and that doesn't sound like the easiest spell to cast.'

'It's not done with a spell; it's done with a potion. I read how to do it in a book last night. I'm going to the The Enchanted Cove after school to get the ingredients, do you want to come?'

'I ... don't think that would be a good idea. You really need to reconsider about this, Alf –'

The classroom door opened. Mr Podmore, their form tutor, stuck his bald head out. 'Are you pair going to come in,' he said briskly, 'or are you going to stand in the corridor talking all day?'

Alfie followed Melissa into the room. Then Mr Podmore slammed the door shut behind them, making them both jump. Laughter erupted as most of the pupils found this funny. Alfie realised that everyone was staring at him and Melissa. As the laughter began to fade away, Alfie made for the back of the class and seated himself at his desk. Melissa's desk was across from his. Her chair scraped on the floor as she pulled it out and sat down.

'Can you make any more noise!' Mr Podmore said, spittle flying from his chubby lips.

'Sorry, sir,' Melissa said. 'Won't happen again.'

'Right,' Mr Podmore said, 'perhaps I can get on with calling the register now.' He perched himself on the edge of his desk, then he picked up a hard-cover log and a pen. He resumed calling names and ticking them off. 'Billy Gregory.'

'Yes, sir,' the boy in front of Alfie said.

'Susan Harrow.'

'Yes, sir – here, sir!'

As Mr Podmore continued to call out names, Alfie reached into his bag and pulled out his notepad and Spiderman pencil case. He got a pen out of the case and began scribbling in the pad. Out the corner of his eye he could see Melissa looking over, no doubt wondering what he was writing. When he'd finished, he tore the sheet out and held it down low by his hip so she could it:

Please come with me this afternoon

Melissa shook her head.

Disappointed, Alfie scrunched the note up, dropped it in his bag, then wrote another:

I'm doing this with or without you. Are you sure you don't want to come?

Melissa shook her head again and gave Alfie an apologetic look.

Scrunching the note up, Alfie dropped this one into his bag as well.

'Alfie Trotter! Are you hearing me?'

Alfie turned to see Mr Podmore glaring at him.

'S-s-sorry,' Alfie stammered. 'What's up?'

A few of the kids chuckled.

'What did you just put in your bag?' Mr Podmore asked Alfie

'Nothing,' he replied, looking down at the drawings that had been etched into his desk (quite a few of which had been done by himself).

'Do I have fool written on my forehead?' Mr Podmore said.

Alfie was tempted to say yes, just so he could get an outburst from those that'd laughed at him. They'd all get detention and that would be good. What wouldn't be so good was that he'd get detention, too. Maybe this afternoon. And Alfie had somewhere to be this afternoon.

Alfie noticed Leo watching from the other side of the room and gave him an enquiring gaze. Turning away, Leo found something of interest to look at through the window. *He knows how to hold a grudge*, Alfie thought. At the start of the term they had been seated together, but Mr Podmore had separated them, because they kept distracting each other.

'Am I talking to myself again here,' Mr Podmore said to Alfie. 'I'll ask once more: do I have fool written on my forehead?'

'No, sir.'

'Good. So what did you put in the bag?'

Alfie reached down and pulled out the crumpled notes. He handed the notes to Mr Podmore, who un-crumpled them and read them aloud with his top lip curling into a sneer.

'Are you and Ms Tate doing something together this afternoon?' Mr Podmore said, looking at Melissa, then Alfie.

'I am,' Alfie said.

'That's right,' Mr Podmore said, 'you are – you're going to be in detention with me.'

'*What!*' Alfie blurted. 'But I've got plans.'

'You *had* plans,' Mr Podmore corrected. He turned his attention to Melissa. 'Oh,' he said to her, 'and you'll be joining him.'

'Eh!' she said, perplexed. 'Me? Why? I haven't done anything wrong.'

'After school,' Mr Podmore said, turning around and walking back towards his desk. 'In this classroom. Don't keep me waiting.'

Melissa looked at Alfie and he had to look away. He noticed that all the other kids (apart from Leo) were also looking at him. Some of them were grinning. Some were shaking their heads. Alfie wanted the floor around him to turn into quicksand, so he could disappear without a trace.

####

Later that day, at just gone three-thirty, Alfie returned for his detention. Melissa was waiting for him by the door.

'I hope he doesn't keep us long,' she said. 'How many lines do you think he'll give us?'

'God knows,' Alfie replied. 'But the sooner we get in there, the sooner we can leave.'

He opened the door and stepped into the classroom, with Melissa following on his heels.

Mr Podmore was sitting at his desk, hunched over, marking papers. He glanced up and managed a grunt of acknowledgement. He motioned them to take their seats, which they did. Then he kept on marking the papers. After a few minutes, Alfie started to feel frustrated. He glanced at Melissa and she just shrugged.

'My mum will be expecting me home,' Alfie said. 'She'll get worried if I'm not back by four o'clock.'

'My mum will be worried, too,' Melissa added.

'Perhaps you should have thought about that before you began misbehaving in my class,' Mr Podmore said, not even bothering to look up. He carried on marking the papers, his rugged face a picture of grim concentration.

A few more minutes passed, then Mr Podmore grabbed some sheets of paper and two pens. His chair scraped across the floor as he stood up. His footsteps echoed into the emptiness of the classroom as he walked towards Alfie and Melissa.

'One hundred lines,' he said, handing Alfie three sheets and a pen. 'The sooner you do them, the sooner you can go home,' he added, giving Melissa her sheets and pen. He turned his attention back to Alfie. 'What do you think you should write?'

'Erm ...' he said, giving it some thought. 'That I should ... not scribble notes in class.'

Mr Podmore shook his head.

'That he shouldn't distract other pupils whilst in class,' Melissa offered.

'That's more like it,' Mr Podmore said, almost smiling at her. 'And what do you think you should write, Ms Tate?'

'That I shouldn't allow myself to *be* distracted,' Melissa said with no hesitation.

'Bingo!' Mr Podmore said, leaving them to it.

He went back to his desk and seated himself. He pulled a drawer open and got a book out. He began reading. The cover caught Alfie's eye: it showed a three-headed dragon emerging from a cave. The dragon had bright green eyes and fire billowing from its nostrils. Alfie noted the title – *Into the Dragon's Lair*.

Then he noticed that Melissa had already written four lines. Determined to catch her up, he got to work. As he wrote line after line, he cast the odd glance towards the clock on the wall. He thought: *as long as I'm out of here by quarter past four at the latest, I should make it to The Enchanted Cove in good time.* (He was working on the assumption that the shop would close at five: the same as most other shops.) But the lines took him longer than he'd anticipated. By the time he was halfway through, his fingers were aching. This slowed him down. And a short while after, when Melissa got up and handed her lines to Mr Podmore, Alfie still had about twenty-five to do. As she was leaving, he looked at her, as if to say: how did you finish so fast? In response, she just smiled and gave him a little wave goodbye.

When the door clicked shut behind her, Alfie got back to work. He didn't like being alone with his teacher, so he scribbled as fast as he could. After he'd written the last line, he handed his work in and Mr Podmore said, 'I hope you've learned your lesson, Mr Trotter.'

'I have,' Alfie assured him.

As he was leaving, he stopped and looked back. Mr Podmore was still hungrily working his way through the book.

'That must be a good book,' Alfie said.

'It's excellent,' Mr Podmore replied, not taking his eyes off the page he was reading. 'Do yourself a favour and get a copy. You won't regret it.'

'I might just do that,' Alfie said.

He noted the time before he left: 4.25.

Out of the building he went and across the field as fast as his legs would take him. Usually it took him fifteen minutes to get home. Not today. He made it there in half that time. When he burst through the front door, Mrs Trotter appeared in the hallway. She did not look pleased.

'Where have you been?' she demanded to know.

She folded her arms across her chest.

Alfie had already thought up a fib. 'Leo was playing football after school,' he said, out of breath. 'I stayed to watch him.'

'Did you now,' Mrs Trotter replied. 'The next time you're going to do that, can you please let me know?'

'I will,' Alfie said.

He rushed past his mother and up the stairs to his bedroom.

'What's the hurry?' she called up. 'Are you going out again?'

'Yes,' Alfie called back. 'I'm going to Leo's; we're going to ... play football in his garden.'

Getting changed, he slipped on a pair of jeans and a black top.

Then he snatched his piggy-bank off the windowsill and emptied the contents onto his bed. He counted out the pound coins and silver: £10.85. Estimating that he had about two pounds in coppers, he filled his pockets with all the coins. Remembering the list he'd hidden in his drawer, he pocketed that as well. When he went back down the stairs, Mrs Trotter was still standing in the hallway, her arms still folded across her chest.

'You're jingle-jangling,' she said. 'Your pockets are full and you're jingle-jangling, which means you've raided your piggy-bank. Why?'

'Erm ...' Alfie said, thinking fast. 'I'm going to the toy shop in town. I saw some new Lego sets in the window when I was passing yesterday and I want to check them out.'

'I thought you said you were going to Leo's,' Mrs Trotter said, giving Alfie a suspicious look.

'I am. But first I want to go to the shop.'

'I thought you were saving for some big set that costs fifty pounds. I don't know how much you've got in your pockets, but I'm guessing it's nowhere near that.'

'You guess correctly, oh wise mother. I'm just taking my money in case I see something that's a must-have. I *really* need to go now, because the shop will be shutting soon.'

He made for the front door. But before he could disappear through it, Mrs Trotter said, 'Don't be late home; I want you back in by seven, at the latest. Oh, and if you're going on your bike, wear your protective gear; I don't want to have to tell you again. And I'll leave your dinner in the microwave.'

'My bike's busted, remember,' Alfie said. He considered asking if he could borrow Eddie's, but didn't bother. His brother wasn't home, which meant he was probably out on it somewhere anyway. And even if he wasn't, Alfie was sure his mother would say no, because she knew Eddie could be protective where his prized possession was concerned.

Not wanting to waste another second, Alfie said goodbye and left the house. Mrs Trotter waved to him from the kitchen window as he walked briskly down the street. Once he was out of view, he broke into a jog, the change bouncing up and down in his pocket. He hoped with all his might that he could make it to The Enchanted Cove before it shut.

####

By the time he got there he was badly out of breath and it was three minutes to five.

He'd always been amazed by the mural painted on the side of the shop, which depicted a purple dragon swooping down out of a stormy sky to attack a castle. Today, however, because he was in such a hurry, he gave the mural no more than a cursory glance. Making for the door, he was happy to see that the sign behind the glass still said **OPEN**. But he was not so happy when he tried to enter and found that the door was locked. The lights were still on though, so that was a promising sign that someone might still be in there. Putting his face to the glass so he could see inside, Alfie cupped his hands to the sides of his head to cut out the glare. He couldn't see anybody. A sign in the display window listed the opening and closing times. Today's closing time was 5pm, as Alfie had suspected, which meant that someone had closed up early (either that or Alfie's watch was running fast).

He knocked. Then he waited. He knocked again. Louder this time. And then he waited. Just as despair was about to set in, he saw a shadow move across the far wall. A stout, round-faced woman dressed in blue robes came into view. She was wearing thick-lensed glasses, which she adjusted on her button nose as she leaned forwards to get a better look at who was outside.

'We're closed,' she said.

'That's not what your sign says,' Alfie responded, pointing.

The woman looked at the sign. 'Oh, I'm always forgetting that,' she said, turning it around.

Alfie had written one hundred lines as fast as he could, wormed his way past his mother, lying through his teeth in the process, then jogged all the way here, only to be denied at the last second by somebody who'd shut up early. Not happening.

'When I arrived, it was three minutes to five,' Alfie said. 'It says on your sign that you close at *five*.'

The woman unlocked the door. A bell jingled as she opened it.

'Normally I wouldn't close early,' she said, 'but I have somewhere I need to be. So what is it you're after, exactly? If it's something I can grab quickly, then fine. Otherwise you'll have to wait until tomorrow, my dear.'

Alfie pulled the list from his pocket and handed it to the woman.

'Hmm,' she said, scanning it over. 'Essence of Nightshade ... drops of Moonsickles ... Akunite Seeds ...' She looked over the top of her glasses, her gaze enquiring. 'You're making an invisibility potion. Why?'

Alfie shrugged. 'Because ... it sounds cool.'

'That's the daftest question I've asked today.' The woman gave Alfie another enquiring look. 'I've a good memory for faces and I'm sure I've not seen you before. New to magic, are you?'

'Yes,' Alfie confirmed. 'New and enthusiastic.'

'How old are you?'

'Twelve.'

'Hmm,' the woman said. 'An invisibility potion is not easy to make and Moonsickle Drops are *very* rare, *very* expensive.'

'How expensive?' Alfie said, pulling a handful of change from his pocket. 'I have money. Maybe I've got enough.' He wasn't optimistic.

'I seriously doubt it,' the woman said. 'There's also the safety aspect to consider. If you add a little too much of one ingredient and not enough of another ...' She raised her hands, simulating an explosion. 'You could disappear forever, up in a cloud of smoke.'

'Ah,' Alfie said. 'Better make sure I get it right, then, hadn't I?'

'I'm sorry,' the woman said, 'I have to go in a minute, so I haven't got time for this.'

She went to close the door and Alfie stopped her with his foot.

'I'll give you all the money I've got,' he said. 'Every penny.'

He put his hand in his other pocket and pulled out another handful of change.

'That's a lot of coins you've got there, but no where near enough' she said. 'Not even in the vicinity of close. Now can you please remove your foot so I can shut up and be gone.'

Alfie knew he would have to come back here the following day, so there were good reasons not to annoy this woman. Number one, she would tell his mother that he had been here and what he'd been up to. Number two, he didn't want to get barred from the shop that supplied the things he needed for his magical studies. Alfie didn't know if there were any other shops like the The Enchanted Cove in the area, so he withdrew his foot and took a step backwards.

'Thank you,' the woman said.

She went to shut the door ...

'Is there anywhere else around here that'll sell what I need?' Alfie said. 'Somewhere that stays open late?' He knew this was a long-shot, but he felt he had to ask anyway. Just to be sure.

'Only a specialist store like this one will have the ingredients you need. The closest is in Castle Meadows, about twenty miles away, and I'd imagine they're shut already. And even if they were open, I doubt they'd have the Moonsickle Drops. Like I said, they're *very* rare, *very* expensive.'

'Okay,' Alfie said, feeling dejected.

Making full use of his big blue eyes, he gave the woman his best pleading look: the one he always gave his mother when he was trying to worm something out of her. Mrs Trotter called it the wounded rabbit look. Sometimes it worked, sometimes it didn't. More often than not, it was her mood that determined whether it was a yes or no.

'I can't help you, I'm sorry,' the woman said. 'Now I really must get a move on.'

The door clicked shut in Alfie's face. The rabbit look had failed him this time, it seemed. He lingered there for a few seconds, his shoulders slumping in disappointment. He wondered how he was going to get around this situation. If he went snooping at the academy without taking the potion, he risked being spotted. He knew he should abandon the idea, but curiosity was eating away at him.

As he was walking away, still thinking things through, he heard the shop door open and the bell jangle. The woman emerged wearing a waterproof mack. She locked up, then looked skywards.

'You should have worn a coat,' she said to Alfie. 'It's going to come down heavy in a bit.'

Alfie craned his neck to look up and saw a blue sky, broken by the odd scattering of clouds. He had seen the weather forecast in the morning, before he'd gone to school, and there'd been no mention of rain.

'Here,' the woman said, reaching into her pocket and pulling out a small glass vial full of liquid. 'There's enough in there to keep you invisible for fifteen minutes, give or take. Use it responsibly.'

'Thanks,' Alfie replied, grinning.

'I always keep some pre-made potions aside for my own personal use, but I don't normally give them to people, because I think you should make your own. It's the only way you'll learn, so don't expect this again, especially with such a rare concoction as that. I'd ask you what you really want it for, but I haven't got time. You look like a sensible boy, so I'll trust my instincts. You're just lucky you've caught me in a *very* good mood. ' The woman checked her watch. 'Oh mi gosh, I really do need to go. I'm going to be *late late late!*'

'How much?' Alfie said, reaching into his pockets, grabbing a handful of change.

'I'm not counting that lot out,' the woman said. 'It won't go anywhere near to covering the cost, believe me. It's on the house. Call it a … promotional gift.'

As she was ambling away, Alfie said: 'How long does it take before it starts to work?'

'Less than a minute, that's all,' the woman called back. 'It's a weird sensation, watching yourself disappear. Don't worry, though; you'll come back. I've been making potions for years and I haven't miss-brewed one yet. Honest.'

Alfie watched her scurry along, muttering to herself about being late. Rounding a corner, she disappeared from view.

Alfie looked at the vial and smiled. The wounded rabbit look had worked, after all.

After he asked a man what the time was – 5.18, matey – he pocketed the vial and set off walking. Job done and not a penny spent. Now *that* was a result.

By the time he got to the academy, it was pushing 5:35 and he was once again out of breath. There was only one car in the car park. He had hoped to be the first person here, but it didn't matter; he was quite confident that he could still do what needed to be done without getting busted. Making his way up the driveway, he glanced towards the largest tower and almost expected to see Mr Pendred watching him. There was no one there, though. The only eyes upon him, as far as he could see, were those of the stone gargoyles. The silent guardians above the door, who'd been there for hundreds of years, regarded Alfie with their unflinching gaze. He noted a pink BMX chained to a drainpipe at the side of the building. He wondered whether the owner had left it there overnight or if it belonged to another early arrival. Just before Alfie entered through the front door, he noted something else: there was now a sign by the slug-eating plants, warning people to steer clear.

Inside, Alfie went up the stairs to the library. He entered and noticed a boy and man browsing down one of the aisles. Other than that, Alfie couldn't see anyone else. Taking another aisle, Alfie walked to the far end of the room and made for what he believed to be the Off-limits Section. Something was telling him that this was a good place to start. Call it intrigue, a hunch, gut feeling, magical intuition (or a combination of all these), Alfie felt sure there was more than books hidden behind that door.

He tried to open it and, as expected, it was locked.

'You must have done something wrong when you mixed your potion,' a familiar voice said, 'because I can see you clear as day.'

Alfie turned to see Melissa standing there. With her arms folded across her chest, she was looking him up and down, shaking her head.

Alfie felt like his heart had jumped into his throat. 'I haven't taken it yet.'

'Why?'

'Because I'm not somewhere I'm not supposed to be ... yet,' Alfie said. 'And keep your voice down. Remember where we are.'

'Of course,' Melissa replied. 'Nice and quiet. I'll be the mistress of whispers, if it makes you happy.'

'It will,' Alfie assured her. 'What are you doing here?'

'I want to see what you're up to ...'

'You know what I'm up to.'

'... and I want to make sure you don't get caught.'

'I won't get caught.'

'You better hope so. And if you're going to start searching the academy, I'd suggest you begin soon. The closer it gets to half-six, the busier this place will be.'

'I think what I'm looking for is in here,' Alfie said, motioning towards the door. 'I think this is the Off-limits Section.'

As if in response, from behind the door, there came a tapping sound.

'I heard that noise before,' Alfie said. 'When I was standing here with my mum.'

'A ghost?' Melissa said. She pulled a face and her red lips stretched to a thin line of anguish.

'Hopefully not,' Alfie said. 'But there's only one way to find out. 'I may need your help opening this door, but I'll try and do it on my own first.'

'I haven't got a wand with me.'

'Neither have I. Keep an eye out. If you see anyone coming, let me know.'

Taking a step back, Alfie lined himself up with the door. He focused on the lock. He concentrated with all his might. It turned out to be easier than he'd expected. There was a click as the lock disengaged. And then Melissa moved forwards and opened the door.

'I don't know anyone who could do that so fast,' she said in awe. 'There's plenty that wouldn't be able to do it at all. Not without a wand.'

Grasping the handful of change in his pocket, Alfie gave it to Melissa.

'What do I want with this?' she said, looking at the change in her palm. 'Is this a gift? Ah, you shouldn't have. You're so kind.'

'Just look after it for me, so I don't jangle about while I'm invisible,' Alfie said, walking past her, entering the room. 'And keep an eye out. Make sure no one comes in.'

'What about Mr Pendred? I can hardly say no to him.'

'It doesn't matter; he won't be able to see me.'

'But he'll know something is wrong if he tries the door and it's unlocked.'

'If you see him coming, give a knock. Then move away. There's no point you getting in trouble.'

Reaching into his pocket, Alfie pulled out the vial and removed the stopper. He swallowed the contents and winced. Then he put the empty vial back in his pocket.

'It's bitter,' he said, wiping his lips. He shuddered from the after-taste.

'I can hear people coming,' Melissa said. 'Go on, get yourself in there before you vanish in front of someone.'

'Or throw up.'

Alfie went through the door. He shut it behind him.

The room he found himself in was like a miniaturized version of the main library: less than half as long and half as wide. There were three aisles, instead of seven. The middle one was marked: Dark Magic. Intrigued, he moved forwards and noted some of the titles on the spines of the books: *A History of Dark Wizards*; *Dark Magic – All You Need to Know*; *Potions for the Wicked* …

Alfie went to grab the potions one, then reconsidered. There was no time for browsing books. Not when he was somewhere he shouldn't be. Continuing along the aisle, he reached the end of the room and paused to look through a window.

Alfie had expected to see a garden of some description, with a housing estate beyond. What he saw instead took his breath away, quite literally. Nearest to the rear of the academy was a cobblestoned courtyard, with stone archways that gave onto a neatly-trimmed lawn (*I bet they fly the broomsticks above there*, he thought). Beyond this was a scrubland area, populated with bushes, tangles of weeds and other low-lying vegetation. And beyond that, past an expansive wooded area, Alfie could see white-tipped mountains in the far distance.

'Whoa!' he said, taking it all in.

Tap, tap, tap …

Looking to his right, Alfie noticed an old-fashioned typewriter with a plain sheet of paper protruding from the top. The typewriter was set on a small table, which had a pile of paper beneath it. Next to this set-up was a giant metallic door with a dial on the front and a handle set above it. He knew a walk-in safe when he saw one. Once, on a school trip, his class had visited a manor house and there'd been one in the cellar. *Well*, Alfie thought, *if you're going to hide something and want it to be secure, what better place than a safe.*

Tap, tap, tap ...

Alfie stared in disbelief as the keys on the typewriter began to go up and down. Words appeared on the paper. A short, curt warning: **Please get out.**

A sliver of goose-flesh ran down Alfie's spine. He stared, slack-jawed, at the typescript, wondering what to make of it.

It's a ghost, he thought – *it's a ghost that's doing that.*

Tap, tap, tap …

The keys went up and down again. And another message appeared: **Not a ghost.**

Looking down at himself, Alfie realised something – he wasn't invisible. If he could see himself, then so could anyone else. Had the woman from the The Enchanted Cove given him the wrong potion? Or was it just slow to work for some reason?

Alfie remembered what Mr Pendred had said to one of the parents during the first lesson: *We have a telepathic typewriter called Doris. Would that be magical enough for you? You can use her, if you like?*

Alfie had thought that Mr Pendred had been joking. Apparently, he had not.

Are you telepathic? Alfie thought. *Can you really read minds?*

Tap, tap, tap …

Yes.

More tapping ...

And I can also see invisible people.

Alfie's mouth dropped open in surprise. So the potion had worked, after all. He assumed that he must be able to see himself, but others could not. Apart from Doris, of course; she could see him. Clear as day.

'Do you know the combination for the safe?' Alfie asked Doris.

Yes. But I'm not giving it to you.

'Why?'

You're smart, Alfie Trotter. Figure it out for yourself.

'It's because only certain people are allowed in there, isn't it?'

There you go; I told you you were smart.

'Are you going to tell him that I've been in here?'

There was a pause before Doris gave her reply.

If you leave now, I'll forget I saw you. I'm here to protect what's in this safe against serious threats. You, little boy, are not a serious threat. You're just … curious, mischievous, poking your nose where it doesn't belong. Are you still here?

'I just want to know what's in there, that's all. Something called the Stormbringer?'

I know you want to know what it is, but it's nothing that concerns you. You obviously don't understand the concept of "LEAVE NOW".

'Okay, okay, I'm going,' Alfie said.

Just as he was about to leave, however, there was a knock at the door.

Someone's coming, he thought, looking for another way out. But there was no other way out. Then Alfie remembered he was invisible, so it didn't matter. All he would do, he decided, was wait until whoever was coming had left, then get out of here. But Doris had told Alfie to "LEAVE NOW" (the capital letters emphasizing the sternness of the warning). No time to worry about that. Alfie would just have to hope that the typewriter appreciated his predicament and didn't rat on him.

Hearing the door open, Alfie positioned himself at the far end of the middle aisle so he could see who had entered: Mr Pendred and another man who Alfie recognized – Mr Langford. Alfie watched with intrigue as he wondered what his pot-bellied maths teacher from school was doing here at the academy.

'Hmm,' Mr Pendred said, looking puzzled, 'I'm *sure* I locked this door.'

'You think someone's been in here?' Mr Langford said, looking along the aisles to see if anyone might still be lurking. He was wearing black robes: standard academy issue.

'It seems so,' Mr Pendred replied. 'I'm not one hundred percent certain, but there's an easy way to find out.'

He's going to ask Doris, Alfie thought, panicking. *He's going to ask her and she's going tell him. Then I'll be expelled …*

Mr Pendred and Mr Langford disappeared from view, making their way along the aisle to Alfie's left. So Alfie focused his attention on Doris, trying to convey the message: *please don't tell them, please don't tell them, please don't tell them …*

As he was doing this, however, he noticed that the piece of paper with her side of the conversation they'd had was still protruding from the top. Mr Pendred would only have to read a few lines and he would *definitely* know there was an intruder. And then, in the blink of an eye, the paper disappeared. Alfie breathed a heavy sigh of relief and thought: *thank you*.

Then Mr Pendred and Mr Langford came into view. Mr Pendred's first concern was the safe. He turned the dial, as if doing this would yield some clues.

'All seems secure,' he said, happy enough. He turned his attention to Doris. 'Any intruders since I was last here?'

A sheet of paper from the stack beneath the table floated into the air, then loaded itself into the typewriter.

Tap, tap, tap …

No, came the reply. **All has been quiet, sir.**

'Old age must finally be getting to me,' Mr Pendred said, shaking his head.

Alfie could see from the look on his face that he still had doubts, though.

'I wouldn't worry about it,' Mr Langford said. 'It's is still in the vault and that's all that counts.'

'Best check to make certain,' Mr Pendred said.

With a quick twirl of his fingers he turned the dial on the safe to the left, then the right, to the left, once more to the left, then to the right again. He pulled the handle and the metal door opened with a squeak. Both men stepped inside.

Alfie couldn't see well enough from his vantage point, so he edged forwards, careful to be as soundless as possible. As he was doing this, he kept an eye on Doris, wary that she might type a warning. About a metre away from the entrance to the safe, Alfie stopped and watched as Mr Pendred picked up a thin, narrow, box off one of the many shelves that lined the walls. Opening it, he pulled out what looked to be a wand. There were other boxes on the shelves and curious-looking things. But it was a purple jewel, displayed on a stand, that caught his eye. *That's got to be worth a lot*, he thought. Alfie wondered which item Mr Pendred was so eager to protect: the wand or the jewel (or both? Or something else?). Alfie assumed it was probably the jewel, just because it looked expensive.

'There you go,' Mr Langford said, 'nothing to worry about; the Stormbringer is exactly where it should be.'

'I'll worry less when it's away from here and with Ullin,' Mr Pendred said.

'You think it will be truly safe with your friend?' Mr Langford said. 'Renwald tracked it here, so who's to say he won't find it again. Surely the most secure place is here, under lock and key, protected by the most powerful wizard I know.'

'Whether or not I'm the most powerful wizard or not is debatable,' Mr Pendred said, clearly not comfortable with having that title bestowed upon him. 'What is not debatable is that the wand cannot stay at the academy. I can't stay here twenty-four hours a day, every day, protecting it. He will wait for the right moment and then he will strike. Him and his followers.'

So it's the wand that needs protecting, Alfie thought.

'This safe is protected by hexes cast by yourself, is it not?' Mr Langford said to Mr Pendred. 'Ones that identify friend or foe?'

'Correct.'

'And there's Doris, too. With her on guard, that's double protection.'

How on earth is a typewriter supposed to stop anyone stealing anything? Alfie thought. He looked at Doris and willed her not to respond: *please don't type a reply ...*

'Renwald will get past any obstacles I put in his way,' Mr Pendred said. 'They will only slow him down. The only true way to protect the Stormbringer is to move it around. Keeping it in one place is foolish. As you know, it cannot be destroyed. Such was the power of the magic that forged it.'

'The bottom of the ocean is the best place for it, in my humble opinion.'

'Even at the bottom of the deepest trench, at the bottom of the deepest ocean, someone would find it, because it radiates so much power.' Mr Pendred held the wand out for Mr Langford to hold, but Mr Langford just looked at it apprehensively.

'Here,' Mr Pendred said, continuing to hold the Stormbringer out. 'It won't hurt you.'

Mr Langford took it. Then he shuddered.

'Ooh, I felt that,' he said.

'The tingling sensation?'

Mr Langford nodded. 'Like electricity through my fingers – a static shock.'

'*Yes*,' Mr Pendred said, his voice a purr. 'You get used to it, eventually.'

'I'm sure I would,' Mr Langford said, placing the wand back in the box.

Mr Pendred placed the box back on the shelf, then both men walked out of the safe.

Alfie backed up a few steps.

'Powerful as it is,' Mr Langford said, 'that wand is more trouble than it's worth.'

'Agreed,' Mr Pendred said. 'Which is why it is where it is.' He closed the huge metal door, then turned the dial back and forth a few times. 'Thank you for agreeing to teach the lesson for me, Graham. And apologies for asking at such short notice.'

Alfie remembered back to the conversation he'd overheard between Charles and Mr Pendred. He recalled snatches of what'd been said: *Not many people are aware that it's being kept at the academy … Graham wouldn't betray you like that. He's a friend of yours, sir. He teaches here at the school sometimes, so I really can't see that being the case …*

Alfie hadn't been aware that Mr Langford's name was Graham. He'd always known him as Mr Langford (as he knew other teachers as Mr this and Mrs that). Everything made sense now.

The only question was, of course, who had ratted about the location of the wand? Alfie was sure that he could rule out Mr Pendred, who was determined to keep the Stormbringer out of the clutches of someone called Renwald (another wizard?). Then there was Charles, who Alfie hadn't known that long. Prior to a few weeks before, Alfie had only spoken to him a few times in passing. But he had been so nice to Alfie since enlisting him at the academy. And he'd saved Alfie from a beating at the hands of Ryan Salter. This did not seem like the actions of someone who would want to help an evil wizard get his hands on a powerful wand. Mr Langford had also saved Alfie from a beating by Salter. He had always been nice to Alfie, going above and beyond to help him with his school work, so he didn't seem a likely candidate for devious shenanigans. This just left Ullin and some others who were helping him out. Alfie had no idea who Ullin was, but he did know that he had given the wand to Mr Pendred to look after. If Ullin wanted the wand to fall into the clutches of Renwald, wouldn't he have just given it to him? Why bother with the charade of handing it to Mr Pendred and then giving away its location? That just didn't make sense. The only possible solution Alfie could think of was that it must be one of Ullin's trusted helpers. The question was, who? Since Alfie had no idea who any of them were, there was no point giving this any further consideration. Not at the moment, anyway. Not until he'd gained more information about what was going on.

Mr Pendred was now telling Mr Langford what to teach in tonight's class.

'We were due to have flying lessons this evening, but you can do something else, if you wish. The students will be disappointed, because they always look forward to it. Just tell them we'll do it next week, instead.'

'I don't mind flying,' Mr Langford said. 'It's been some years since I rode a broomstick and I know I'm a bit on the weighty side,' he tapped his portly belly with the palm of his hand, 'but I don't like to disappoint – and I'm up for it.'

'Thank you for agreeing to cover for me while I take care of some business,' Mr Pendred said, giving his stand-in a pat on the shoulder. 'I'll leave things in your more than capable hands.'

'It's always a pleasure to teach one of your classes,' Mr Langford went on. 'The students here are a dream to deal with compared to some of the scallywags at Eldon Road.'

Looking down at himself, Alfie wondered how long it would be before he became visible. The woman at The Enchanted Cove had told him the potion was good for about fifteen minutes. Alfie wasn't sure how long he'd been standing here and he didn't want to just suddenly appear out of nowhere. Not only would he be in trouble, but Doris would also be in trouble as well. Mr Pendred would know she'd been covering for Alfie. So, with this in mind, Alfie edged quietly backwards. He hid down the aisle at the far end. Then he listened as the two men talked to each other as they exited the room.

'I would still like to know how Renwald found out that Stormbringer is being kept here,' Mr Pendred said.

'Well, as I told you before, I had nothing to do with that. You said yourself that someone would find the wand, even if it was at the bottom of the ocean, because it emits so much power.'

'I wasn't accusing you, Graham, and I apologize if I've offended you. But I had to ask. You understand that, yes?'

'Of course, of course. Along with you, I'm not the only one who knows it's here, though.'

'Charles would never betray my trust.'

'Are you certain of that?'

'*Absolutely* certain.'

'As unlikely as it sounds, there's always Ullin to consider.'

Alfie heard the door open and close. The sound of a key being inserted into a lock, then turning. Mr Pendred and Mr Langford's voices faded away ...

Let's just hope I can get out of here in a minute, Alfie thought, *when the coast is clear*.

Tap, tap, tap ...

Doris was typing a message again, so Alfie went to take a look.

Don't worry, I'll let you out.

'Thanks,' Alfie said in a low voice. 'I keep forgetting that you're telepathic.'

That's one of my many talents.

Alfie was curious what those talents might be. But he didn't ask and Doris didn't offer to tell him.

'Am I still invisible?' Alfie inquired. Then he remembered that the typewriter could see him anyway (this was one of the other talents she'd mentioned, Alfie realised).

I can still see you but others cannot. I'd advise getting out of here while this is still the case.

'Oh, okay, yes – good idea.' Alfie went to leave, but before he did he thanked Doris once again for not ratting on him.

Not a problem, came the reply. **Don't let me see you in here again, though. Next time I might not be so accommodating (unless you've got permission to look in the Off-limits Section, of course :)).**

The smiley made Alfie smile.

As he walked away he glanced over his shoulder and saw that the piece of paper that'd been in the top of the typewriter had already disappeared. Reaching the other end of the room, Alfie heard a click and assumed it must be the lock disengaging. As it turned out, it was. He opened the door a little. Just enough so he could peak out. He couldn't see anyone, so he slipped back into the library and closed the door behind him. *Click!* The lock re-engaged. Then Melissa appeared, holding a book titled: *Palm reading – a Handy Guide*.

'What took you so long?' she said quietly.

Alfie looked down at himself. 'It's must have just worn off,' he said, also keeping his voice low, 'because Doris told me I was still invisible.'

'Doris?' Melissa said, looking perplexed. 'Who's she?'

'Remember when Mr Pendred mentioned that he had a telepathic typewriter?'

'Yes. I assumed he was pulling our legs.'

'He wasn't; he really *has* got one and I've just been speaking to her. Well, not actually speaking to her. I spoke and she typed out responses. It's her job to protect the safe and make sure no one tries to break into it.'

Cocking her head to one side, Melissa regarded Alfie with a disbelieving look.

'Now is not a time for jokes,' she said. 'I thought you'd get caught when Mr Pendred went in there.'

'I'm not joking. She *is* in there and she *is* telepathic.'

'Whatever you say, Alfie. Like a typewriter is going to be able to stop anyone from doing anything anyway.'

'I think she's capable of doing a lot more than you'd expect.'

Alfie glanced down the middle aisle to see if anyone else was about.

'Everyone's gone to class,' Melissa said, 'so we've got the room to ourselves.'

'Did you see who Mr Pendred was with?' Alfie said. 'Mr Langford from school. From what I could gather, he covers for Mr Pendred when he's got things to sort out. So Mr Langford is a wizard. Who would have thought it?'

Melissa did not seem surprised at all.

'You knew?' Alfie said.

'My dad is friends with him; they go bowling together on Saturdays.'

Alfie once again found himself wondering how many witches and wizards were out there in the world. Some probably walked past him every day and he didn't realise.

'Life is full of surprises at the moment,' he mused.

'Life is always full of surprises,' Melissa said. 'Now tell me what happened in there? Are you any closer to finding out what you want to know? Or did you just risk getting expelled for nothing?'

Alfie explained about the safe and what was inside. 'Somebody called Renwald is trying to get hold of it and that's why Mr Pendred is so eager to move it. Do you think Mr Pendred would leave Doris guarding the wand if she wasn't capable of protecting it? No, I don't think so either. Have you heard of the Stormbringer? And what about Renwald, have you heard of him?'

'Who hasn't heard of them.'

'Erm, me. And only me, it seems.'

'Haven't your parents told you anything about the history of magic? About the Realms?'

'Nope,' Alfie said, shaking his head. 'I didn't even know I was magical until a few weeks ago. If it was down to my dad I wouldn't even be here. I'd still think I was an odd boy who could do odd things. Unnatural things.'

'Look, I'll tell you anything you want to know,' Melissa said, making sure there was still nobody else in earshot, 'but we need to get out of here first.'

She gave Alfie his change back and he pocketed it.

As she led the way, Alfie said, 'Were you just pretending to read that book, or are you taking it with you?'

'I picked it up and pretended to read it when I saw them coming. As luck would have it, I've been looking for a good book about palmistry. We'll be learning about that, you know. Plus, I thought it might look less dodgy if I carried something out with me. Perhaps you should grab one, too.'

'I would but I'm at my limit of four.'

'We don't have to log them out, so how is anyone going to know you've borrowed more than four?'

'Maybe Doris will be able to tell; she is telepathic, after all. Or maybe one of the ghosts will appear out of nowhere and scream like a banshee if you try and get a fifth book past the door.'

As they were about to leave the library, Alfie paused in the doorway and said, 'Are the ghosts *really* real? Have you seen one?'

'I haven't, because I'd never been to the academy before the first lesson. But my mum has. When she was studying here, she saw a few. This place has been here for hundreds of years, from what I can gather. I think the ghost that most people see is of Mr Keward, who ran this place before Mr Pendred. You'll know if you run into him, because he's got wild eyes and a shock of white, grey hair. Looks *verrry* scary, apparently.'

'The slightest glimpse of him and I'm out of here.'

'I wouldn't be too concerned. Most old buildings have ghost stories attached to them and this one's no different. What you need to remember is that ghosts can't harm you. My mum says that if you do see one, it's just a snapshot from the past. She used a word ... oh, what was it ...' Melissa snapped her fingers together. 'Residue – that was it. Basically, what that means is that when someone dies in a place that was special to them, a part of their being remains there, even after they're gone. My mum also said that it's not the dead you should worry about; it's the living. Because they're the ones who can hurt you.'

'I'd still rather not see a spook, thank you very much.'

'Never mind that, anyway. Let's get out of here before someone takes an interest in us.'

Passing the classroom, they heard Mr Langford talking about broomsticks and how safety was paramount when riding one.

'Oh, man,' Alfie said, exiting the building with Melissa, 'I can't wait to ride a broomstick. Have you ever been on one?'

'A couple of times, yes. With my parents supervising me, of course. The problem is visibility. The academy is the only place you can practice without fear of being spotted by non-magical folk.'

'How come?'

'The airspace above and around the academy has been enchanted so no one can see us when we're up there.'

At the side of the building, Melissa tucked the book under her arm. Then she went to the pink BMX and wheeled it away from the wall.

'That's yours?' Alfie said, surprised.

'It sure is,' Melissa replied. 'Why, is there a problem with that?'

'No, it's just that … you don't often see a girl with a BMX. It's kind of cool.'

'I'll show you some bunny hops in a bit, if you want? When we're clear of here.'

'You might just be the coolest girl I've ever met.'

Glancing skywards, Melissa said, 'It's gone very overcast. Looks like it's going to tip it down in a bit, so we better get moving.'

Alfie remembered what the woman from The Enchanted Cove had said: You should have worn a coat, it's going to come down heavy in a bit. *How could she have known?* he thought. Then a single word popped into his head: magic. *She's probably got some sort of enchanted barometer, which tells her what's happening with the weather.* Alfie decided that, if this was the case, he would get himself one of those devices, because it would be a useful thing to have.

Alfie walked with Melissa as she cycled slowly down the driveway. Through the gate they went and down the road.

When they were a safe distance away from the academy, Alfie stopped and said, 'So who is this Renwald and why does he want the ...' he clicked his fingers together, trying to remember the name of the wand. 'The ...'

'Stormbringer.'

'That's the one. What's the big deal with it? I mean, I get that it's a powerful wand – *the* most powerful one – but what does he plan on doing with it, exactly?'

Melissa had a second to herself before she replied. She looked like she was deep in thought, wondering how best to explain everything to Alfie. Then she said, 'Our existence, the world we live in – it's not the only one ...'

'I know that,' Alfie replied, interrupting. 'I've read books about the universe and everything. I know all the planets in the solar system and that there are stars and planets millions of miles away from us. But what's that got to do with this Renwald guy and the Stormbringer?'

'Has anyone ever told you that it's rude to interrupt someone when they're talking?' Melissa said, looking annoyed.

'Erm, my mum has – on quite a few occasions. Sorry, it's a bad habit. Carry on. I'll keep my gob zipped until you finish, I promise.'

Melissa breathed deeply, composing herself. Then she resumed. 'As I was saying, there is another world beyond this one. A magical place with knights and castles, kings and queens. A place that's as dangerous as it is beautiful. A place where fantastic creatures and beasts exist: ogres, trolls, giants, dragons, amongst others ... Oh, and witches and wizards, of course. You can't have a magical world without those, now, can you?'

Not sure whether he should respond, Alfie looked at Melissa and waited to see if she would continue. He didn't want to say something, only to be accused of interrupting her again. Best to keep quiet. *Safer* to do so.

And then she did continue. 'Kordoba consists of five Realms. The west is controlled by King Greyhawk. The east belongs King Sandford. The north is the stronghold of King Faverham. And the Southern Realm, which is as big as the other three combined, is home to King Godfrey, who commands largest army. And for a good reason. Because beyond the Southern Realm lies the Darklands, which is where the evil wizard Renwald is from. His one burning desire is to rule all the realms, which is why he wants the Stormbringer.'

'Crikey,' Alfie said, feeling a little overawed by all this information. 'You're not joking, are you? This place really does exist, yeah?'

'I'm not joking,' Melissa replied. 'It *definitely* exists.'

'But how would he get here? How would Renwald get to our world to steal the Stormbringer?'

'My guess is that he'll use an Emoruld: a rare gem that allows someone to travel between worlds.'

'What does it look like, this stone?'

'It's purple – about the size of a baby's clenched fist.'

'Oh,' Alfie said, 'I think I saw one of those in the safe, on a shelf.'

'Really?' Melissa said, looking surprised. She thought about it for a second, then didn't seem surprised at all. 'Well, I suppose it's only fitting that the most powerful wizard in the land should own one. I wonder if he uses it to travel to Kordoba, or if he just keeps it locked away so others can't.'

'I was just about to ask you that.'

'My parents have educated me well about magical history and all aspects of the craft, but I don't know the answer to that one, I'm afraid.'

'I know someone who would know. But he won't tell me.'

'Who's that?' Melissa asked, intrigued.

'Remember Charles from the first lesson?' Alfie said. 'The boy who was helping Mr Pendred?'

'Yes, of course; I know him quite well from the after-school chess group that I go to sometimes. He lives on Welbeck Road, not far from me.'

'Do you know what number? I might not see him at school tomorrow and I'd really like to talk to him. I'll probably be wasting my breath. It's worth a shot, though.'

Melissa mulled this over, then said, 'I'm not sure which number, but his house is on the left if you come in from the Casterton Avenue end. You can't miss it – it's the only one that has an extension on the side. What do you want to discuss with him?'

'*Everything!*' Alfie said. 'I want to know all about the Emoruld stone and how Mr Pendred came to own it. I want to know how to get to Kordoba. Does it just whisk you off to this place when you hold it, or do you have to say some magical words as well? If so, what are they? I want to know who this Ullin guy is and how he came to be in possession of the Stormbringer. And then there's Renwald. How did he rise to power and why is he so determined to control all the Realms? I'm sure there's other stuff I'd like to mention, but that's all I can think of on the spur of the moment.'

'Whoa! *Whoa!*' Melissa said, tucking her book under her arm and making a time-out gesture. Look, as far as the Emoruld is concerned, you don't have to say any magical words, I'm quite sure. It just allows you to pass through a portal that leads to Kordoba. All the other stuff you're blabbing about, I can't help you with – I'm just as clueless as you. Why are you so fixated on these things and so determined to get involved in something that doesn't concern you? If you're planning on somehow trying to get to Kordoba, then you're out of your mind. It's not Neverland, you know. It's a place full of dangerous creatures and warring factions. You've already risked enough by entering the Off-limits Section without permission, Alfie. So why would you want to take things to a whole new level of silliness?'

'Because it sounds like … fun. And I think it would cool to go to this place. Just to have a look around, if anything. The first sign of trouble and I'd be out of there, believe me.'

Melissa shook her head in disbelief. 'Well don't expect me to help you out, because you're on your own with that one.'

'I haven't asked for your help. You mentioned a portal. Where would I find one of those.'

'You've just been to one. The only one. The academy.'

'The academy is a gateway to another word?' Alfie said, amazed. This threw up a whole load of new questions, far too many for him to process. He felt like his brain was going to explode with all the information he was learning. 'How can that be? Is there a special room or something?'

'The gateway – entrance – whatever you want to call it – is at the rear, beyond the lawn area and through the trees. My mum told me all about it. Back in the old days – we're talking hundreds of years ago, here – they used to have student outings to Kordoba. How cool is that?'

Uber cool, Alfie thought, stunned into silence.

Looking skywards, he felt drops of rain dapple his cheeks. The branches of nearby trees rustled, swaying back and forth as the wind began to pick up. Alfie watched leaves skitter along the pavement while he mulled over what Melissa had said. *Maybe she's right*, he thought. *Maybe I am being silly.* But he was still determined to speak to Charles. Determined to try and worm any information out of him that he could …

'It's going to belt it down in a minute and it's getting dark,' Melissa said, 'so I'm going home.'

'Okay,' Alfie said. 'Well, I'll see you tomorrow at school, yeah?'

'Yes,' Melissa replied, cycling away, 'I'm sure you will.'

Alfie remembered that she was going to show him some bunny-hops. He went to shout after her. But before he could, she disappeared around the corner, out of sight.

Then the rain starting coming down heavy, so Alfie forgot about bunny-hops and anything to do with magic. He just took off, running as fast as he could with the change jingling in his pockets. By the time he got home he was soaked. And his mother was suitably angry when he traipsed wet footprints through the hallway.

'How many times have I told you to take your shoes off in the porch!' she seethed.

'Sorry,' Alfie apologized, stomping back into the porch and kicking off his trainers.

'I take it you didn't see anything at the shop that caught your eye.'

For a moment Alfie thought she was talking about The Enchanted Cove. He was about to ask her how she knew he had been there, then he remembered he'd told her that he was going to the toy shop.

'Your pockets are still full of change,' Mrs Trotter went on, 'so I'm assuming there weren't any Lego kits that caught your eye.'

'There were some, but nothing I could afford.'

'Thought that might be the case. Make sure you put that money back in your piggy-bank, otherwise it'll end up all over the place.'

'I will,' Alfie assured her. 'Is my dinner still in the microwave?'

'It is,' Mrs Trotter said. 'But first you need to get out of those wet clothes. Go on, upstairs. You're dripping water all over my carpet.'

Alfie bounded up the stairs and into his bedroom.

'Oh,' Mrs Trotter called after him, 'and remember that it's your school trip tomorrow, so you don't need to go in your uniform.'

Alfie had forgotten all about that. He and his class were visiting Whitewood Farm in Earlsfield. This was a trip that he'd been looking forward to for some time: if only so he could spend a day away from school. A farm didn't sound like the most interesting of places, but it would be a lot more interesting than maths or English, he was sure.

Alfie emptied his pockets of change out onto his bed, along with the empty vial that'd been filled with invisibility potion. He tucked it underneath his mattress, out of sight. Then he studiously inserted the coins back into his piggy-bank, each one making a hollow thud as it hit the bottom. When Alfie was done, he got changed. Downstairs, at the living room table, he gulped his dinner down – chips, sausages and beans – like he hadn't eaten for a week. And all the time, as he chewed on each mouthful, his thoughts were of the Stormbringer and the Emoruld and Kordoba ...

CHAPTER 6
(The Enchanted Cove - Revisited)

The following day, when Alfie was on his way to school, he kept an eye out for Charles. But he didn't see him. During breaks and at dinnertime, Alfie kept an eye out for him. But he didn't see him. It wasn't until home time that he finally caught a glimpse of him, walking across the field at a brisk pace.

'Hey!' Alfie shouted. 'Wait up! I want to talk to you!'

Charles looked over his shoulder, but he kept moving.

'*Hey!*' Alfie shouted again. Louder, this time. '*I want to talk to you!*'

'Sorry,' Charles called back. 'I haven't got time – I'm in a rush.'

With that, he broke into a jog and then a sprint with his Adidas bag bobbing about on his back. He disappeared across the field and was out of sight before Alfie could even contemplate chasing after him. Alfie wondered if he would have time to visit Charles at his house. "Persistence pays off" was a phrase that Alfie's father liked to use. But Alfie was going to The Enchanted Cove with his mother this afternoon, so he was sure there wouldn't be time. *You are going to tell me what I want to know*, he thought. *One way or another, I'll worm it out of you.*

####

Pulling onto Thurland Street, Mrs Trotter parked her VW Beetle outside The Enchanted Cove and Alfie looked out of the passenger side, admiring the mural on the front of the building.

'Check out the dragon and castle,' Alfie said.

Mrs Trotter leaned over him to get a better look. 'That's good, isn't it?' she said in awe. 'The dragon is swooping down for an attack. I would not want to get in its way – it looks *hungry*.' Something in the front window of the shop caught her eye and she pointed. 'Ooh, there's a Dreamcatcher; I got one of those on holiday once, when me and your father went to Tenerife. It's that wooden hoop that has spider-like webbing inside of it.'

'What's dangling from the bottom?' Alfie asked. 'Are they feathers?'

'That's right,' Mrs Trotter confirmed. 'Feathers and beads, to be precise. North American Indians used to hang it above where they sleeping. The webbing in the middle is supposed to catch the bad dreams and let the good ones through.'

'Does it work? Have you still got it?'

'Well, I can't recall having any nightmares while it was above mine and your father's bed, so maybe it does. It might be in the garage, or we might have thrown it away.'

'If it isn't in the garage, can I have one?'

'I think we're going to be spending enough money today without factoring in anything else, don't you?'

'Okay,' Alfie said, his voice full of disappointment.

'Come on,' Mrs Trotter said, throwing her handbag over her shoulder as she got out of the car, 'let's get in there and relieve my purse of some weight.'

Alfie made sure he'd got his list and followed his mother into the shop. The bell jangled above the door as they entered, then they stood around waiting for someone to serve them. When no one appeared, Alfie picked up a porcelain statue of a Raven perched on a rock. He gave it a quick once-over, then he put it back.

He wondered if the woman from yesterday would be serving again today. If so, would she recognise him and ask him how he'd got on with his invisibility potion? That would put him in trouble with his mother. And, of course, the questions would begin. Why did you lie to me? What do you want with an invisibility potion? What mischief have you been getting up to this time, Alfie Trotter?

On a shelf marked **DIVINATION**, he saw some purple stones in a bowl. They had strange yellow markings. Scooping some up, he asked Mrs Trotter what they were used for and what divination was.

'I'm as clueless as you,' she said.

'They're Runes,' someone said. 'And they can be used to tell the future.'

Alfie recognised the voice and wasn't surprised to see the woman who'd served him the day before. This time she was dressed in colourful robes as she appeared from the rear of the shop, shuffling into view. Her round face brightened as she laid eyes on her customers. She looked at Alfie for a second, a glint of recognition flashing across her face.

Please don't dob me in, he thought. *Please don't dob me in …*

And she didn't.

Alfie focused his attention on the runes. 'I'm pretty sure I need these,' he said, scanning down his list to make sure. 'Yep, I do.'

'Ah, you must be Mrs Tippings,' Mrs Trotter said to the woman.

'I am, indeed,' Mrs Tippings said with a warm smile. 'Guilty as charged.'

'Mr Pendred had nothing but good things to say about you,' Mrs Trotter said, 'and your shop is every bit the wondrous cavern we thought it would be.'

'Thank you very much,' Mrs Tippings said. 'You'll be in good hands with Mr Pendred. His academy is the finest in the area – perhaps the country – and his students are always *very* welcome here.'

'There are more academies around here?' Alfie said.

'Of course,' Mrs Tippings said. 'There are two not far from here: one in Billingforth, near Derby, and one not far from Newark, in Gosford. Plus countless others scattered throughout the country – and the rest of the world. There are more wizards and witches than you realise, young man. You probably pass some in the street every day and you don't even realise it.'

'You have lots to learn,' Mrs Trotter said to Alfie.

'Indeed he does,' Mrs Tippings said. 'So let's set him on his way.'

Alfie held the list out to her. 'Do you need this?'

'No-no-no,' Mrs Tippings replied with a brisk shake of her head. 'Honestly, I don't know why Mr Pendred bothers handing those out. His students have been coming here for years, so I know *exactly* what they need. You're in the beginners' class, I take it?'

Alfie nodded. Then he folded his list up and put it in his pocket.

'Let's start with the easiest things first,' Mrs Tippings said. 'Follow me, please.'

She led them to a section that had clothing rails full of black robes. Then she looked Alfie up and down, her eyes wide and disk-like behind her glasses.

'A size five, I think,' she said pulling some robes off one of the rails and handing them to Alfie. 'Here, try this on. I'm usually good at guessing, but I have been known to get it wrong.'

Alfie pulled the robes over his head and they fit perfectly.

'Well that's that sorted,' Mrs Tippings said. She gave Alfie another set of robes, then disappeared and returned with a cauldron. 'Medium sized: made from quality cast iron.' Placing it on the floor, she removed the lid and showed them what was inside. Two books: *Potions for Beginners* by Charlie Pepwick and *Entry Level Spells* by Miranda Clutterbuck.

Alfie placed the runes and both sets of robes in the cauldron and Mrs Tippings put the lid back on. 'Follow me, please,' she said again, leading them to the rear of the shop: to a stand that had broomsticks displayed on it.

'Now,' Mrs Tippings said, 'as a beginner you're allowed either a Grade 1 or slightly faster grade 2.'

'Can I have the faster one?' Alfie asked his mother.

'Depends on the price difference,' she replied.

'The Grade 2 is twenty-five pounds more,' Mrs Tippings said. 'They're both excellent broomsticks, though. Very sturdy. Good for learning on.'

'You're going to bankrupt me and your father at this rate,' Mrs Trotter said to Alfie.

'Does that mean I can have the quicker one, Mum?' Alfie said.

'Yes,' Mrs Trotter said, giving Mrs Tippings a look of resignation.

Mrs Tippings gave Alfie one of the Grade 2s and he stared at it in awe, admiring the red lightening bolt that ran its length.

'Don't even think about trying to fly that thing around in the back garden,' Mrs Trotter said to him. 'You fall off it from high up and you'll kill yourself.'

His eyes brightened as a cunning smile spread across his face

'I mean it, Alfie,' Mrs Trotter warned. 'Disobey me once on this and I'll … I'll burn that broomstick, I swear.'

'You wouldn't dare!' he said.

'Oh, I would,' Mrs Trotter said. 'You've been warned.'

'Your mother speaks wise words and you'd do well to heed them,' Mrs Tippings said. 'I believe we have one more thing to sort. The most important thing: your wand.'

She showed them into a side room, which was full of shelves with wands displayed on them. Some were long and thin, others were shorter and thicker. Alfie wondered what the difference could be. A wand was just a wand, wasn't it? You pointed it at something, said some magical words and …

'It's important that we find the right one for you,' Mrs Tippings said to Alfie, 'so you can maximise your power and reach your full potential. If I give you the wrong one, you may not be able to do the more powerful spells and even the easier ones will have less oomph. Hmm – now let me see, which one shall we try first.' She selected a thin one and handed it to Alfie. 'This one's made from hazel, give it a go. Which spells did you learn during your first lesson?'

'Just how to make fire,' Alfie said, resting his broomstick against the wall.

'Oh,' Mrs Tippings replied. 'Better not do that one, then. Don't want the shop burning down, now, do we.' She caressed her chin with her finger as she thought of a spell Alfie could try.

'There is another one I know,' he said.

'What's that?' Mrs Trotter asked curiously.

'When I met Charles at the lake, he showed me how to make things shake.'

'That will do,' Mrs Tippings said.

She disappeared from the room, then returned with a green, leafy plant and a wooden stool.

'This is a Lucky Bamboo,' she said, placing the plant on the stool in front of Alfie. 'It's meant to bring the owner health, wealth and good fortune.'

'And does it?' Mrs Trotter asked.

'I would like to think so,' Mrs Tippings replied. 'I have one at home and I'm doing just fine.'

'I'll have one of those,' Mrs Trotter said.

'So we can't afford a Dream-catcher, but we can afford a Lucky Bamboo,' Alfie said.

'Just get on with what you're supposed to be doing,' Mrs Trotter said to him.

Raising the wand, Alfie pointed it at the plant and tried to remember the magical words. Then he said, 'Excutite Wancadum!'

And … nothing happened.

Shoulders slumping, Alfie looked on in despair. A sigh of frustration slipped out of him.

'It's Wincantum, not Wincandum,' Mrs Tippings said with an encouraging smile.

Composing himself and taking a deep breath, Alfie raised his wand again, then said, 'Excutite Wincantum!'

And … this time it worked. But only just. The leaves on the plant shook a little and then were still.

'Hmm, clearly not the one,' Mrs Tippings said, taking the wand from him and handing him another, which was shorter and thicker. 'Made from willow, this one. Give it go – give it a go.'

This time, when Alfie cast the spell, the leaves shook vigorously – then the plant shot off the stool and hit the wall, spraying soil everywhere. The pot it was in shattered to pieces and the plant itself hit the floor with a thump.

'Oh dear,' Mrs Tippings said. '*Definitely* not the one.' She looked along the shelves, taking some time to decide which wand Alfie should try next. 'Ah-hah!' she exclaimed, picking one up and handing it to him. 'Oak – long and slender – could do the trick.'

As Alfie took the wand, his fingers began to prickle. 'Whoo!' he said. 'That was like a static shock.'

'That's a good sign,' Mrs Tippings said. She disappeared from the room and returned with another Lucky Bamboo. She placed it on the stool, then stepped aside.

Alfie said the magical words and this time he made the leaves shake with a good rustle.

'Superb!' Mrs Tippings exclaimed, clapping. 'I think we've found the one.'

The bell jangled, signalling that someone else had entered the shop.

Alfie heard a girl say, 'I'm not going to find a wand in here that's as good as mine.'

A woman replied, 'I'm sure you won't, dear.'

Alfie recognised the girl's voice. *Great*, he thought, *Amelia – why did she have to come in here now, while I'm being served?*

'Sounds like I've got more customers,' Mrs Tippings said. 'Are you happy with that wand, Alfie? You look happy.'

'I am,' he replied, clutching it tightly and savouring the smoothness of the wood.

'Bet you feel like a real wizard now, don't you?' Mrs Trotter said to him.

'Not quite,' Alfie replied. 'I've got a lot of training to do before I feel like a *real* wizard.'

'Were you serious when you said you wanted a Lucky Bamboo for yourself?' Mrs Tippings asked Mrs Trotter.

'As long as it's not too expensive,' she said.

'They're only eight pounds,' Mrs Tippings said. 'And they do bloom with lovely flowers.'

'Plus it might bring us some luck,' Alfie pointed out.

'Oh go on then,' Mrs Trotter said.

Mrs Tippings gave her the one off the stool.

'It can be kept in water or soil,' Mrs Tippings said. 'Anything else you need to know, just read the label on the side. It tells you everything about caring for it.' She regarded the plant by the wall with a sorrowful glance. 'I'll have to re-pot that and hope for the best.'

'*Service!*' Amelia called out. 'Hullo! Is anyone at home! *Serviccce!*'

'Impatience is not a virtue I have much time for,' Mrs Tippings said, looking ruffled.

Alfie picked up his broomstick.

Mrs Tippings led him and Mrs Trotter back to the front of the shop, then to the till.

'I remember you from class,' Amelia said. 'Is that your new wand? What's it made from? It looks like oak.'

'It is,' Alfie said proudly.

Wrinkling her nose in a disdainful way, Amelia opened her mouth to say something, but Mrs Tippings cut her off. 'It is indeed an oak,' she said. 'And it's every bit as good as that willow one that you're holding, my little miss. The power comes from the wizard or witch, not the wand. Always remember that.'

But what about the Stormbringer? Alfie thought. He assumed this must be an exception to the rule.

Amelia looked towards her mother for support, but she was browsing the shelves, picking things up and examining them.

Mrs Tippings fingered the keys on the till and it opened with a *ping!* She said to Mrs Trotter: 'That comes to one hundred and eighty-five pounds and forty-seven pence, please.'

Opening her purse, Mrs Trotter pulled out a wad of money, removed a twenty pound note, then handed the rest to Mrs Tippings.

'Well that was less than I thought it would be,' Mrs Trotter said, looking relieved.

Mrs Tippings gave her some change. 'Just check you've got everything before you go, won't you,' she said.

Alfie put his broomstick and wand aside. He went to where he'd left the cauldron, then removed the lid and checked inside. Everything he needed was in there, as far as he could see.

'Are we set, then?' Mrs Trotter asked him. 'All accounted for?'

'Yes,' Alfie replied. 'All accounted for.'

Mrs Tippings bid them good day and thanked them for coming to her shop.

Mrs Trotter said that it'd been a pleasure and that they would no doubt see each other again, probably when Alfie enrolled for the intermediate level at Pendred's.

On the way out, Alfie smiled at Amelia and was surprised when she returned the gesture (even though it looked like it was an effort to do so).

####

When Alfie arrived home, Eddie was first to greet him at the door.

'You've got it all, then,' he said, eyeing the things that Alfie and Mrs Trotter were carrying into the hallway. 'A cauldron? Aren't creepy old witches supposed to have those?'

'You've been watching too many b-grade horror movies,' Alfie replied. 'All witches and wizards have them. I'll show you one of the books I borrowed from the academy library and you'll see the nifty potions I can make.'

'Do not go getting up to any mischief!' Mrs Trotter warned, placing the broomstick against the wall. 'I mean it, you pair. Don't even *think* about it.'

Eddie put a hand on his chest, feigning insult.'Mischief? What, me and Alfie? As if we would.'

'You've been warned,' Mrs Trotter said, disappearing into the kitchen with her bamboo plant and placing it on the sideboard.

'Another thing you'd expect a witch to own,' Eddie said, picking up the broomstick and giving it a once-over. He whispered to Alfie: 'You've gotta take me up on this when you've learnt how to ride it, yeah?'

'Now that *would* get us in trouble if we got caught,' Alfie said.

'*What* would get you in trouble?' Mrs Trotter said from the kitchen. 'I can hear you in here, you know; I'm not deaf!'

'I was just saying that we should be careful not to do anything that'll get us thrown in the doghouse,' Eddie replied, giving Alfie a wink.

'Of course you were,' Mrs Trotter said.

Alfie heard the clink of a glass being removed from the cupboard in the kitchen, then the sound of a tap being turned and water running.

'So what do you reckon to my wand?' Alfie said, showing it to Eddie.

'Looks like just a stick to me,' Eddie said.

'A stick with some very special powers,' Alfie said.

Eddie went into the kitchen and began talking to Mrs Trotter about some new clothes he wanted. Alfie caught the opening bit of what he was saying: 'If he's had all those things bought for him, does this mean I can get a new pair of trainers and a new top?'

Then Mr Trotter appeared from the living room. Dressed in stripy blue pyjamas with matching fluffy slippers, he had a cup of tea in one hand and a copy of the *Daily Mail* newspaper in the other. 'The power comes from the wizard or witch, not the wand,' he said.

Alfie found himself once again thinking of the Stormbringer and how it must be different to other wands. He wondered how this had come to be. More questions, questions, questions ...

Mr Trotter took in all of Alfie's new acquisitions. 'Brings back some memories, looking at that lot. I can remember being just as excited as you are, son. Perhaps even more so. Make sure you use it all responsibly.'

'I will,' Alfie assured him.

Mr Trotter went to go back into the living room. So Alfie asked him a question to try and keep him engaged: 'Can you remember any of the spells you learned when you were younger?'

'Of course,' he said. 'I used to have my favourites.'

'Can you show me some?' Alfie asked, not feeling hopeful.

Mr Trotter closed his eyes for a second, then exhaled deeply through his nose. When he opened his eyes, Alfie thought he was about to tell him off. But he didn't.

'You're not going to let this go, are you?' Mr Trotter said. 'One way or another, either directly or indirectly, you're going to keep pestering me until I get involved, aren't you?'

'He is,' Eddie said, chirping in.

Mrs Trotter came out of the kitchen, sipping from a glass of water. 'He certainly is,' she said. 'You know what he's like. I don't call him Mr Persistence for nothing.'

'You're right,' Alfie said, 'I won't stop pestering you. Not until you give me the support I need for my studies. It's not fair on Mum that she should have to take me every week. She's not the magical one. I'm sure I was one of the only ones there without a magical family member ...'

'All right, *all right!*' Mr Trotter said, holding his newspaper in the air, like a man at an auction who wants to place a bid. 'I can see how happy it'll make you, so we'll go together. We'll learn together and we'll practice *together*. Anything to stop you badgering me ... There, you've got what you wanted. Now can I read my newspaper in peace?'

He didn't wait for a reply. He just turned around and went back into the living room, pushing the door shut behind him.

'I don't want him to come just so he can stop me bothering him,' Alfie said, looking from Eddie to his mother. 'I want him to come because he *wants* to come and *wants* to see me learn.'

'Oh, Alfie,' Mrs Trotter said, giving his cheek an affectionate touch with her fingers, 'I think he does want to come; he's just not willing to admit it. Give him time and you'll see. Before you know it you'll be casting spells together and brewing potions.'

'And for the time being,' Eddie said, 'while you're waiting for Dad to get a grip, you can practice casting spells and making potions with me. Whaddaya say, bro?'

'*Eddie!*' Mrs Trotter said, giving him a playful clip round the ear.

Later that evening, whilst Alfie was lying in bed, he skimmed through the books he had borrowed from the academy library, squinting in the glow of his bedside lamp. Then he skimmed through the two beginner level ones he'd got from The Enchanted Cove. He wanted to read through all of them, every word, front to back. But he knew he wouldn't have time to read more than a few sections of one, so he decided to concentrate on the beginner level books as this would give him a head-start with his studies.

In *Entry Level Spells*, he found some spells that caught his eye. One allowed you to shrink things, so you could hide them. A friendship one made Alfie think: *I could do with using that on Leo.* And there was a dieting one which he was sure that his mother would be interested in (assuming he could find a way to tactfully tell her about it without getting a clip round the ear, of course).

In *Potions for Beginners*, Alfie found potions that peeked his interest. There was one that induced uncontrollable laughter (Alfie would love to have given a double-dose of this to Amelia). There was a hair-regrowth potion and Alfie could think of quite a few men who would benefit from that. But the potion Alfie was most interested in was the one that made someone tell the truth.

The first name that popped into his head was Eddie. He'd got Alfie in trouble quite a few times by telling porky pies: the most recent occasion being when Eddie had eaten all the cupcakes and blamed it on his younger brother. Eddie had owned up in the end, but only because Alfie had badgered him for days.

And then Alfie thought about Charles: *now there's someone who I could* definitely *use a truth potion on*. Not that Charles was lying to him, of course; he just wasn't telling Alfie anything about what was going on. Alfie pondered how he could get him to drink some truth potion. *I could try and sit with him during dinner time, then pour some into his drink*. But what if Charles noticed? What would happen? Would he tell Mr Pendred? Alfie decided that he would pester Charles one more time. Then, if that didn't work, he'd resort to more drastic measures.

The only problem was that the Stormbringer was being moved tomorrow and Alfie wanted answers before then. He had a feeling, a kind of intuition, deep in his gut, that something was going to go wrong. Alfie knew that the wand was being moved in the evening, between six and seven o'clock. He was due to return from his school trip at 3.45pm, so that would give him time to go to Charles' house, then get to the academy afterwards.

'I could do with more invisibility potion,' Alfie whispered to himself. He was sure that he would have time to pull in a trip to The Enchanted Cove. But he didn't think that Mrs Tippings would give him another pre-made vial again and he couldn't afford to buy the rare ingredient: Moonsickle Drops . What was it she'd said to him when he was last there?: I always keep some pre-made potions aside for my own personal use, but I don't normally give them to people, because I think you should make your own. Alfie wasn't confident that he'd be able to worm a pre-made one out of her (assuming she had more). Not for a second time. It was worth a try, though. The worst she could do was say no. Well, actually, that *wasn't* the worst she could do. She could start asking questions about why Alfie wanted to be invisible again. And if she did, he would just have to tell her that it was for private, *very* important business. This wasn't a lie, but not exactly the sort of response that would make Mrs Tippings part with any of her pre-made vials. It was the best lie Alfie could think of, though, so it would have to do.

Alfie placed his books by the side of his bed. He switched his lamp off. Darkness sucked in around him. A short while later, he fell into a deep, dreamless sleep.

CHAPTER 7
(The School Trip & the New Boy)

Alfie got up late in the morning. For some reason, his digital alarm clock hadn't sounded. Getting dressed as fast as possible, he slipped on a pair of jeans and yanked a Pokemon t-shirt over his head, then a Star Wars jumper (one of the great things about school trips was that you didn't have to wear a uniform). Alfie rushed downstairs to find Mrs Trotter eating toast in the kitchen.

'My alarm didn't go off,' he said, putting some Weetabix in a bowl and pouring milk over them. 'Why didn't you wake me up?'

'I'm in a bit of a rush, myself,' Mrs Trotter replied. 'I'm not your personal alarm clock. You're old enough to get yourself out of bed for school now, me laddo. And just for your information, I was going to give it five more minutes then give you a shout. I've made you a pack lunch, just in case you were wondering. Cheese and onion sandwiches. Plus there's a drink of Vimto and a banana. Will that be enough?'

'Yes, Mum, thanks.'

'I've put five pounds in your box, as well; just in case you want to buy something,' Mrs Trotter said, peering out the window. 'Oh, well, at least the weather looks like it's going to be nice. Check out that blue sky.'

By the time Alfie got to school, the coach was ready to go and Mr Langford looked like he was about to explode.

'What time do you call this?' he blustered, jabbing a finger at his watch.

'Sorry, sir,' Alfie said, walking past him with his head lowered.

'You're fifteen minutes late!' Mr Langford seethed. 'Another five and we'd have left without you! And then you'd have had to sit in the Headmaster's office all day, reading texts and writing reports!'

Alfie stepped onto the coach with the teacher's harsh words ringing in his ears. And Mr Langford wasn't the only one who was annoyed with him. As Alfie moved down the aisle, searching for a free seat, some of his classmates gave him dirty looks.

'Oversleep, didya?' one boy sneered.

'Getcha yourself seated, yeh numnit!' another one jeered.

Alfie saw Leo, but someone else was next to him.

'Over here,' Alfie heard someone say.

He looked to his right and saw Melissa. She put her hand up, so he shuffled along and plonked himself next to her.

'I see you're not winning any popularity contests again today,' she said, offering him a slight smile.

'Nothing new there, then,' he responded.

Along with Mr Langford, two other teachers were tasked with monitoring the children (classes 7a and 7b) on their trip.

Apart from being heckled because he was late, Alfie had a nice time. He got to see lots of different animals: ponies, donkeys, goats, cows, geese, chickens, pigs, deer, and llamas. Mr Langford advised caution around the llamas. He told everyone how he'd annoyed one when he was a kid and that it'd spat on him. Alfie enjoyed feeding the goats (even though they slobbered on his palm as they licked up the pellets). There was an adventure playground, too, which was a bonus. As Alfie was scaling the climbing frame with Melissa, he kept trying to catch Leo's eye. But Leo wasn't interested. Melissa noticed and asked him why they weren't speaking to each other.

'I haven't played with him much lately,' Alfie replied, shielding his eyes against the sun, 'and I think he's taken it personally.'

'Why haven't you been playing with him?'

'Ever since I learned that I'm a wizard, I've been too busy. What with enrolling at the academy and buying all the stuff I need and browsing through books and ...'

'Snooping around parts of the academy you're not supposed to be in and making yourself invisible and trying to find things like powerful wands and Emorulds and ...'

'Hey!' Alfie said, giving Melissa a playful punch on the arm. 'You did some snooping yourself, too, remember?'

'That was because you pestered me to. And I only watched out for you because I didn't want you to get in trouble. You need to make up with Leo. He's your best friend and you pair were inseparable until a week ago.'

'I will,' Alfie assured Melissa. 'I'll pop over and see him this weekend. And I won't stop pestering him until he comes around, even if it means I have to grovel.'

'From the looks Leo has been giving you, that may be what you'll have to do.'

'Yeah,' Alfie said. 'Anyone would think I'd kidnapped his pet Chihuahua.'

'You should never ditch your friends, Alfie; because you never know when you might need them.'

'That's the sort of thing my mother would say.'

'She sounds like a wise woman.'

'Oh, that reminds me,' Alfie said. 'I won't be coming with her for the next lesson, because my dad has agreed to take me.'

'That's great news,' Melissa said. 'How did you manage to persuade him?'

'Persistence pays off,' Alfie replied with a sly smile.

'Ah-hah! So you badgered him into submission.'

'I did indeed.'

'Sometimes it's the only way,' Melissa said, giving Alfie a knowing nod.

He looked skywards, turning his face towards the sun, relishing the warmth on his skin.

Then Mr Langford came striding into the playground, clapping his hands together and saying, 'Okay, okay, if you'd all like to make your way to the gift shop now please. That's it, come on – no faffing around, get those feet moving.'

In the shop, Alfie considered buying himself some packs of marbles, but he changed his mind when he saw a Nigella Lawson recipe book that he thought his mother would like. Mrs Trotter loved to cook and she was a big fan of Nigella.

'I'm guessing that's not for you,' Melissa said, peeking over Alfie's shoulder as he thumbed through the pages.

'You guess rightly,' he replied, taking the book to the checkout and parting with his five pounds.

For the coach ride back, Alfie sat next to Melissa again. Once they got onto an open stretch of road, he leaned to his left, resting his head against the glass. He stared blankly out the window, watching the countryside roll past: the fields of yellow and green; the thatched cottages and farmhouses; the narrow country lanes which spiralled into the distance.

Alfie found the steady motion of the coach quite hypnotic. So much so that he was falling asleep, his eyelids slowly shutting. But then Melissa asked him a question, which brought him round with a start.

'You're going to the academy tomorrow, aren't you?' she said, careful to keep her voice low. 'You're going to watch them move the Stormbringer ... aren't you?'

'I might be,' Alfie said groggily, giving Melissa a searching sideways glance.

'That's a yes, then,' she said.

'I guess it is,' Alfie admitted. 'And so what if I am.'

Melissa shook her head. 'I'm not even going to bother warning you not to do it,' she said, 'because you won't listen. You're the most pig-headed, stubborn person I've *ever* met, do you know that?'

'I'm hoping to get some more invisibility potion, but I don't like my chances. One of the ingredients is very rare and very expensive. I was lucky to get some the first time, so who knows, maybe I'll be lucky again. If I can get enough to make us both invisible, would be interested in coming to the academy with me. You won't get seen.'

'I told you that I wasn't helping you out anymore. If you want to get expelled from the academy, then that's your look-out. Just don't rope me in on it. I'm not interested.'

'Okay, okay,' Alfie said, wishing he hadn't involved Melissa in any way. 'I'll do it on my own. Just don't don't go asking me any questions tomorrow. Because I won't tell you *anything*.'

Melissa gave him a reproachful look. Then she folded her arms and turned away from him. Following suit, Alfie folded his arms and shuffled in his seat, showing Melissa his back. They didn't talk to each other for the rest of the journey. And when they arrived back at the school, Melissa got up and stepped off the coach without acknowledging Alfie. *I'm going to end up with no friends at this rate*, he thought.

But he didn't hang around worrying about this. He got himself off the coach and was making his way across the field at pace when he heard someone call his name, then issue an insult. Not bothering to stop, Alfie kept walking as he craned his neck around to see who was behind him.

Ryan Salter. And he wasn't alone. Two others were with him: Mason and the huge new kid that Alfie had noticed at the beginning of the week. From the aggressive looks on their faces and the rate at which they were closing on Alfie, he guessed they weren't wanting to have a friendly chat. So Alfie broke into a sprint. He out-paced Salter and the big kid with ease. He put some distance between him and them in no time at all. And Alfie would have got away if it hadn't been for Mason. No matter how fast Alfie ran, he couldn't lose Mason. Reaching the edge of the field, with his bag bouncing up and down on his back, Alfie made for the road in the hope that he could get home before he was caught. Every few seconds Alfie would look over his shoulder and see that Mason had gained ground on him. Until eventually, when Alfie reached the end of his road, he turned and saw Mason's grinning face bearing down on him. And then a hand seized Alfie by the shoulder and shoved him to the ground. Alfie grazed his hands on the concrete as he went sprawling.

'You're pretty fast,' Mason said, looming over him. 'But not fast enough.'

'What do you …' Alfie began to say, out of breath. 'What do you want now?'

'I don't want anything,' Mason replied. He pointed down the street, towards Salter and the other boy. 'They do, though.'

Snatching glances around, Alfie wondered if there was some way he could get away without Mason catching him.

'Just stay where you are, dumbo!' Mason advised. 'Things will work out better for you if you just *stay where you are.*'

Salter was the first to reach them. He looked as out of breath as Alfie felt. And then the big boy arrived, huffing and puffing.

'How rude!' Salter exclaimed. 'Legging it like that when all we want to do is introduce our new friend to you.' He gave the big boy a pat on the shoulder. 'This,' Salter said with a grin, 'is our new buddy. He's the newest member of our gang and his name's Harrison. He can crush a tin of beans with one hand, can't you Harrison?'

'With ease,' he replied, grinning down at Alfie through gapped teeth.

'Since this is the first time you pair have met,' Salter said, 'I think you should shake hands with each other. Because that's what you're supposed to do when you meet someone, isn't it?'

'It sure is,' Mason agreed.

'Can't we just say hello?' Alfie said, trying to sound light-hearted.

'What's up, don't you want to shake Harrison's hand?' Salter said. He put an arm around his big new friend. 'Don't you want to be buddies with him, Trotter?'

Alfie got to his feet. 'It's not that,' he said. 'It's just the whole can-crushing thing that's putting me off.'

People were walking past on the other side of the street. A man with a poodle, which was pulling at the leash because it'd spotted a cat. A young couple were merrily bouncing along, too busy giving each other lovey-dovey smiles to notice what was happening with the boys. Alfie wondered if any of them would come to his aid if he asked them for help.

'Be nice,' Salter said to him, 'and shake hands with Harrison.' He waited a few seconds, then added: 'I won't ask you again.'

A surge of anger ran through Alfie. *If I concentrate hard enough,* he thought, focusing his attention on Salter, *I could HURT you.* And then what would happen? Salter's friends would most likely run away, screaming. Then, at school, the following day, they would tell everyone how Alfie had used his powers to attack them. And then what would happen? Every kid in school would be afraid of Alfie and no one would want to come near him. Eddie would get wind of this and so would Charles (and so would Mr Langford, come to think of it). Which meant that Mr Pendred would surely get wind of what'd happened, as well. This, of course, would be bad. *Very* bad.

'Looks like he doesn't want to be friendly,' Harrison said, cracking his knuckles.

'I do!' Alfie said, offering his left hand.

Harrison grinned, then he took the offered hand and clasped it so hard that it made Alfie screech in pain.

'Okay!' Alfie said, grimacing. 'You can let go now!'

But Harrison didn't let go. He squeezed harder. And he grinned harder. And this time it was Alfie's knuckles that cracked. He wilted to one knee, trying as hard as he could to escape Harrison' grasp. It was no good, though; the big boy was just *too* strong.

'Your brother really thinks he's something. doesn't he?' Salter said, going to one knee beside Alfie. 'He *really* thinks he's some sorta tough guy, doesn't he?'

'He was just … *protecting me!*' Alfie screeched. Along with the pain, he could feel a tingling sensation in his fingers as the blood began to leave his hand.

'Do you know what he did to me?' Salter asked. 'Did he tell you?'

'No! No … he didn't!'

'Now why don't I believe you. I bet you pair had a right laugh about it. Well, you're not laughing now, are you? Hanging me from a tree trunk by my pants! Do you know how long I was up there before some man helped me down? Must have been thirty minutes, at least! I couldn't sit down for an hour after that, 'cause my bum was red raw.'

'*I'm sorry!*' Alfie said, grimacing more than ever. '*Really, I am sorrrry!*'

But he wasn't. Not in the slightest.

Alfie summoned every bit of strength in his body as he tried to free himself from Harrison's death grip. Alfie could feel anger surging inside of him again. Boiling up like a column of hot steam. Any second now he was going to erupt and something bad would happen. He looked up at Harrison, focusing his energy, his *power*. Harrison's eyes widened and his stone-like expression started to crack. His grip loosened.

That's when a fist crashed into the side of Alfie's face. And the world around him began to swim, colours dancing across his vision …

How am I going to explain this? Alfie thought, caressing the lump that was forming beneath his left eye as he walked home – *Mum and Dad will go ballistic!* And Eddie, too. Alfie realised that his brother would want revenge and he didn't like the idea of him messing with Harrison. Eddie was tough, no doubt about that. But Harrison was too big, even for him.

One thing was for sure, though: Alfie needed to get in and out of the house quickly. If any of his family noticed his face, then that would be it. No way would his parents let him go out again after that. Not this evening, anyway.

With his shoulders slumped and his head low, Alfie hurried along Burrow Street, hoping none of the neighbours would notice him. He slunk into the house as quietly as he could, leaving his bag in the hallway. He could hear the TV on low volume in the living room, so he tip-toed up the stairs and into his bedroom. Not wasting a second, he emptied the contents of his piggy-bank onto the bed, then filled both of his pockets with coins. Back down the stairs Alfie went, into the hallway (he was careful to put his hands over his pockets to stop the coins jingle-jangling). He opened the front door to leave ...

And that's when Mrs Trotter called out, 'Is that you, Alfie? Are you off out already?'

'Yes,' he replied. 'I'm ... going to Leo's again. I won't be late.'

'But what about your dinner! I'm cooking sausage, chips and beans. It won't be the same warmed up in the microwave.'

Alfie heard the springs clink as Mrs Trotter got up off the settee. He heard slippered footsteps as she walked towards the hallway.

'I don't mind it warmed up,' Alfie said, slipping back out through the front door and closing it behind him before she came into view.

Alfie set off down the road without even so much as a backwards glance. Even after his run-in with Salter and his cronies, Alfie still sure that he had plenty of time to get to The Enchanted Cove before it shut. The swelling beneath his eye was becoming more pronounced now. Just touching it with his fingers made Alfie wince in pain. He wanted to see what he looked like, so he stopped next to a row of terraced houses and checked out his reflection in one of the windows.

'Oh, that's not good,' he said, feeling more and more deflated.

Then a face appeared on the other side of the glass: an old man scowling at him. This made Alfie jump. He was already on edge because of what'd happened and what was going to happen this evening, so this he could do without.

The old man opened a side sash and said, 'Can I help you?'

'I'm sorry,' Alfie apologized. He explained what he'd been doing and the old man's initial look of worry turned to one of concern.

'Now that *is* a nasty lump you've got coming there,' he said. 'What happened to your face, son? Have you been scrappin'?'

'Not exactly scrapping, no. More like being used as a punch bag.'

'Bullies, eh?'

'Yup,' Alfie said, nodding.

'All bigger than you, I bet?'

'Yup.'

The old man's bloodshot eyes narrowed as he said, 'They always say that the best way to deal with these sorts of things is to fight fire with fire, which is a bit of a daft suggestion, don't ya think? I mean, who ever put a fire out with more fire, eh? No, what ya gotta do is dowse those flames – extinguish 'em! Violence just breeds more violence, so you've gotta use this ...' he tapped a gnarled finger to the side of his gnarled head, 'and outsmart 'em. You get me?'

'I do,' Alfie replied. 'So how do I outsmart them?'

'Good question. And I have no idea. But you're a smart boy; I can tell just by lookin' atcha, so you'll think of summink. I'll tell ya somethin' for nothin', though; it's the leader ya need to take care of, ya get me? 'Cause there's always a leader in a gang and if you can put him in his place, the others'll be wary of yeh.'

'I thought he already had been put in his place,' Alfie muttered.

'Sorry,' the old man said, cupping a hand to his ear, 'whadja say?'

'Nothing,' Alfie said. 'I was just thinking out loud. I will put the leader in his place. Somehow, some way.'

'That's the spirit,' the old man said. 'Now go home and get some ice on that eye of yours; it'll bring down the swellin'.'

'I will,' Alfie said, lying. There was no time for that. The sooner he got to The Enchanted Cove, the better, as far as he was concerned.

He once again apologized to the old man for suddenly appearing at his window and startling him. The old man told him it was okay – not a problem – and that he'd had much worse scares in his life.

As Alfie walked to the shop, he wondered what he could do to Salter – without badly hurting him – that would prevent another ambush. He couldn't think of anything, though. Not off the top of his head. This didn't bother him, however, because he was sure something would come to him. And he was sure of something else, too: that it would involve magic.

Arriving at the shop, Alfie went inside. The bell above the door jangled, sounding his entry. Mrs Tippings was sitting behind the counter, knitting something or other, the needles in her hands dancing a merry a jig – up and down, up and down. She looked up, over the top rim of her glasses …

'My word,' she said, her face aghast, 'what in the name of the Lord has happened to you?'

The lump beneath Alfie's eye had bloomed to a red, swollen pillow and was beginning to blacken over. He flexed the fingers of the hand that Harrison had crushed and was relieved when it didn't hurt. No bones were broken, which was something, Alfie supposed. His hand was just a bit sore, that was all.

'Have you had an accident, or has someone beaten you up?' Mrs Tippings asked.

'I tripped over. Hit my face on a lamppost as I was going down.'

'Oooh, I bet that hurt, you poor thing,' Mrs Tippings said with a pained expression on her face.

She put her knitting aside and went to Alfie so she could get a closer look. 'Have you been to the Walk-in Centre? Has a nurse or doctor examined you?'

Alfie shook his head. 'No.'

'You could have a concussion. Especially if you hit your head on a lamppost. Have your parents seen the state of you?'

Questions, questions, questions, Alfie thought. 'No.'

'Don't you think you should go home? You've obviously come here because you need something, but what's more important than your health, young sir?'

'I, erm, was wondering if you had any more of that pre-bottled invisibility potion? Now I know what you're going to say: that I should make my own and that it's the only way I'll learn and that one of the ingredients is rare and expensive, but ...'

Mrs Tippings held a hand up, halting Alfie mid-sentence. 'You're right, making your own *is* the only way you'll learn. But I couldn't give you any more even if I wanted to, because I don't have any more.'

'Oh,' Alfie said. *Well that's that idea crushed*, he thought.

'What do you want it for? I want to know what's so pressing that you'd come here to get it before seeking medical attention or letting your parents see what a state you're in? Why are you hankering after more invisibility potion?'

'Err ...' Alfie replied. He tried to think of a plausible lie. He cursed himself for not anticipating that she would ask this question. The best he could come up with was: 'To have fun, scare my mates.'

'*Very* pressing,' Mrs Tippings said, not looking at all impressed. 'As I told you, though, I don't have any more to give you. The only Moonsickle Drops I had were used to make that potion, so I have nothing to give you.'

Alfie thanked her for her time, then turned to leave.

'Actually,' she said, 'I have got something for you. Wait here a second.'

She disappeared into the back room and Alfie felt his hopes rise. He was sure that she'd changed her mind: that she'd taken pity on him because of his accident and the nasty swelling beneath his eye. And in a way he was right; she had taken pity on him. But not in the way he had hoped.

'Here, take this – on the house,' she said, giving him a vial full of potion. 'Swallow it in one quick gulp. It'll bring the swelling and bruising down. You should still see a doctor, though; because you really may a have a concussion and I haven't got anything made-up that can help you with that.'

Mrs Tippings seated herself behind the counter again and picked up her needles. She resumed knitting. After a few seconds, she looked up over the rim of her glasses and said, 'Are you still here?'

'I really appreciate what you've given me,' Alfie said. 'That's the second time you've gifted me a free potion.'

Mrs Tippings smiled. 'I don't normally give stuff away free. You caught me in a good mood the first time and I could hardly let you go home looking like that, now, could I. Yes, giving potions away for free is not good for business, so don't expect this to be a regular thing. Now, if you don't mind, I want to get this top finished by tonight. It's my niece's birthday tomorrow and I'm sure she'll love this; she's been asking me to knit her one for a long time and I don't intend to disappoint.'

Alfie thanked Mrs Tippings for the potion, said goodbye, then slipped the vial into his pocket.

'Well that didn't go as I'd hoped,' he muttered as he left the shop.

He got walking, knowing now, more than ever, that he would have to be careful in the hours ahead. Without the potion he would be visible to anyone and everyone, which meant there was a much greater risk of being spotted.

Thinking ahead, Alfie tried to formulate a plausible explanation for him being at the academy this evening (he was determined to be better prepared than he had been for his trip to The Enchanted Cove). But the academy wasn't open to students on Fridays, so the gates would most likely be locked. This meant that Alfie would have to use his magical willpower to once again open them. So what possible explanation could he give for being on academy grounds on a non-student day? The answer was simple: none. It would be obvious what Alfie was up to, should he get caught. *Better not get caught then*, he thought with determination.

He was in no rush. Mr Pendred had told Mr Langford that the Stormbringer was being moved between six and seven o'clock, which gave Alfie plenty of time to get to Charles' house and then to the academy. So he walked along, lost in his thoughts.

Twenty-five minutes later, he rounded the corner that took him from Casterton Avenue onto Welbeck Road. Melissa had said that Charles' house would be on Alfie's left if he approached from this end and that he couldn't miss it because it was the only one with an extension on the side. And she was right; Alfie spotted the house straight away.

Alfie noted there was a red Ford Fiesta on the driveway, which meant someone could be home. He also noted something else: that the downstairs curtains were drawn, despite it still being daylight. He made his way down the driveway, then knocked on the front door. The top half of the door was filled with obscure glass. Alfie could see the hallway beyond. He waited a few seconds, but there was no sign of movement yet and no noises in the background. *No Oboe barking and jumping up*, Alfie thought. *Charles is probably out walking him somewhere.* Alfie knocked again: this time giving the glass a good rap with his knuckles. And he waited again. But still he heard nothing. He was just beginning to think no one was home when a loud *thud* from upstairs made him jump. *Ah-hah!* he thought. *Either someone* is *home, or there's a poltergeist on the loose.*

Kneeling down, Alfie called through the letterbox, 'Hullo! I know you're in there, so there's no point hiding!'

But there was no response.

He called through again, '*Hullllo!* I'm not deaf, you know; I heard the bang. What happened, did you knock something over? There's no point hiding now – you may as well come down, 'cause I'm not going away 'till you do!'

No response.

It suddenly occurred to Alfie that he may have been presumptuous. He'd assumed it was Charles upstairs, but what if it wasn't? What if it was one of Charles' parents. Maybe his mum had just stepped out of the shower and been startled enough to knock something over when she'd heard Alfie calling through the letterbox. Or perhaps Charles' dad had been taking a nap on his bed and had sprung up like he was spring-loaded, then fell out of bed. Then Alfie decided it couldn't be either of Charles' parents because they would most likely be at the door by now, telling him off for causing such a ruckus (or at least someone would have called down, shouting something along the lines of: 'Who in the blue blazes is making all that noise!). But no one had come to the door or called down, so Alfie concluded that it must be Charles who'd made the noise.

Alfie said through the letterbox, 'I know you're in there, Charles. I'm not going away 'till I've talked to you.' When no reply came, he added, 'If you don't show yourself I'm going to start singing through your letterbox. It'll be painful to listen to 'cause I can't sing (or, at least, that's what Mum keeps telling me).' Alfie counted to ten, then thought of a song that would annoy Charles. And then it came to him. 'Okay, here it goes ...'

Alfie broke into a very shrill and out of tune version of *Let it Go*: the theme tune from the movie *Frozen*.

'All right, all right,' a voice called down, 'Just gimme a second, will you!'

Bingo! Through the letterbox, Alfie saw feet descending the stairs. Standing up, he backed away and watched as a figure approached through the obscure glass. Then Charles unlocked the door and opened it.

'Your mother is right,' he said. 'Your singing *is* painful to listen to ... Crikey, what's happened to your face?'

'I had a run-in with Salter and his mates. He's team up with a new boy in school, who just happens to be huge and throws a meaty right hook. His name's Harrison.'

'I've seen him around. Wouldn't want to mess with him.'

'I didn't want to, but they gave me no choice.'

'You need to do something about that situation, because it's only going to get worse. Who knows what they'll do to you next time.'

'I thought I *had* done something about it (or rather Eddie).' Alfie explained how his brother had hung Salter from a branch by his underpants.

Charles chuckled. 'Ha-hah – no wonder he's so out to get you.'

'Forget about my face and the school bullies,' Alfie said. 'I'll deal with that situation one way or another. How come you took so long to answer the door?'

'I had my headphones on,' Charles explained. 'I was listening to some heavy rock, so that's why I didn't hear you.'

'Really? So you weren't hiding?'

Charles shook his head a little too vehemently for Alfie. 'No, I wasn't.'

'I drank a magical potion, which means I can detect lies.'

Charles gave Alfie a doubtful look. 'I don't know of any potion that can make the taker detect lies. And I haven't taken a potion and I'm detecting one.'

'Ditto,' Alfie replied simply.

Averting his gaze away from Alfie, Charles took an interest in something along the road.

'Is it that obvious?' Charles asked.

'You're about as good at lying as my brother. So what was the bang? What did you knock over?'

'I've got a huge Darth Vader figure by my bed. I got up to close the door so I wouldn't have to listen to you going on and I caught my hip on his lightsaber.'

'So you're a Star Wars fan, eh? I hope you didn't break Darth.'

'He's okay. Still in one piece. I've got every figure and every vehicle there is to collect; I'm not ashamed to admit that I'm an obsessive fan.'

'I've got a few figures myself, but I've always been more into Lego.'

'Oh I've got Lego, as well. Star Wars Lego, of course.' Charles smiled, then said, 'Okay, enough of the small talk; how can I help you, Alfie?'

Charles was being to the point, so Alfie did the same. 'Why have you been avoiding me for the last week?'

'I haven't,' Charles replied. But there was no strength in his denial.

'Oh come on; every time I've tried to talk to you, you've scurried away like your bottom was on fire. Why?'

'I … I've had family issues I've had to deal with. I've fallen out with my parents. And don't ask me why, because it's private. To say that things have been stressful recently would be a bit of an understatement. I'm sure you understand.'

'No, I don't. You're still lying to me.'

'I'm *not* lying.'

'Not about the being stressed part; I believe you about that. And you might have fallen out with your mum and dad, but that's not why you're sweating. That's not why you've avoided me like I'm a leper. And that's not why you want to shut the door in my face. It's because of what's happening tonight, isn't it? It's because of what's Mr P. is trying to relocate?'

'You know about tonight, don't you? You know exactly what's happening?'

'I do,' Alfie confirmed.

Stepping out, Charles took him by the arm and led him inside, then into the living room. Because the curtains were closed, it was quite dark in here.

'Who told you?' Charles said. 'I know you were ear-wigging outside the door, because you've already admitted it. But who's given you specifics? Who's filled in the blanks?'

'Let's just say I did some snooping. I know about the Stormbringer and who you're so desperate to hide it from: Renwald – an evil wizard from Kordoba.

'You know about the Stormbringer and Renwald?' Charles said, looking more surprised than ever. 'Just exactly what sort of snooping have you been doing?'

'Let's just say it involved some invisibility potion and some more ear-wigging.'

'You've only just enrolled at the academy and you're creeping around the place like a ninja, poking your nose into things that doesn't concern you. You're messing in dangerous business, Alfie; you need to know that.'

'I *do* know that,' he said. 'And it's exciting, isn't it?'

Charles stared blankly at him, his mouth slightly open.

There was a red L-shaped settee in the corner of the room. Backing up and without even a glance over his shoulder, Charles slumped onto it like he was exhausted. He let out a sigh which sounded like a deflating tyre.

'Exciting,' Charles said, talking more to himself than Alfie. 'Exciting, he says!'

'Where are your parents?' Alfie asked as he walked around the room, picking up ornaments and looking at them.

'They've gone for a walk to visit some friends. Taken Oboe with them … No! *No!* Put that down!'

Alfie had picked up a framed photo off the mantelpiece above the fireplace. It showed a baby with the toothiest grin and wildest curly hair he'd ever seen. Charles snatched it from him and put it back, careful to place it exactly where it'd been before.

'That's my mum and dad's favourite photo of me,' Charles said. 'They'd go mad if it got damaged.'

'You were very cute. I wouldn't worry too much, though; I'm sure there must be a spell for fixing broken things … isn't there?'

'There is. Given how things have been going for me lately, I'd probably mess up the spell somehow and make things worse.'

Slumping into an armchair, Alfie made himself at home. 'Well, I'll agree not to touch anything else if you tell me why you've been avoiding me. And don't say that I already know, because I don't. There's something else you're not telling me. You've looked worried and been on edge all week. Way too worried and on edge for this Stormbringer business to be the only thing that's stressing you. I mean, it's not like you're having to do anything to get rid of it. Mr P. is taking care of everything. Am I right in thinking you won't be at the academy when the wand is moved?'

Charles confirmed that he wouldn't. 'But that doesn't mean that I'm not concerned that something will go wrong.'

'A little too concerned for my liking.' Alfie mulled things over for a few seconds. 'Unless ...' he said, clicking his fingers together, then taking an educated stab in the smog. 'Unless you *know* that something's going to go wrong. Is that it? There's going to be an ambush. You know about it, but you're not going to warn Mr Pendred. Why?'

Charles did not reply.

'My mum always says that silence speaks volumes. Are you going to spill? I'm staying rooted in this chair until you do.'

'You can stay rooted as long as you like. Or until my parents get back and they tell you to leave. My father is not someone you want to annoy, though. Just thought you better know that. And Mr Pendred might like to know about this conversation. I'm sure he'd be interested to hear what you've been up to.'

Charles' threat didn't worry Alfie. 'You're not telling anyone anything. You've been up to no good yourself and I'm sure it's not something you'd want Mr Pendred to find out about. Or anyone else, for that matter.'

'You have no idea what you're talking about.'

'No idea? Oh, I think I have. It's got something to do with this Renwald guy and the Stormbringer being moved this afternoon. I was right when I guessed that he knows everything, wasn't I? That's why you didn't deny it. And you haven't told Mr Pendred. So I'll ask you again – why?'

This time it was Charles' turn to slump into an armchair. He looked lost for a few seconds, like he didn't know what to say. Then he put his head in his hands and erupted into tears. 'I had no choice!' he blurted. 'He was going to harm my parents, so I had *no choice!*' His shoulders hitched up and down as he continued to wail, tears streaming through his fingers.

Springing up out of his seat, Alfie went to him. He put a hand on Charles' arm and could feel how much he was shaking.

'You need to calm down and tell me everything,' Alfie said. 'Every little detail. A problem shared is a problem halved and all that.'

He gave Charles a moment to get himself under control.

Slowly, the crying and hitching began to subside – until, finally, he looked up at Alfie and nodded. 'Okay,' he said, his eyes glistening. 'Every little detail.'

Alfie went back to his armchair and seated himself. Then he listened.

'O-kay,' Charles said, taking a deep breath and explaining: 'You're not the only one who likes sneaking around and being places you're not supposed to be. Until a few weeks ago, once or twice a week, I'd turn up early so I could access the library and browse the books. Or, at least, that's what I wanted people to think I was doing. Except it wasn't really books I was interested in – it was the Emoruld. Other than Graham, I'm the only other person who's entrusted with a key to the Off-limits Section. Getting past Doris wasn't a problem; she knows who's allowed into the safe and who isn't ...'

'But she's telepathic, so she'd know what you were up to' Alfie interrupted. 'When she saw me, she knew immediately what my intentions were. And I was invisible, too. Yet she could *still* see me.'

'She can do a lot more than you'd think. Her primary job is to guard the Stormbringer. She obviously didn't think you were a threat. And she was right, wasn't she? You weren't there to steal the wand, were you? You were just nosing around.'

'I was.'

'Anyway, where was I? Ah, yes – the Emoruld. D'you know what they're used for?'

'You hold one and it allows you to enter some magical place. I can't remember what it's called ... Kormoda ... Korboda ...'

'Kordoba.'

'That's it! Melissa told me about that place. You know her from school, don't you? She's in my class. Got curly blonde hair and a spring in her step. She knows you.'

'I've said hello to her a few times.'

'She says that Kordoba is a fantastic place full of magical creatures, wizards and witches, knights and fantastic creatures.'

'It is. And it's a dangerous place, as well. I've been there many times, so I should know.'

Alfie remembered Melissa saying the same thing: that it was a dangerous place.

He shuffled forwards in his seat, all ears.

'I remember the first time I went there,' Charles said with a wistful look on his face. 'About four months ago, this was. I came to the academy early one study night, because Mr Pendred had given me permission to look in the Off-limits Section. I was trying to find a rare book about ancient magical practices that somebody had recommended (Mr Pendred was sure he'd seen it in the History Section, but he wasn't certain). I turned up at half-five, on the dot. I'd never been in the restricted area and I was determined to make the most of it. But when I arrived at the academy, I couldn't find Mr Pendred anywhere. He's usually either in the classroom, preparing for the lesson, or he's in his turret office, sorting paperwork. After about five minutes of searching, I gave up and went to the library. The door to the Off-limits Section is always locked, so you can imagine how surprised I was when I saw it open. I didn't know there was a safe in there. One of those big walk-in ones. The door to it was open, as well. Then I noticed Doris on a table nearby, which struck me as strange. I'd seen her before, in Mr Pendred's office. He dictates letters to her without even having to speak.'

'She scared me silly when she read my thoughts and started tapping out responses onto a piece of paper.'

'Yes, it can be unnerving to have your thoughts read, but you can guard against this. You'll learn how as part of the advanced level training. And she did start tapping out messages when she saw me. Mr Pendred was in the safe and she was trying to warn him that I was there, but he just told her that he'd be with her in a minute.'

Hearing the gentle screech of brakes and the sound of a car pulling onto a driveway, Charles got up to investigate. 'It's okay,' he said, pulling back the curtains and looking relieved, 'it's just next door. I forgot that my parents didn't take the car.' He seated himself again. 'At first Mr Pendred had his back to me, so I couldn't see what he was doing. Then he turned around and I saw it: the Stormbringer. I've seen pictures of it in books, so I recognized it straight away. I don't know of any other wand that's that long and gnarled. He had forgotten that he'd given me permission to be in the Off-limits Section. It's the only time I've ever seen him look worried.'

'And I'm guessing that's when you saw the Emoruld.'

'You guess correctly. It was just sitting there on one of the shelves, all pretty and pink. As with the wand, I knew exactly what I'd laid eyes on. Anyone but the newest of beginners to magic knows what an Emoruld looks like. And anyone but a newb would know what it was for. There were other curiosities in the safe, but Mr Pendred didn't seem concerned about me seeing those; it was the Stormbringer he was concerned about. And that was when he confided in me, telling me all about it and how it'd come to be in his safe. You see, the wand emits so much power that it leaves a trace. Think of a slug when it moves around: how it leaves a gooey trail, which eventually fades. But that's not the only problem with the Stormbringer. Because it emits so much power, it acts like a homing beacon. Wizards and witches are drawn to it like a moth to a flame. And this is why the wand is moved around all the time and it can never be kept in one place for too long. Mr Pendred told me that he'd been in possession of it for six months (which *was* too long, he said with some degree of urgency). Previously, a wizard named Ullin from Kordoba had been looking after it.'

'I remember that name from when I was ear-wigging outside the classroom door. Mr P said that he wasn't ruling anyone out when it came to who'd given away the location of the wand. Which brings us back to what you were saying before. You said you had no choice and that someone had threatened to harm your parents. Would I be right in thinking that that someone is Renwald?'

'Yes,' Charles confirmed sullenly. He looked tearful again as he began to explain: 'When you pass through the portal, it brings you out near a village called Albernay. On my first trip to Kordoba I kept well clear of that place and I didn't venture far. Some of the Albernay men look quite scary and I was sure they wouldn't greet a stranger warmly (especially one dressed in weird clothes). It was on my third visit that I got a bit braver. I heard a lot of shouting and cheering coming from the village, so I went to investigate. Keeping myself hidden in the trees, I saw some children sword-fighting with sticks. It was nice to see them playing. They were whacking each other quite hard and even the girls were joining in. I was so engrossed in watching them that I didn't notice someone sneaking up behind me. I heard a twig snap, so I turned around and saw a girl – very pretty, with long, flowing red hair – just standing there by a tree. She looked at me and I looked at her. I was sure she was going to scream or call for help, so I got ready to run. But she didn't scream or call for help. She asked me why I was dressed so funny and I couldn't give her an answer. So she just looked at me again and I looked at her. Then I finally found my voice. I asked her what her name was and she said Hulda. She asked me what my name was and things just went from there –'

'You've got a girlfriend from another world?'

'Yes,' Charles said, blushing slightly in the dimness, 'I guess I have. But that's not what I'm trying to tell you. Whenever I go to Kordoba, I hang out with Hulda and we talk about stuff. She's told me all about her world and I've told her all about ours. She got me some clothes to wear, so I won't look so out of place, but I still stayed away from the village, because I knew no one would recognize me. We have this favourite spot where we sit, down by the lake. Hulda loves it there and I do, too. Sometimes we sit there for hours, talking and skimming stones across the water. What we didn't know was that Hulda's little brother, Godrick, had been spying on us for a while. He'd got curious about where she was going and followed her one day. We had no idea about this until Hulda got home that day and her father was waiting for her. Godrick had told him what he'd overheard us talking about;which wasn't good, because we'd been discussing the Stormbringer. When and where it was being moved from: times and dates, *everything*. Obviously I had no idea about any of this until I visited Kordoba again the following week. Hulda and I had agreed to meet by the lake, so I began to get concerned when she didn't turn up. I waited at our usual spot for fifteen minutes, getting more and more worried as every minute passed. I was just about to set off towards the village when *he* showed up – '

'Who?' Alfie said. 'The father?'

Charles nodded. 'Yes, *him:* Aldred.' Just muttering the man's name made Charles look like he'd swallowed a sour grape. 'He must have made her tell him everything: all about me and where I'm from. He told me that I was to stay away from his daughter and that he never wanted to see me again. He also told me that if he did ever see me again, I'd regret it. But that wasn't the worst of it. When he stepped aside, there was a man in black hooded robes standing behind him ... Renwald.'

'*Renwald?*' Alfie said, shocked. 'As in the evil wizard?'

'Yep – the one and only.'

'What was he doing there?'

'I can only assume that Hulda's father told him. What connection he's got with Renwald ...' Charles shrugged and shook his head, 'I have no idea. As for Renwald ... oh, man, he is the creepiest looking man I've ever seen. He's got these dark eyes that bore into you when he staring at you. And there's this smile that plays at the corners of his mouth, like he knows something you don't. Something that isn't good.'

'Did you run? I think I'd have run.'

'I was about to, but then he pointed his wand at me. He was about to cast a spell, so I told him that he better not kill me, because I had friends who knew where I was. Friends who would tell Mr Pendred that I was missing. That was only time I saw that smile falter, just for the briefest moment. Then Renwald said that Mr P. wouldn't know what'd happened to me: he'd only know I was missing. So I said that Mr P. would find out, one way or another. I pointed out that Mr P. isn't known as being one of the greatest wizards of all time for no good reason.'

'And what did he say to that?' Alfie asked, lapping up every detail of Charles' story.

'He thought things through for a second and obviously saw sense in what I was saying. Then he warned me not to say anything to Mr P. (or anyone else, for that matter). He told me that if I *did* give away the fact that he knows when and where the Stormbringer is being moved from, he'd kill my parents.'

'What, no! But how could he even know where you live?'

'I told Hulda the name of the street I live on and what our house looks like.'

'But even then,' Alfie said, 'Renwald would need an Emoruld to come into our world. And he'd have to pass through academy grounds, right under Mr P.'s nose. He wouldn't dare, would he?'

'He might have an Emoruld and he might not. But where my mum and dad are concerned, I'm not taking any chances. I feel like I've betrayed Mr P by not telling him, but what other option did I have? Family comes first and always should.'

Alfie felt thankful that he hadn't been put in such a difficult position. 'You shouldn't feel too bad about not telling him, because I'd have done the same. It's not too late to give him a heads up, though. He might know of a way that this can work out well for everyone but Renwald.'

Not even giving this suggestion a moment's consideration, Charles shook his head and said, 'No – no chances. I love my parents too much to risk their lives.' Clearly wanting to change the subject, he focused his attention on Alfie's ever-swelling eye. 'That's beginning to look quite nasty. You can get a potion that'll put you back right again.'

'I know,' Alfie said, producing the vial from his pocket and swallowing the contents in one bitter gulp, 'I've already got it. I went to The Enchanted Cove to get something and Mrs Tippings took pity on me. That's the second potion I've got for free.'

'And what do you plan on doing about Salter? He isn't going to stop terrorizing you just because he's given you a beating.'

'It was actually Harrison who gave me the beating, but, yeah, you're right, something has got to be done. The question is, what?'

Charles took a second to think things through, then he said, 'Sometimes, on Monday evenings, I go to the Westby Road Sports Centre to play squash. I always see Salter there, queuing to get into the main hall, so he can play football.' He smiled, his eyes glinting mischievously in the gloom of the room. 'Now, I know we're not supposed to use magic outside the academy (except under supervision), but I think this situation calls for a slight bending of the rules. I've got a plan.'

Shifting forwards in his seat, Alfie was all ears. 'I'm liking the sound of this already.'

Charles told him all about the plan. 'And he's always on his own when he walks home.'

'I'm *really* liking the sound of this,' Alfie said, grinning. 'So he leaves at seven-thirty, you say?'

'Yep. And we're gonna be ready, waiting for him.'

'Cool – uber cool.'

'Hey, you said that you went to The Cove for something. What was it?'

'Err ... nothing important.'

Charles gave him a suspicious look. 'Nothing important, eh? Why do I get the impression you're telling me fibs.'

'No, I'm not lying. I ... erm ... wanted to mix a skin potion that would make my mum look younger, but Mrs Tippings didn't have all the ingredients in stock.'

'You're about as good at lying as I am,' Charles said, not taking his eyes off Alfie. 'You may as well just tell me now, otherwise I'm just going to keep asking you until you do. You're not fooling anyone.'

Alfie considered continuing the facade, but couldn't see the point. Charles was right: he wasn't fooling anyone. 'I ... I was hoping to get some pre-made invisibility potion from Mrs Tippings, so I could go snooping at the academy this afternoon. She gave me some the time before when I went, because I caught her in a good mood.'

'And what do you hope to achieve with this snooping?'

Alfie shrugged. That was a good question. What *did* he hope to achieve?

'I just want to see what happens,' he said. 'Plus, I figured that if I was invisible, I could somehow help out if at all goes wrong, which it most certainly will.'

Charles did not look happy at all. 'You're not going anywhere near that academy. If you try and interfere in what's happening, you'll put my parents' lives at risk. If Renwald so much as gets a whiff that anyone I know is involved in trying to stop him getting that wand ...' He shook his head, unable to comprehend the aftermath. 'And just how exactly do you hope to "help out"? You hardly know any magic. You'll just get yourself hurt, invisible or not.'

'But what about Mr Pendred? What if he gets hurt or killed?'

'Don't you think I haven't thought about that. He's been so kind and helpful towards me since I began studying at the academy.' Charles shook his head. He looked close to tears again. 'It's tearing me up inside, knowing what might happen – but what other alternative is there?'

'You could tell Mr P. and have some faith that he'll be able to sort this mess out for you. If he's the great wizard that everyone says he is, then everything could turn out well all around.'

'The key word there is "could", as opposed to "would". I'm not gambling where my parents' lives are concerned. And that's that.'

Trying to imagine himself in the same predicament, Alfie was sure that he'd do the same as Charles and not risk the safety of loved ones.

Charles got up out of his seat. 'My mum and dad will be back soon, so it's probably best you get going. They don't like it when I have friends in while they're out. I'm sure they think I'm going to hold a party or something. I should be so lucky.'

'Oh, right,' Alfie said, standing up and suddenly feeling a little unwelcome.

'Promise me you'll go home now, Alfie,' Charles said, escorting him to the front door. 'Give me your word that you'll go home.'

'I give you my word,' Alfie said as he stepped outside.

'I'll find out how things went soon enough. I think Mr P will be fine, because Renwald will wait until the Stormbringer is away from the academy before he strikes.'

'Who's transporting it and where's it being transported to?'

'Ullin and some others are moving it back to Kordoba . Where exactly in the Kordoba, I don't know.'

'And will they be fine?'

Looking decidedly ruffled, Charles did not answer this question. He told Alfie to take his potion to sort his eye out, then bid him good day and shut the door.

####

Walking home, Alfie decided to take a detour past the academy. *I'll just look through the gate*, he thought as he made his way down Mysterium Road. He had given his word to Charles that he would go home, which was what he intended to do. A little peek wouldn't hurt. He probably wouldn't be able to to see anything because of the trees and how the driveway curved to the right, but curiosity was eating away at him. Reaching the gate, he pressed his face against the bars. And that's when a familiar voice spoke up behind him.

'Well, it looks like I arrived just in time.'

Alfie turned to see Melissa on her BMX. 'Has someone hit you?' Your eye looks swollen.'

'It's not as bad as it was,' Alfie said, touching the swelling beneath his eye, which now felt less pronounced. 'I got a potion from the Enchanted Cove and it seems to be doing its thing.' He explained how he'd come by his injury.

'Salter is such a bully,' Melissa said, shaking her head. 'And now he's going to be even worse with that new kid to back him up. Honestly, I've never seen anyone so big for their age. You need to watch your back, Alfie; they've targeted you this time, so they'll do it again.'

'Oh I've got something planned for Ryan Salter. Something that'll keep him and his bruisers away from me.'

'Nothing that'll get you in trouble, I hope,' Melissa said. 'Trouble seems to find you like flies find a light.'

Alfie couldn't help but grin as he explained everything to her. 'Charles is coming with me and I can't wait or Monday night.'

'Can I come, too?'

'I don't see why not.'

'Well then I'm looking forward to Monday night, as well.'

They both grinned and then Melissa turned her attention towards the academy. She looked through the gate, then at Alfie.

'Did you get your invisibility potion?' she said. 'Are you still planning on going through with this?'

'Mrs Tippings told me she didn't have any more. Not that she'd have given me any if she did. She asked me what I wanted it for and obviously I couldn't tell her.'

'I hope that puts an end to any silly ideas you had about watching what's going to happen.'

'I'm not going to try and get in there. But not because I don't have the potion.' He told Melissa about the conversation he'd had with Charles and everything they'd discussed.

'So Charles knows that there's *definitely* going to be an attack and he hasn't told Mr Pendred,' Melissa said, looking stunned.

'Yes. Because Renwald has threatened to kill Charles' parents if he blabs.'

'Yeah, I got that bit. But ... still, this is Mr P we're talking about here. He could get hurt or killed.'

'I know. I pointed that out to Charles and he was pretty sure that the attack would take place away from the academy, when the Stormbringer had been moved back into Kordoba.'

Melissa thought this through for a second and came to the same conclusion Alfie had. 'So whoever's transporting it will get killed or injured instead. I'm not sure I'm comfortable with knowing that and knowing that I could prevent it.'

'You and me both,' Alfie said, offering a shrug.

'Perhaps we should just tell Mr Pendred. Let him sort it out. He has a right to know if he or anyone who's helping him is in danger.'

'That's exactly what I said to Charles and all he's concerned about is making sure his parents don't get killed.'

'Quite understandable. I'm sure we'd both be doing what he's doing in this situation.'

'We just have to sit back, do nothing and hope for the best.'

Resting her elbows on the handlebars of her BMX, Melissa went quiet again as she thought things through some more.

Alfie gave her a moment, then said, 'There's no way around this. No matter what we do, someone is in danger of getting hurt. So the best thing we can do is nothing – and hope for the best.'

Although Melissa was clearly not comfortable with the idea of doing nothing, she came to the same conclusion as Alfie. 'Talk about being put in a tricky situation,' she said, shaking her head.

'Come on,' Alfie said, walking away, 'it's getting dark and if we linger here any longer we might get noticed.'

Pedalling after him, Melissa said, 'Oh, and just so you know, I came here to try and persuade you not to go in there.'

'Really?' Alfie said. 'So you wouldn't have been tempted to go in if I'd got the invisibility potion?'

'No,' Melissa said. 'Of course not.'

But Alfie wasn't so sure that this would have been the case.

On the way home, they passed the park on Gretton Way and decided to spend some time in the playground.

####

When Alfie arrived home, Mrs Trotter greeted him at the door with a less than cordial smile.

'Been out having fun, have we?' she said.

'Sorry,' Alfie apologized. 'I lost track of time. Won't happen again. I promise.'

157

'Any later and I was going to send your father out searching for you in the car, young man.'

'Soon as I realised what the time was, I head back as fast as I could.'

'Oh yes, I'm sure you did.' Mrs Trotter's gaze lingered on Alfie, making him feel uncomfortable. He wondered if the swelling beneath his eye was still visible. Before leaving the park, Melissa had assured him it wasn't.

'Your dinner's in the microwave,' Mrs Trotter said, allowing Alfie to relax a little.

He was starving. The mere mention of the D word had made his tummy rumble. As he was sitting in front of the TV, wolfing down the sausages, chips and beans, he heard Eddie coming down the stairs, humming to himself. He sounded chirpy.

Because Alfie's wounds had healed, he'd had no intention of telling his brother about his run-in with Salter and his cronies. Alfie had thought it through and initially come to the conclusion that Eddie would want to get revenge. He would seek out Salter, not knowing that he had a new best buddy, who happened to be the biggest, meanest boy in school. Alfie didn't want to send Eddie – as annoying as he could be – into a situation where he could get beaten up. But the more Alfie had mulled things over, the more certain he was that he *should* tell his brother. Eddie had humiliated Salter and Salter wasn't the sort to let that slide (especially now he was friends with Harrison). So Alfie wanted his brother to be prepared for whatever trouble might come his way.

Eddie entered the room and gave Alfie a nod of acknowledgement.

Alfie nodded back. He continued to eat his dinner.

'Is it okay if I turn the TV over in a five minutes?' Eddie asked, slouching on the settee. 'Lord of the Rings is on, if you're up for a three hour marathon of coolness?'

'I don't mind. But I'm not too sure Mum will agree to that. Some of her favourite programs are on tonight, so good luck with that one.'

'She's already okayed it (although she did say I'd have to go to bed as soon as it's finished).'

'Where's Dad?'

'He nipped out about half an hour ago. Gone to the snooker club to play a few frames with his mate, I think.'

Leaning forwards, Alfie looked down the hallway and into the kitchen, to see if Mrs Trotter was within earshot. She was standing in front of the sink, humming to herself as she washed some pots. She seemed to be lost in her thoughts, but Alfie didn't want to take any chances. His mother had a way of hearing things, even when she appeared to be tuned out, in a way that all mothers seem to be able to do.

'Can I have word with you upstairs?' Alfie said to Eddie in a low voice.

'I don't want to miss the beginning of the film.'

'It's important. It's about Salter.'

'Eh?' Eddie said, pulling a strange face. 'What could you possibly have to tell me about that fool that could be important?'

'Come upstairs and you'll find out.'

'I'm too comfortable to move now, bro. Just tell me here. Spit it out.'

Alfie cast another glance down hallway, to make sure his mother was still washing the pots. She was.

'*Please,*' Alfie said. 'It'll only take a minute. I'm pretty sure Salter plans on getting revenge on you.'

Eddie pulled another strange face, not even bothering to take his eyes off the TV screen. 'Ooh, I'm quaking in my boots.'

'He beat me up earlier. Him and his friends.'

This time Eddie took notice. He shot a glance Alfie's way, studying his face. 'If that's the case, how come you haven't got a mark on you?'

'I used a potion to heal my wounds. I would have had a nasty black eye otherwise.'

'All right,' Eddie said, springing up off the settee. 'Upstairs, now. I want to know everything.'

Once they were in Alfie's bedroom, he shut the door to make sure they could have some privacy. Then he told Eddie everything: about how he'd been jumped on the way home from school and how Salter had teamed up with the big, new boy.

Eddie's face twisted in anger. 'You wait 'till I get my hands on him,' he said, clenching his fists. 'This time I'll *really* teach him a lesson.'

'No, no, *no* – don't lay a finger on him. Let me deal with this.'

'Oh, please, Alfie – what are you gonna do? Tickle him into submission?'

Alfie shook his head. 'I'm going to use magic.'

'Ah, of course,' Eddie said, his mouth breaking slowly into a wide, toothy smile. 'I should have known.'

'Nobody needs to get hurt.'

'Really?' Eddie looked disappointed. 'So what have you got planned?'

Alfie filled him in with all the details.

'That sounds awesome. Let's just hope it works, otherwise I'll be getting involved. Salter doesn't scare me in the slightest. I'm surprised that he's brave enough to pick on you again after what I did to him last time.'

'Well, he is best friends with the new boy now, so he's got some hefty back-up. I'd be brave if I had him with me. Salter told me what you did to him. I wish I could have been there to see it.'

'After you told me what he'd done to you, I waited for him after school. I followed him as he walked home. When he reached Cavendish Road, he cut under the bridge and went down by the river. And that's when I pounced. At first I adopted the nicely-nicely approach. I explained who I was and asked him to stop bothering you. He laughed in my face and told me to get lost.'

'Not a wise move.'

'Nope, not a wise move. I had to use all my powers of restraint not to punch him in the eye. After taking a very deep breath, I gave him another chance to be nice and he told me to keep walking if I knew what was good for me. So I grabbed him,

picked him up by his pants and gave him a wedgie. As I
bounced him up and down, I asked him if he'd be giving you
any trouble again. He didn't respond, so I bounced him more
vigorously, then asked him the question again. He told me to get
lost. So I hung him from a tree by his pants. Oh man, you should
have seen his face; I've never seen anyone go so red; I thought
his head was gonna explode.' Reminiscing, Eddie chuckled to
himself. 'So, once more, I asked him the question: are you gonna
give my bro any trouble again. I thought he'd break at that point,
but he didn't; he told me to get him down or else. So I went to
walk away, and *that's* when he buckled. "No no no," he begged,
"don't leave me here – you *can't* leave me here!". "Oh yes I can,"
I said, and went to walk away again. "*Okay, okay!*" he screamed,
"*I won't pick on your brother anymore!*". And that's how I made
that bully squeal like a pig.'

'Your intimidation tactic worked for a while, until Salter
paired up with that giant. It's like Salter's got his own henchman
now. One who can swing a mean punch and probably crush my
head with one of his shovel-sized hands.'

Eddie ruffled his hair and pinched his cheek. 'But you're
gonna get this sorted, right? You're gonna do some hocus-pocus
on him, yeah? I tried the humiliation route and it didn't do the
trick. I think you're right about taking it down the scare tactics
route this time. Make him so afraid he can't even bring himself to
look at you again.'

'Oh I will, don't you worry.'

Alfie considered telling Eddie about where he'd been this
afternoon and what'd happened. He didn't, though; because he
couldn't see the point. When it came to bullies, his brother was
an authority on how to deal with those. But Eddie would not be
so comfortable dealing with magical issues. He would probably
say the same as Charles and Melissa: there's nothing you can do,
so just forget about it. But Alfie couldn't forget about it. He just
couldn't.

'Is there anything else you want to talk to me about?' Eddie
asked. 'You look like you're deep in thought.'

161

'No, nothing else.'

'Okay, I can hear the opening credits to the film,' Eddie said. 'Are you coming down to watch?'

Daft question. Of course he was. Troubles or no troubles, Alfie wasn't about to miss the *Lord of the Rings*. Three hours of coolness would be just the trick to take his mind off things.

Later that night, as Alfie sat up in bed, reading under the glow of his gooseneck lamp, he skimmed through the index of the potions book he borrowed from the library. He was looking for the potion Charles had suggested. He found the appropriate page and turned to it. 'Fun and games,' he said, chuckling to himself. 'Fun and *games*.'

CHAPTER 8
(Friends Again & the Impromptu Broomstick Ride)

Normally, on a Saturday, Alfie would have a lie-in and Mrs Trotter would have to badger him out of bed. Not this morning. At seven-thirty, he was downstairs eating toast in the kitchen when his father entered the room. Slouched over, Mr Trotter was clutching a piping hot cup of tea in one hand. In the other, he was holding a folded over copy of the Guardian newspaper, which he was reading as he shuffled along.

'Yeh, gads,' Mr Trotter said, stopping dead in his slippers. 'I thought I was seeing things for a second there. What are you doing up so early? Have you wet the bed?'

'Dad, I haven't wet the bed since I was about four.'

'So how come you're up so early?'

'There's somewhere I need to be and I want to make sure I get there before someone goes out.'

'And who is this someone? Leo?'

'Yep.'

'He hasn't been round this week. You pair are usually inseparable. You haven't fallen out with him, have you?'

'No, I haven't fallen out with him.'

Alfie was thankful that Mr Trotter didn't possess Mrs Trotter's ability to detect porky pies. Alfie wasn't interested in getting into a long conversation about why he'd fallen out with Leo. Mr Trotter would want to know every detail and Alfie just wanted to be gone.

'Your mum mentioned that you haven't done any chores to pay for the broken wheel on your bike,' Mr Trotter said. 'So I thought, with it being the weekend and my car needing a good wash, you could make that your first chore. What do you say, son?'

'Yeah, okay,' Alfie said. 'Tell Mum I'll be back for Lunch.' He wolfed the rest of his toast down, then brushed past his father as he exited the kitchen. He nipped upstairs, got everything he needed, then made for the front door.

On the way to Leo's, as Alfie walked along at a brisk pace, he wondered what he could say to his best friend to end the frosty winter that'd settled in-between them. The truth? *Should I tell him that I've found out I'm a wizard?* he thought. Leo wouldn't believe him, no doubt. If the situation were reversed, Alfie would think that his friend was pulling his leg and most likely trying to make him look a fool in the process. *I could show him; I could make something happen.* But hadn't he already done that anyway? Yes, of course he had: when he'd jumped ridiculous distances on his bike and skimmed stones across the pond, all the way to the other side. Achieving these feats was one thing, though. Producing a wand and making fire with it was a different kettle of Mackerel (not that Alfie had his wand with him, of course; but he could go home and get it if needs be). Alfie wasn't sure how Leo would react to him being able to do such things. Would he think it was cool, or would he think it was unnatural and be scared of Alfie?

'Heaven only knows,' Alfie muttered to himself as he kept walking.

He decided he'd just see how things went and deal with the situation as it panned out.

Arriving at Leo's street, Alfie regarded the houses on both sides of Sherwood Close with more than a tinge of jealousy. All of them were big, modern and spacious, with long driveways and expansive gardens. Alfie knew he would have to work hard when he was older if he wanted to afford an expensive property and he was determined to do so (even though he had no idea what he wanted to do when he left school).

Reaching Leo's, he made his way down the driveway, past Mr Parkes' grey Volvo estate, and stopped by the side door. He went to knock, hesitated, then rapped on the glass with his knuckles. After waiting a few seconds, he knocked again and waited. And then, in the kitchen beyond, a petite-framed shape appeared on the other side of the glass: Mrs Parkes.

When she opened the door, she greeted Alfie with a warm smile. 'Oh hello there, you're here early. Shouldn't you be lying in and vegging out. I didn't think kids your age knew the world existed before ten a.m. on a weekend.'

'Neither did I,' Alfie said.

'Speaking of lying in, that's exactly where Leo is. I'll get him up for you. Back in a tick.'

Into the hallway she went, out of view, her thin legs moving fast, fast, *fast*.

'LEOOOOO!' Alfie heard her call. 'ALFIE'S HERE!'

Alfie was always amazed at how Mrs Parkes could get such a boom in her voice, considering how small she was.

'*LEOOOOOO!*' she bellowed again. '*GET YOURSELF UP! ALFIE'S HERE!*'

'I'm coming!' came the faint, groggy reply.

Mrs Parkes returned to the kitchen and said, 'He'll be down in a tick.'

'Thanks,' Alfie said.

Great, he thought, *he's probably going to be annoyed with me for getting him out of bed.*

As Mrs Parkes busied herself cleaning down the work surfaces with a wet rag, she engaged Alfie in small talk.

'I haven't seen you at all this week,' she said. 'Have you been all right? Or have you just been busy with one thing and another?'

'Things have been hectic for me over the last few days. It's been all go.'

'Life keeping you on your toes, is it?'

'You could say that.'

'That's good. Much better for you like that than being stuck around doing nothing, twiddling your thumbs.'

'If only you knew,' Alfie whispered.

'What's that, sorry?' Mrs Parkes said. 'I didn't catch you there.'

Alfie did some quick thinking. 'I said that I've also had a touch of the flu.' He winced slightly as he said it. 'But I'm feeling better now.'

'Ooh, don't get too close to me then,' Mrs Parkes said. 'The last thing I need is to be catching the flu. Too much to do and so little time to do it all in, if you know what I mean … *LEO, ARE YOU COMING OR WHAT! ALFIE'S WAITING!'*

Shuffling into view, dressed in a Spiderman dressing gown, Leo greeted Alfie with a look he couldn't judge.

'Hello,' Alfie said, offering a smile. 'I'm sorry I came so early; I should have known you'd still be asleep.'

Wiping gunk from his eyes, Leo said, 'It's okay; I'm sure Mum would have got me out of bed soon anyway. She gets up at the crack of dawn every day and bangs around, doing jobs. She's like a busy bee, buzzing around the place. She never stops.'

'I think most mums are like that,' Alfie said.

'They are,' Mrs Parkes agreed, 'because little boys and girls are so adept at making mess, we mothers need to be adept at cleaning mess up. And I can only keep on top of things by keeping busy busy busy.' She tossed the rag in the sink and opened the oven door. 'You see,' she said, gesturing towards the inside, 'look at the state of this. Cheese all over the bottom. And that's not even a child who's made *that* mess – it's my adorable husband, who doesn't seem to know how to clean up after himself either. In some ways, he's a bigger kid than you pair. Men! Do they ever grow up? I don't think so.' She shook her head in dismay.

Meanwhile, Alfie and Leo just looked at each other, not sure what to say.

After a moment of silence descended, Mrs Parkes got the hint.

'I've got some things I can be getting on with upstairs,' she said, whistling a tune as she disappeared down the hallway.

When Leo was satisfied she was out of earshot, he said, 'I'm glad you've come around, Alfie, 'cause I've been meaning to speak to you. The thing is … erm, err … Well, what I'm trying to say is ... (if I can just get my words out without stammering like a fool) ... I think I've been a bit of a twit over the last week. So what I'm trying to say is that I'm ... erm ... sorry, I guess.'

This wasn't what Alfie had expected. As he had waited for Leo to get out of bed, he'd become convinced that Leo would not be pleased to see him. So this was a nice surprise. It threw Alfie a little, making him stammer and stutter himself.

'You ... err ... You don't need to apologize,' he said. 'I'm the one who's been too busy to go anywhere or do anything with his best friend. Things have just been pretty hectic for me over the last week or so, which is why I'm here now, to make up for it. Are you doing anything today? If not, do you fancy going go-carting?'

Leo's face brightened. He didn't look at all sleepy now. 'Oh yeah!' he said. And then he frowned. 'But I don't think I can go, 'cause I'm broke. I spent all my pocket money yesterday on sweets.'

'*YOU CAN GO!*' Mrs Parkes bellowed from somewhere inside the house. '*I'LL GIVE YOU THE MONEY! ANYTHING TO GET YOU OUT FROM UNDER MY FEET FOR A FEW HOURS SO I CAN GET SOME JOBS DONE!*'

'Honestly,' Leo said, shaking his head, 'I don't think she knows the meaning of the word privacy.'

'*I HEARD THAT!*' Mrs Parkes bellowed.

Leo leaned forwards and whispered to Alfie: 'The walls have ears in this house.'

'Yes, they do,' Alfie said, closing his hands into fists and shaking them excitedly. 'But ... *we're going to the go-cart park!*'

'Woo-*hoooo!*' Leo said, mimicking his friends fist-shakes. '*Yesssss!*'

'The earlier we get there, the more chance there'll be of us having the place to ourselves, like last time.'

'Where's your bike?' Leo said, looking past him, scanning the yard. 'You always come on it.'

Alfie explained about the accident he'd had and how he'd buckled the wheel. 'I've got to do chores to pay for the repairs, starting with washing my dad's car this afternoon.'

'I hope you didn't hurt yourself.'

'I had a few grazes, that's all.'

'You can borrow my old one, if you like. I got my new one for my birthday.'

Birthday! Alfie thought. 'Oh poo, I forgot all about that!'

'It's okay,' Leo said. 'Don't worry about it. Easily done when things are hectic.'

'I'll make it up to you. I'll buy you an ice cream. Pay for your go at the go cart park.'

'I'm not going to say no to that.'

Still in his pyjamas, Leo led Alfie to the garage and showed him his new bike: a bright BMX with THUNDER embossed on the frame.

'Awesome,' Alfie said, feeling a tinge of jealousy.

Thirty minutes later they were on the bikes, zooming down the road, side by side.

'Can you remember the last time we went and you crashed into those tyres, then flipped over and landed upside down.'

'How could I forget. It hurt. A lot.'

'And the guy that runs the place looked like he wanted to murder you.'

'I apologized. What more could I do?'

'If you'd have damaged the go-cart, I think he would have banned us.'

'In my defence, it had been raining that day and the track was waterlogged in places. And that's why I lost it on that corner.'

'Well, it's not raining today. Looks as if it's going to be a good 'un, so no excuses this time.'

'It'll be you that needs the excuses.'

Alfie looked skywards. Leo was right: it did look like it was going to be a good 'un. The day had started chilly, but now the sun was rising and it was warming up nicely. A scattering of bubble-shaped clouds was the only thing to mar an otherwise perfect morning.

The boys rounded a corner and Leo asked the inevitable question: 'So, what is that you've been busy doing over the last week? What have you been up to, Alfie?'

Alfie was faced one of two possible options: tell the truth or tell a lie. A lie seemed the safest option, but Alfie had only just patched things up with Leo and didn't want to do anything that would jeopardize their friendship again. Plus, Alfie was such a useless liar that he was sure Leo would see right through it. So it would have to be the truth, then …

Alfie brought his bike to a stop and Leo pulled up next to him.

'What have you stopped for?' Leo asked. 'I thought we were going to try and get there early.'

How best to say this, Alfie thought, looking around to see who was about. The street they were on was quiet enough: a back road full of terraced houses. The curtains were still closed in most of them. The only other person Alfie could see was a man getting into his car farther down the street. Once the man had driven away, Alfie produced his wand from inside his jacket.

'That's a nice stick,' Leo said, looking confused. 'What do you plan on doing with it?'

'I could tell you, but it's better to show. The only thing is where. I can't do it here and I need some paper or something.'

'Do what?' Leo replied, looking more and more confused. 'And what do you need paper for? If it's to showcase your Origami skills, don't bother, 'cause that sort of thing doesn't impress me.'

Spotting a bin at the end of the street, Alfie took off towards it, with Leo following behind. Reaching the bin, Alfie pulled along side it and put his hand inside. He rummaged and pulled out a takeaway menu.

As Leo caught up with him, he said, 'Isn't it a little early for a Chicken Chow Mein? If you're hungry we can go to a café, if you want? I know one that does a mean Full English: two rashers of

169

bacon, two eggs, two sausages, fried bread … the works! Crikey, I ate before I left and this is making me feel hungry.'

'This isn't about food.'

Alfie made sure the coast was clear, then he held his wand over the menu and said the magic words: 'Lucidum Elevare!'

The menu burst into flames so fast that it caught Alfie by surprise.

He dropped it on the pavement and stamped on it until the flames were extinguished.

'*Whoa!*' Leo said, taking a step back. 'That's a neat trick. How did you do that?'

'It's not a trick; it's magic.'

'Magic is all about tricking people. So how did you do it? Is there a lighter in the end of that wand? Let me have a look.'

Leo went to grab the wand, so Alfie stowed it behind his back, out of reach.

'It wouldn't work for you. It … only works for certain people.'

Leo gave Alfie a reproachful look. '*Really?*' Leo said. 'And I thought we were friends again. You can't show me something like that and not let me have a go. I mean, come on – be fair.'

Alfie opened his mouth to explain. But before he could say anything, a man dressed in pyjamas and fluffy slippers appeared on the other side of the road.

'*Hey!*' he roared. 'I saw what you just did! That's dangerous, lighting fires in the street!'

'Time to go,' Leo said.

Alfie placed the wand back inside his jacket. Then the two of them rode away as fast as they could, with the man's voice ringing in their ears. When they were a safe distance away, they stopped and continued their conversation.

'Come on,' Leo said, rubbing his fingers together, 'hand it over; it's my turn now. Is there a switch on it that makes the flame.'

'Fine, you want to look, here you go,'' Alfie said, giving him the wand. He watched with amusement as Leo tried to find a switch. 'I wish I knew some more spells so I could do more with it, but I've only had one lesson at the academy and that's all Mr Pendred has shown us so far.'

'Lessons?' Leo said. 'What are you talking about? What's this academy you've been to and who's Mr Pendred?'

Alfie was excited and getting ahead of himself, so he explained things in a more logical fashion. He began with the day when Salter and his friends had challenged them in the nature reserve car park. He told Leo how Charles had seen him jump farther than seemed possible and why he was able to do it. He told Leo about his first day at the academy and all the things he'd bought from The Enchanted Cove. He told him about the Emoruld and Kordoba and the things that could be found there. He told him about the Stormbringer and Renwald's attempt to steal it (had he been successful? This was a question Alfie couldn't help but keep asking himself). He told him about invisibility potions and levitation spells and flying broomsticks and all manner of other weird, wonderful, magical things. And he even told him about Doris.

'A telepathic typewriter?' Leo said, pulling a strange face. 'This is quite some leg-pull that you're trying here. Which I'm not falling for, by the way. Do I have mug written on my forehead, or what? *And* you're trying to tell me that Charles is a wizard. I've known him for a few years and he's about as magical as a teapot, I can tell you.'

'I'm telling the truth.'

'Of course you are.'

'Nice try, but I'm not falling for it,' Leo said. 'Come on, we can still be the first to get to the go-cart park if we get a move-on.' He went to cycle away, so Alfie grabbed him by the arm.

'I don't need a wand to perform magic,' Alfie said. 'I can make things happen just by thinking it.'

'Really?' Leo replied. 'Okay.' He looked up and down the street, then focused his attention on a street lamp. 'You can do stuff *just* by thinking it, eh? Make it flicker on and off, like a disco light.' He folded his arms and waited.

'Oh, please, you could at least give me a challenge.'

Looking up, determined to impress his friend, Alfie focused on the street lamp and concentrated hard. He imagined it burning so bright that it would hurt your eyes if you looked at it.

BOOM! The lamp exploded, showering the pavement with bits of glass and plastic.

'WHOA!' Leo said, recoiling and putting his hands up to protect his face. 'Did you … did you just do that?'

'I wanted to make it flicker on and off; I didn't mean to make it explode.'

With eyes as big a saucers, Leo regarded Alfie with a look of awe.

'*Now* do you believe me?' Alfie said.

Leo's look of awe changed to one of fear. 'Remind me not to annoy you,' he said. 'I'd hate to think of what you could do to someone if they annoyed you.'

'You've seen me do other stuff before; you just haven't realised it. Like at the reserve, when I jumped further than anyone else. At the lake, when I skim stones across the surface: that's why I can do that. Because I'm *willing* it to happen. Because I'm using *magic*.'

'Can you remember when we were walking through Woodland Park one night and it was dark and scary? The wind was up and howling through the trees. We were both scared ...'

'You were scared.'

'We were *both* scared. The lights by the path weren't working and I said that I wished they were, then, just after that, they all flickered on. That was you, wasn't it?'

'Probably. Either that or it was a major coincidence.'

'That's highly unlikely.'

From houses up and down the street, people began to appear, wondering what the noise was: sleepy-looking people dressed in nightgowns and pyjamas. A fat, bald, hairy man who was wearing only a pair of y-fronts came striding towards Alfie and Leo, so they took to the road, pedalling away at speed.

'*OI!*' the bald man shouted after them, balling his nicotine-stained fingers into a fist and brandishing it at the boys. '*COME BACK 'ERE YOU PAIR!*'

When Alfie and Leo were a safe distance away, they stopped again.

'I think we need to cut out the magic for now,' Alfie said, 'before we get ourselves in trouble. I'm not supposed to do it outside of the academy without proper supervision.'

Slightly out of breath, Leo fixed his friend with a searching look. 'If I hadn't seen you do that, I wouldn't have believed it.'

'If I was in your position, neither would I,' Alfie said, wiping sweat from his brow.

Shaking his head slowly, Leo took a few seconds to process everything that'd happened in the last few minutes. Then he said, 'So what did your parents say when you told them that you wanted to enrol at a magic academy? I bet they were even more sceptical than I was. And I bet they thought you were joking, yeah?'

'No, they knew I was a wizard; they just hadn't told me about it.'

'How did they know? It's because they've seen you do weird things like making lights explode and making fire from nothing, yeah?'

'No, it's because my dad's a wizard, too.'

Now Leo really *did* look shocked. 'Your *dad's* one? What about the rest of your family? Your mum? Eddie? They've got to be, I s'ppose.'

'Nope, that's not how it works. Mum and Eddie are just normal. They're ...' Alfie was about to say "just like you", but he thought better of it. When Eddie had found out his brother was a wizard (as opposed to being just an oddball with strange powers), his initial reaction had been one of jealousy. Alfie was concerned that Leo might be a bit jealous as well. He didn't want to blurt out anything that might put their friendship in jeopardy again; especially when they'd only just patched things up. So he chose his next words carefully.

'They're not magical,' he said. 'It's hit and miss through the generations of a family. It's a bit of a lucky draw, really.'

'You certainly lucked out: being able to do what you can do. I wish I had that sort of power. I can think of a few kids at school I'd like to cast spells upon.'

This got Alfie thinking about Salter and how he was going to get revenge on him.

'Why are you smiling?' Leo said. 'I take it there's someone you'd like to zap with your wand.'

'Can you guess who?'

'Ooh, err … now let me see … Salter!'

'Bingo. Got it in one.'

Alfie explained how Salter and his friends had jumped him whilst he was walking home. He told him how he'd been punched in the eye by Harrison.

'For a big kid, he doesn't punch very hard,' Leo said. 'You haven't got a mark on you.'

'I had a nasty red mark and swelling. And it would have blossomed into a juicy black eye if I hadn't taken a potion.'

Now Leo was angry. 'I wish I'd have been there to even things up a bit. I'd have probably got beaten up too, but I would have made sure Salter didn't get away unmarked, I can tell you that.'

It warmed Alfie's heart to see that his friend still cared enough to be so protective. As he explained to Leo how he planned on getting revenge, Leo's mouth gradually widened into a huge grin.

'I've got to be there to see that. Tell me I can come along … please … *please.*'

'You can come.'

'*Yes!*' Leo said, punching the air.

'I'll be at yours for about quarter to seven. Make sure you're ready.'

'Oh, I'll be ready, don't worry about that. I wouldn't miss it for nothing,' Leo said. 'Hey, where is this academy you mentioned? I don't know of one around here (or anywhere else, come to think of it).'

Alfie told him where it was and how only magical people could see it.

'Well, that explains why I haven't noticed it before. Oh man, I can't believe that Charles is a wizard as well and I've been none the wiser. I'm beginning to feel distinctly left out here. How many kids are magical at our school, d'you think?'

'Not that many, I'm sure,' Alfie said, once again wondering the exact same thing himself. 'Come on, let's get moving.'

Once again, they set off on their bikes. For the remainder of the journey, Leo was full of questions about magic. Alfie answered each one patiently, as best he could:

Can you make things disappear? Yes, I've done it quite a few times.

Can you make yourself super strong? I dunno … maybe.

Can you make money from nothing? That would *awesome*. But I have no idea.

On and on it went, until the boys finally reached the go-cart park. Despite all the delays, they were still the first customers to arrive. They wasted no time taking to the track, which was a figure of eight shape. Alfie promised Leo that he wouldn't use magic to make his go-kart move faster. Leo won four races and Alfie won three. Neither of them crashed, which was good. By the time they left, Alfie's legs were aching from pedalling and he was out of breath. Leo, on the other hand, looked like he could have another seven races and barely break a sweat.

'Who needs magic,' Leo said as they were leaving, 'when you can rip up the track like I do.'

'Careful now,' Alfie replied. 'If your head swells much more, you won't be able to get it through the front door when you get home.'

Leo went quiet for a moment and Alfie could see he was deep in thought, mulling something over.

'What's on your mind?' Alfie asked.

'I keep thinking about that wand – what's it called? The Stormbringer?'

'That's it. What about it?'

'I keep wondering whether that evil wizard got his hands on it or not.'

'I'm almost certain he did.'

'How do you know?'

'I don't know, not for sure; it's just a gut feeling – a *strong* gut feeling.'

'That sounds bad.'

'It is bad. Perhaps not for us at the moment, but for those that live in Kordoba ...' Alfie didn't want to contemplate the consequences.

'So ...' Leo said, 'what are we going to do about it?'

'What are *we* going to do about it?'

'Yeah. We. Us. You and me. We're still a team, I take it? Just 'cause I can't do magic, doesn't mean I can't help you out.'

'I've already discussed this with Melissa and Charles. They said that there was nothing we could do and, now I've thought about it, I agree with them. There is nothing we can do until we know for sure whether Renwald got the wand or not.'

'You said you were certain he did.'

'*Almost* certain. But I'd still like to know for sure.'

'And when will that be?'

'My next lesson is on Tuesday, so I guess it'll be then, if I don't see him before. Charles will find out, one way or another. Until then, we need to concentrate on Salter and making sure he doesn't bother either of us anymore. Hey, how would you like to come to The Enchanted Cove on Monday, after school? It's where I got my wand and all the other stuff I need for the academy. I need to get some ingredients for the potion I'm going to brew.'

'I'm sure I've heard of that place,' Leo said. 'Is it that kooky shop on Thurland Street with weird ornaments and things in the window?'

'That's it,' Alfie replied. 'You coming?'

Leo gave him a thumbs up. 'I'd like to see someone try and stop me. I could help you mix the potion, if you want? That's assuming someone without magical power *can* mix a potion.'

'You can check that I put the right ingredients into the cauldron and do some stirring. I'm sure that won't be a problem.'

'Cool – I can't wait!'

'Me, neither.'

Once again, the boys took to their bikes. They raced along roads, overtaking each other and zooming up and down pavements. Alfie suggested that they go to the skate park, so they could bust some moves on the ramps.

An hour and a half later, feeling quite exhausted, Alfie then suggested they go back to his house for lunch because he was hungry. Leo also thought this was a great idea because Mrs Trotter often offered him cake when he came for lunch. Last time he'd devoured a slice of home-baked jam sponge, which he'd made disappear in seconds (as if by magic – *poof!*). And she didn't disappoint this time, either. She offered Leo some caramel slices and he couldn't scoff them fast enough.

The boys spent the rest of the day in the garden. First they played penalties. Leo went in goal first and Alfie scored five out of ten shots. Then they switched around and Leo had his turn at shooting. After nine attempts and with things tied at five a piece, it came down to the last penalty. If Leo scored, he would win. If not, things would go to sudden death where they'd take one penalty each until someone missed.

'Are you ready?' Leo asked, placing the football down and readying himself.

'As ready as I'll ever be,' Alfie responded.

Smiling as he took two steps forwards, Leo struck the ball with the side of his foot. It hit the top of the crossbar, making the entire goal shudder, then disappeared over next door, out of sight.

'Oh, great!' Alfie said. He looked over the fence to see where the ball had gone. 'It's all the way on the other side, in the vegetable patch.'

'I'll climb over and get it.'

Leo went to do so, but a loud bang on the kitchen window stopped him. Mrs Trotter glared down at him and shook her head.

She opened the side sash and said, ' If Mrs Draper sees you clambering over his fence, it'll give him a heart attack. If you want that ball back, you need to go around and get it.' Pulling the sash shut, she disappeared from view.

'If he sees us traipsing through his vegetable patch to get our ball, he'll do his nut as well. He's a right miserable old duffer who loves any excuse to moan. Last time I asked for my ball back he had a right go at me. He's got one eye bigger than the other. It's bloodshot and bulges out.'

Leo screwed his face up, looking disgusted. 'Err, maybe we should leave the ball where it is. I'm tired of playing football anyway. I'm sure the old guy'll throw it back when he finds it. Want to call it a draw?'

He'll probably throw it in the bin, Alfie thought. But he was happy to call it a draw.

'Want to check out my magic books and other stuff?' he asked Leo.

'Oh yeah! Now *that* would be awesome.'

In Alfie's bedroom, the boys sat on the bed and examined all the magical bits and bobs. Alfie had laid them all out on the carpet in front of them.

There was an Iron Man poster on the back of the door. Pointing the wand at it, Leo said, 'Abracadabra!'

'Abracadabra,' Alfie said. 'Really?'

'It's what they say in the movies. Why don't you show me something cool. You've got all your books here, so we can look up a spell.'

'I'm not supposed to do magic unless I'm supervised by an experienced wizard or witch. That's what Mr Pendred told me. Also, we're only supposed to fly over academy grounds, so we won't get seen.'

'And how is he going to know you've been flying your broom?'

'*He* probably won't. But my mum might. How would we sneak it out without her noticing? Not to mention the neighbours. Can you imagine what would happen if Mrs Draper next door saw me floating around in mid air. She'd most likely collapse from a heart attack, or something.'

'No, he'd most likely just think he was seeing things.'

'There's no way I'm risking my mum seeing me riding my broomstick,' Alfie said, hoping this would close the subject.

Then Mrs Trotter called up the stairs: 'I'm off out to do a bit of shopping and post a letter. I'll be about half an hour. Be good, you pair. There's chocolate cake on the kitchen sideboard, so help yourselves. And if you make any mess, clear it up!'

Alfie went to the door and replied: 'We will.'

When he turned to look back at Leo, he wasn't surprised to see him smiling.

'I hope that smile is because of the cake.'

'Partly.'

Leo was still smiling. Still looking at Alfie expectantly.

'No,' Alfie said flatly.

'Oh, come on. You don't have to go flying over the houses on it. Just hover above the ground a bit, that's all.'

'No – I've never ridden one before. My dad's playing golf, so he'll be out for ages, but I don't know where Eddie is and he could come back any time.'

'He wouldn't snitch on you, would he?'

'Probably not. But I don't want to take any chances.'

They heard the jangle of keys, then the front door opened and closed as Mrs Trotter left the house.

Leo gave Alfie another enquiring look. Leo's eyes twinkled with mischief.

'What part of the word no don't you understand?'

'It must tell you how to ride a broomstick in one of these,' Leo replied, picking up a book and skimming through it.

'That one's about potions.' Alfie hoped that changing the subject would divert the conversation away from any madness about flying. 'There's one near the back that tells you how to mix a potion that'll cure a cold.'

'That's good,' Leo said, uninterested. 'If I get a cold, I know where to come. Now ...' he rubbed his hands together, '... we're wasting time, so let's have it, yeah?'

Alfie closed his eyes, then opened them. He inhaled, then exhaled. *Patience*, he thought. *I just need to be patient.* But he knew Leo would not relent. Not where something like this was concerned. Not where something as *cool* as this was concerned. *If you're going to do this, then best do it quick*, Alfie thought. *Before Mum comes back. Or Eddie.*

'I'm just going to try and make it hover above the ground,' Alfie said, 'and *that's* it.' Laying his hands flat in front of him, he crossed one over the other to emphasize this point. 'Don't ask me to go any higher, because I won't – no matter how much you beg me. Oh, and there's nothing in those books about flying. I know, because I've looked.'

'Right,' Leo said, beaming. 'What are we waiting for? Let's scoff some cake then go outside.'

In the garden, standing in the middle of the lawn, Alfie placed the broomstick in-between his legs and waited. When nothing happened, he looked at Leo and shrugged.

'There's obviously something you should be doing,' Leo said helpfully.

'Duh – obviously! The question is, what?'

This time Leo shrugged. 'Try pushing off from the ground.'

'Like *that's* going to do anything.'

But Alfie gave it a go anyway. He rocked back and forth, tilting the broomstick upwards.

'Go on,' Leo said encouragingly, 'kick off and jump!'

Not having any other ideas about what to do, Alfie did as he suggested. And then he let out an '*Oooooh nooooooo!*' as he shot up into the air faster than a Nerf bullet. The air whooshed past his face, making his eyes water. Looking down, he watched as the earth began to fall away and Leo's upturned, shocked face grew smaller. Keeping a tight grip on the broomstick, Alfie tilted his weight forwards. This slowed his ascent, allowing him to bring the broomstick under some modicum of control. *Don't panic*, he thought, unable to stop himself from doing so. *Deep breathes, deep breathes – keep a cool, calm head.* Tilting his weight forwards a little more, he leant slightly to his right and relief washed over him as he started circling in a wide arc. Alfie had often watched birds and wondered what it would be like to fly. And now he knew. In all his life, he'd never felt so exhilarated as he did now. He had never felt so *alive*.

'*Wooo-hoo!*' he said, continuing to circle.

From up here he could see for miles. He took in the view, wowing at the valley below and the fields in the distance. Easing to his left, he could see the tree tops of the reserve. Some boys were rummaging in the skip in the car park, possibly looking for a ramp to set up for their bikes. Easing more to his left, making himself turn around, Alfie watched the cars on the main road as they passed by. A double decker bus chugged past and a girl on the top level stared slack-jawed in Alfie's direction. She tried to get the attention of another girl seated next to her. But by the time she did, the bus turned a corner and headed off in another direction. Time to get back to ground level, before someone else spotted him.

Guiding the broomstick forwards and downwards, Alfie descended until he was about a metre above the lawn.

'It's easier than it looks,' he said to Leo, 'once you get the hang of it.'

'Oh ... my ... God. When you shot off like that, I thought that was it. I didn't think I was going to see you again. Let's just hope no one saw you.'

'At least one person did. A girl on a bus. You should have seen the look on her face.'

'She might not have been the only one. Hey, there's room on the back there for another bottom. Can I hitch a ride?'

Alfie shook his head vehemently. '*Noooo!* Like I haven't pushed my luck already.'

'Oh come on,' Leo begged. 'Just a quick ride. A minute. Or just a few seconds.'

'I daren't risk it. Someone might see us and my mum could come back early.'

BANG! BANG! BANG!

Alfie's heart leapt up into his throat as he and Leo turned to look at where the noise had come from. Mrs Trotter was standing behind the back door, glaring through the glass at them.

'Ah,' Leo said. 'This could be tricky to explain.'

Alfie's feet felt numb as he landed soundlessly on the lawn.

And then Mrs Trotter snatched the door open and came bounding down the steps towards them. Alfie had seen her angry plenty of times before, but never *this* angry. He was sure he could see steam coming out of her ears.

A few minutes later, after Alfie had been banished to his bedroom, her voice was still ringing in his ears. Mrs Trotter had promised he'd be punished, but she hadn't stated what that would involve. Lying on his bed, he hoped with all his heart that she wouldn't stop him attending magic classes. Even with what he had done, that would be an extreme punishment. He came to the conclusion that he would most likely be grounded: for a week, maybe two.

Leo had been sent home. Soon as Mrs Trotter had ordered him to leave, he had beat a hasty retreat, giving Alfie an apologetic look as he went.

Alfie didn't blame his best friend for what'd happened (well, maybe he did a bit). The main weight of blame, however, was his on his own shoulders. He should have been tougher with Leo. He should have said no and kept saying no. Should-a, would-a, could-a. But the simple fact was that he hadn't. What was done was done and nothing was going to change that now. Lesson learned. Time to move on and accept the consequences. Whatever they might be.

Putting his hands behind his head and lacing his fingers together, he listened as Mrs Trotter crashed about in the kitchen, putting crockery away. She was waiting for Mr Trotter to come home so she could discuss things with him. Alfie considered begging his mum not to tell him, but thought better of it. The way she was raging about downstairs, the best course of action – the *safest* course of action – was to steer clear. Alfie knew this from previous experience.

It was an hour later when Mr Trotter returned home. Mrs Trotter had calmed down a little by this time, but she was still very eager to greet him in the hallway and fill him in on what'd happened. Sat at the top of the stairs, Alfie listened to the conversation. He was sure he would be summoned before them, but they moved into the living room. Alfie heard the door slam shut, so he could no longer make out what they were saying. After a while, the door opened and Alfie scrambled back into his bedroom, He waited to be called. And he waited. And he waited some more. But his father didn't call up to him for another hour. By this time Alfie was back on his bed, flat out, browsing through his potions book. The mattress *pinged* as he put the book aside and sprang up, eager to get this over and done with.

Downstairs, in the living room, Alfie seated himself on the settee. Mr and Mrs loomed over him as the inevitable tirade began.

'What were you thinking?' Mr Trotter said.

'Anyone could have seen you!' Mrs Trotter seethed.

'Whose idea was that?' Mrs Trotter said. 'Yours or Leo's?'

'What difference does it make whose idea it was!' Mr Trotter said, turning on her. 'He shouldn't have done it anyway.'

'Don't you have a go at me!' she spat back at him.

On and on it went, with Mr and Mrs Trotter arguing with each other and intermittently venting their frustrations towards Alfie – until, finally, Alfie had had enough.

He stood up and said, 'Oh just shut up, the both of you!'

He didn't know who was more surprised: him or his parents. They stared at him, open-mouthed, slack-jawed.

'I'm sorry,' Alfie apologized. 'Sorry for telling you to shut up and sorry for flying on my broomstick.' He threw his hands up in frustration. 'What else do you want me to say? I can't take back what I've done, so just punish me and be done with it. I promise that something like this won't happen again – '

'We've heard your promises before,' Mrs Trotter said, cutting him off. 'They mean nothing. You gave us your word you wouldn't do something like this and you've done it anyway. So why should we believe you this time?'

Alfie mulled this over for a second, then offered a solution. 'I can't ride a broomstick if I don't have one. For now, maybe you should lock it away and I'll only take it to the academy if I need it for class.'

'That's sounds like a good start,' Mrs Trotter said.

She looked at Mr Trotter, who gave an approving nod.

'We'll confiscate the wand, too,' Mr Trotter said. 'Until you can prove you're mature enough to have it outside of academy time.'

This wasn't exactly unexpected, but Alfie's heart sank nonetheless. 'What about my books? You're not going to lock those away, are you?'

Mrs Trotter said, 'You can keep those; I can't see any problem with that.' She glanced at her husband to check that this was okay with him and he nodded agreement.

'Now,' he said, folding his arms across his narrow chest, 'we need to make a decision on how long you're going to be grounded for.'

'I'm going to be grounded as well!' Alfie said.

'Of course you are,' Mrs Trotter said. 'You didn't think we'd just confiscate a few items and that would be it, did you? Now, I'm thinking that you shouldn't be able to go out for a month.'

'A *month!*' Alfie said, hardly able to believe what he was hearing. The longest punishment he'd received before was a week. 'A month is too much!'

'Too much?' Mr Trotter said. 'After that stunt you played and how you've risked exposing yourself for what you are, do you *really* think that's too much?'

'I suppose not,' Alfie said. He felt tears welling behind his eyes, but he was determined not to cry. 'Will I be able to attend magic classes and are you still going with me on Tuesday, Dad?'

'We won't stop you attending your classes and yes I'll still go with you. But if you do anything like that again then … well, let's not try and think about that, shall we. Because you're *not* going to do anything like that again, are you?'

'No,' Alfie said. 'Never.'

'Hopefully this will teach you a lesson,' Mrs Trotter said. 'And you need to talk to Leo and make sure he doesn't tell anyone about what you are and what you can do. That's very important, Alfie. Maybe I should have word with him myself.'

'*I'll* talk to him,' Alfie said. 'He won't say anything to anyone.'

'You better hope he doesn't,' Mrs Trotter chastised.

Alfie realised that if he was grounded he couldn't go out Monday evening. This meant he wouldn't be able to implement his plan to put Salter in his place. Not for another month. Alfie didn't think he could endure another month of looking over his shoulder, wondering if Salter and his friends were about to pounce.

The front door opened and Eddie came in, full of smiles.

'Ooh, this looks ominous,' he said, noting the gloomy expressions. 'What's going on? What's Alfie done this time?'

'Never mind that,' Mrs Trotter said. 'Alfie, get yourself back to your bedroom; I'll let you know when you can come back down.'

As he left the room, Eddie gave him an enquiring stare. And a smile. Alfie knew he'd have *that* smile on his face: the mocking – oh, boy, you're *sooooo* in trouble again, bro – one.

Back in his bedroom, Alfie didn't know how long he would be here, so he decided to build a house out of Lego. By the time Mrs Trotter called him down for dinner, he'd built walls and fixed windows in and clipped a roof on top. He was reluctant to leave the construction, because it was coming along so well, but he dare not keep his mother waiting. Not after what'd happened.

Dinner was a sombre affair. Eddie sat across from Alfie and kept kicking him in the shins. He kept smiling and pulling faces, too, much to Alfie's annoyance. Mr Trotter was seated across from Mrs Trotter and they both sat in silence, chewing unenthusiastically on their food (thick-cut chips, sausages, beans and eggs, with treacle pudding and custard for afters). Alfie, on the other hand, was wolfing his food down. It would take a lot more than being grounded and having his magical items confiscated to ruin Alfie Trotter's appetite. After he'd licked his plate clean, he waited for the others to finish, then asked if he could be excused.

'Yes,' Mrs Trotter said. 'Be off with you.'

'Can I stay down here now?' Alfie asked.

'Yes,' Mr Trotter said, collecting up the dirty plates, 'but the less we hear from you this afternoon the better, I think.'

Then Alfie remembered the house he'd been building, so he went back to his bedroom anyway. Inevitably, Eddie paid him a visit, trying to establish why his brother was yet again in trouble. Alfie knew that Eddie would badger him until he found out, so he enlightened him straight away.

'You did *what!*' Eddie said, shocked. 'Whoa – you've surpassed yourself this time. Did anyone see you?'

Kneeling on the carpet by his Lego house, Alfie explained about the girl on the bus.

'Hah-hah! She probably won't tell anyone, 'cause she'll convince herself she was just seeing things, I bet. And even if she does tell someone, who'll believe her? No one. They'll think she's, you know ...' he twirled a finger by the side of his head, '... *cuckoo!*'

'I'm the cuckoo one for letting Leo talk me into it.'

'I wish I'd been here to see Mum's face when she caught you. I haven't seen her look this annoyed since you put that big magnet on the TV screen and broke it.'

'The magnet made some pretty colours on the screen as I was moving it around. I didn't know it would wreck the TV and Dad did say it was a good excuse to buy a new big one.'

'Oh, bro!' Eddie said as he left the room. 'When will you ever learn?'

186

Alfie listened to the creak of his brother's footsteps on the stairs. Then he once more busied himself building the Lego house and wondered again how he could possibly get out of the house on Monday evening (and sneak back in) without being noticed. Not to mention the fact that he didn't possess the ingredients for the potion he wanted to brew. How would he obtain those? He'd planned on making a trip to The Enchanted Cove after school, but how would he pull that in if he was grounded?

'No no no,' he muttered to himself. 'Why are you even contemplating this?'

He thought: *when* will *I learn? There must be another way?*

And then it came to him. He would ask one of his friends to do what needed to be done: Charles, Melissa, or ... Leo, who would be more eager than the others, Alfie figured. The only problem with Leo was that he wasn't a wizard, so Alfie wasn't certain the potion he had in mind would work on him. He couldn't see any reason why it shouldn't, but he would make some enquiries before asking Leo to swallow it. Better to be safe than risk blowing your best friend up.

CHAPTER 9

(Revenge)

Sunday was a dull affair for Alfie: a taster of things to come. Unable to leave the house due to his grounding, he spent most of his time camped in front of the TV, munching on snacks and drinking gallons of diet coke. That was until Mr Trotter reminded him that he still hadn't cleaned his car. So Alfie cleaned and polished the Astra until it was gleaming. Then Mrs Trotter decided the lawn needed a late season cut. Another job for Alfie. One that made his arms ache. After he'd finished, he went to his bedroom before his parents could find another for him to do. He stayed there for a good few hours, finishing the Lego castle he'd started.

At school, the following day, he was as alert as ever, eager to avoid a confrontation with Salter. As soon as Leo spotted Alfie in the playground, he came bounding towards him with a football under his arm.

'What happened after I left?' Leo said. 'Did you get grounded?'

'Yes,' Alfie replied. 'For a month.'

'A *month!* That's a bit harsh, isn't it?'

'I know. That's what I said at first. But it isn't harsh. Not really. Not when you consider what I did.'

'Well, no, I s'ppose not.' Leo looked sheepish. 'And it's all my fault. If I hadn't pestered you to do it, you wouldn't have. It should be me who's been grounded, not you. I'm sorry, Alfie. I owe you one. A *big* one.'

'You do,' Alfie agreed. And then he explained what he wanted him to do.

Leo's face brightened with a blossoming smile as he listened. 'Now *that* sounds like fun.' But as he gave it more thought, he began to express concern. 'When you mix this potion, you will get it right, yeah? I don't want to end up being transformed into a goat by accident and find out later that there's no way to turn me back.'

'I won't get it wrong. I'll double-check – triple-check! – as I'm mixing the potion. Are you up for this? You do owe me a big one, after all.'

'I'm up for it,' Leo said, giving a determined nod.

'*Excellent!*'

A boy named Ollie from Alfie and Leo's form called over to them: 'Are you having a game or what?' Ollie was standing with three other boys, who were beckoning them over.

'You up for a game?' Leo asked Alfie.

'Err ...' Alfie said, looking around at the groups of kids that were clustered here and there. 'I think I'll give it a miss.'

'If you're worried about Salter, don't be. We'll both keep an eye out. First sign of that twit and we'll leg it.'

'Oh, okay,' Alfie said, joining in with the fun.

At eleven o'clock, as Alfie was on his way to science class, he had a close call. On the second floor, rounding the corner that took him into the main corridor, he stopped dead when he saw Salter. He was bent over, gurgling as he drank from a water fountain. There was no sign of his friends and there was a good reason for that. As Alfie turned around, ready for a hasty retreat, he came face to face with a wall of school jumper, the embossed hallmark of Eldon Road School centimetres from his nose. Looking up, past the barrel-like chest, the red and blue tie, Alfie knew which face would be looking down at him. There was only one boy *that* big in school. And he wasn't alone. As Alfie stepped back, he noted that Mason and Bradley were behind Harrison, grinning. Alfie got ready to run. He would burst into one of the rooms if necessary, even if it meant being told off by a teacher. That would be preferable to taking another beating.

'In a hurry, are you?' Harrison said. With his head cocking slightly to one side, he looked closely at Alfie's face and Alfie knew what he must be thinking: how come he's got no bruises?

'Ye-yes,' Alfie said, his voice jittery. 'I am in a bit of a hurry. So if you don't mind, I'll be on my way.' He stepped to his left with the intention of walking past the three boys and they stepped to their right in unison, blocking his way.

'Uh-ah,' Mason said. 'We haven't finished talking to you yet. Didn't your mother teach you that it's rude to walk away from people when they're talking to you?'

Didn't your mother teach you that it's cowardly to bully people smaller than you, Alfie thought, but didn't say.

He heard footsteps behind him and knew it was Salter closing in.

Other boys and girls were looking on now, eager to see how this would play out. Alfie was sure none of them would think he was a coward if he ran away – not with four bullies bearing down on him – so that was what Alfie did. Figuring it would be easier to get past one rather than three, Alfie turned and bolted. He went face-first into Salter, head-butting him in the mouth, knocking him back a few steps.

Salter ran his fingers across his bottom lip and looked shocked to see they were bloodied.

'You're gonna suffer for that,' he said, advancing on Alfie.

A door to the right opened. Mr Trent, the fifth year music teacher, stepped out and said, 'What's going on out here? What's all this noise?' He looked at Salter, who had blood dripping down his chin. 'I might have known *you'd* be involved. What's happened to your mouth? Somebody given you a bunch of fives, have they?'

Salter pointed at Alfie. 'He did it. He ran into me on purpose.'

Bradley confirmed this. 'He did, sir. I saw it happen. Clear as day.'

'No I didn't,' Alfie protested. 'You and your bullying friends were ganging up on me and I was just trying to get away.'

'That sounds very plausible,' Mr Trent said. He focused his attention on Salter. 'You're dripping blood all over the floor, boy. Get yourself to the nurse – *now!*'

Salter glared at Alfie as he shoulder-barged past him and whispered, 'This is unfinished business, Trotter.'

Harrison and the other boys also glared at Alfie as they followed Salter down the corridor.

Clapping his hands together, Mr Trent banished all the on-lookers. 'You've got classes to go to!' he bellowed, a vein bulging on his forehead. 'So go on, be gone, the lot of you! *Go!*'

Everyone began filtering away.

'Are those four giving you trouble?' Mr Trent asked Alfie. 'You should let the headmaster know, if that's the case.'

'It's all under control,' Alfie replied as he was walking away. *Or soon will be*, he thought, smiling smugly.

At lunchtime, Alfie caught up with Charles in the dinner hall. The room was alive with the noise of laughter and chatter, so they had to talk loudly to be heard above the din. Alfie asked Charles if it was okay for a non-magical person to swallow a potion and Charles said it was. And then came the inevitable question:

'So what's this potion?' Charles asked. 'And who's this non-magical person you're planning on giving a potion to? And, more importantly, is this person going to be *aware* they're swallowing it? Please tell me you're not planning on slipping it into someone's drink without them knowing, because that would be a very dicey thing to do.'

'I'm not slipping it into anyone's drink. I can't go to the sports centre this evening to do you know what, so ... Leo's agreed to do it for me. Ah, now, don't look at me like that. He's my best friend. If I can't trust him, who can I trust?'

'What did Mr Pendred say to you during the first lesson?'

Alfie recalled what he'd said, word for word: 'As tempted as you might be, do not tell your friends - even your best, most trusted friends – what you can do. That's a dangerous path to slide down. You'll risk everything. Not only for yourself, but for everyone else in the magical community. Don't do it! Are we all clear on this? Do you all understand?'

'Yet you still told Leo,' Charles said, glancing around to make sure no one was listening.

'He's my best friend and he won't say anything to anyone. And even if he did, who would believe him? You know Leo well enough to know he isn't a blabbermouth.'

Charles looked nonplussed. 'Oh, Alfie, you really don't get it, do you? Either that or your just too pigheaded or silly to understand.'

Alfie recoiled like he'd been slapped. 'I'm not silly. He *won't* tell anyone.'

'Most likely he won't, but that's not the point. You've told him, so who's to say *you* won't tell someone else. By letting you study at the academy, Mr Pendred has put his trust in you and you've betrayed that trust. If he gets wind if this, he'll stop you from going. He doesn't mess around where things like this are concerned. I want you to swear you won't tell anyone else. Swear on your mum and dad's lives.'

Alfie didn't like the idea of swearing on his parents' lives, but he did it anyway. Just to show he could be trusted. 'On their lives,' he pledged, meaning it. 'I won't tell another soul.'

'Okay,' Charles said, 'I hope I'm not a fool for believing you.'

'You're not. I won't let you or Mr Pendred down again.'

'Good. Now let's go get some food.'

The boys grabbed themselves a tray each and joined the queue. Charles opted for mashed potato, beans and sausages, plus a drink of orange juice. Alfie plumped for the same. They found a free table. As they were seating themselves, Melissa appeared and said hello.

'Oh, hi,' Alfie replied.

Charles gave her a nod of acknowledgement.

'I'll get my food and then sit with you, if that's all right?' Melissa said.

She didn't wait for a reply. She got herself a tray and went to the back of the queue.

'Have you spoken to Mr Pendred since Friday?' Alfie asked Charles. 'Have you found out what happened yet?'

'I was going to pay him a visit over the weekend, but I couldn't think of a decent excuse to go to the academy. Plus I'm a useless liar, so he'd have probably smelt a rat and began questioning me. We'll just have to wait 'till tomorrow. I'll find out one way or another, don't worry.'

'Don't worry about what?' Leo asked, sliding in next to Charles. 'Is this to do with Salter? Has he been giving you more grief?'

'I had a narrow miss,' Alfie said. 'If Mr Trent hadn't stepped out of his classroom and intervened ...' He didn't want to think about what level of humiliation Salter would have inflicted on him.

'I wouldn't worry about it,' Leo said, giving Alfie a wink, 'we've got it covered, haven't we, Alfie?'

Alfie replied: 'If all goes well, yes. And there's no need for sneaky winks; Charles knows I told you.'

'Oh,' Leo said, giving Charles a wary look. 'You don't need to worry. If anyone finds out, it won't be from me. My lips are sealed.' He pinched his index finger and thumb together, then ran them across his lips to emphasize this point.

As with Alfie, Charles made Leo swear on his parents' lives, which Leo was happy to do.

'I'm sorry, you pair,' Charles said. 'I wouldn't normally ask anyone to do that, but the magical community needs to be protected from being exposed. You understand, yeah?'

'We understand,' Leo said sombrely. 'Don't we, Alfie?'

Alfie nodded. 'We do,' he said, holding Charles' gaze. 'We *do*.'

'I still can't believe you're a wizard, too,' Leo said to Charles.

'Let's not try and broadcast it, shall we,' Alfie said. 'Although ... I do think now is probably a good time to mention that Melissa is magical. She's, erm ... well, she's a witch.'

Shaking his head, Charles gave Alfie a disbelieving look. 'Have you already forgotten the conversation we just had!'

Alfie said, 'He's going to find out soon enough anyway.'

Leo looked overwhelmed. 'You're all magical and I didn't know. Oh man, I really *am* beginning to feel like the odd one out here.'

'Just remember that most people aren't wizard or witches,' Alfie pointed out. 'You're far from alone.'

Charles veered the conversation back towards the potion. 'Listen, I don't trust you pair not to mess this up, so I'm going to do you a favour. I'll mix the potion for you. At least you won't have to worry about getting that wrong and I won't have to worry about you getting it wrong, either.'

'Thanks,' Alfie said, tucking into his dinner.

'I'm pretty sure I've got all the ingredients we'll need in my store at home,' Charles said.

'Think I'll start building up my own stash of ingredients,' Alfie said, 'so I don't have make a trip to The Cove every time I want to knock a potion up.'

'You shouldn't be so ready to mix anything but the simplest ones,' Charles said. 'As I'm sure I've told you before, it can be dangerous if you get it wrong.'

'What's dangerous?' Melissa said, placing her tray on the table and seating herself next to Alfie. 'What are you boys up to now? Something mischievous, no doubt.'

'Just talking about potions,' Charles said. He eyed Melissa's dinner – chicken pie, sweetcorn and mash, covered in parsley sauce – then looked at his own. 'I knew I should have gone for the pie; it looks really nice.'

She spooned some into her mouth. 'It tastes really nice, too.'

Even above the din of noise in the hall, Leo's tummy rumbled loud enough for Alfie to hear.

'I'm going to get some of that pie,' Leo said, disappearing from the table.

After he'd gone, Melissa said, 'What's this potion for then? Something to do with a certain bully and what's happening this evening is my guess.'

'So you know what's happening as well?' Charles said, focusing on Alfie more than Melissa.

'She's my friend *and* she's a witch *and* no one else knows,' Alfie said in his defence. 'Oh, and she wants to be there to see what happens this evening, don't you Melissa? She told me this was something she just couldn't miss.'

'The more the merrier,' Charles said with a look of resignation.

At that moment, Salter and his friends entered the room and began causing a commotion. Harrison and Mason decided to pester a girl, pulling her ponytail. Salter and Bradley decided they would harass three boys who were seated, so they could acquire themselves a table. The harassment worked. The boys got up, taking their trays of food with them. Once they were clear of the danger zone, they looked around for somewhere else to sit. Not an easy task, now all the tables were taken.

Alfie looked on, concerned. He wondered how long it would be before Salter noticed him.

Alfie told Melissa that Leo had volunteered to take the potion.

'Leo?' she said. 'Why have you involved him? He isn't a wizard … is he?'

'Charles has already given me an ear-full for involving Leo,' Alfie said. 'I've given him my word that I won't tell anyone else, so I don't need a lecture from you.' He began eating his dinner a lot faster, whilst snatching occasional glances towards the table where Salter was seated.

'Right-o, not the smartest thing to do: telling non-magical friends,' Melissa said. 'And I won't lecture you about the silliness of what you've done, because I'm sure that's all too obvious now. Not to mention that you've put the magical community at risk of exposure. Plus there's the fact that Mr Pendred might find out about this ...'

As she carried on talking, repeating everything Charles had said, Alfie stared at the wall on the far side, tuning himself out of this situation. When he opened them, he focused his attention on Charles.

'Can you be at my house with the potion for quarter to seven?' he asked him. 'Will you have enough time to brew it?'

'It shouldn't be a problem,' Charles said. 'Some can take days or even weeks to brew, but this one's a thirty minute job, if I remember rightly.'

Alfie told Charles his address, then he cast another glance in Salter's direction. Harrison and Mason had finished harassing the girl and joined him at the table. Salter was rubbing his lips and looking thoughtfully menacing. Alfie didn't have to be a mind-reader to know what he was thinking. And then Salter's gaze shifted in Alfie's direction.

'He won't do anything now,' Melissa said. 'Mr Langford's over there, look. By the door.'

'I wouldn't be so sure,' Alfie said.

He put his knife and fork down, then pushed his plate away. He'd lost his appetite.

Salter got up and for a second Alfie thought he was going to come in his direction. But he didn't. He and Harrison got a tray each and joined the queue. *He'll work his way over here in a minute,* Alfie thought. *He's probably waiting for the teacher to disappear and then he'll pounce.*

Alfie wasn't going to wait around for that to happen.

'I feel a bit sick,' he said, standing up and downing his orange juice in one big, long gulp. 'I need some fresh air.'

The others weren't fooled.

'You can't run and hide every time you see him,' Melissa said.

'She's right,' Charles said, agreeing with her. 'You can't avoid him forever.'

'Just until this evening,' Alfie said.

'And what if your little stunt doesn't work?' Melissa said. 'What if it doesn't have the desired effect? You'll be back to square one tomorrow and things might be worse. Probably *will* be worse.'

'Charles will get the potion right, won't you Charles?' Alfie said.

'I most certainly will,' Charles assured him.

'Then I have nothing to worry about,' Alfie said.

'Are you off?' Leo said, returning with his tray of food and drink.

'He's frightened that Salter's going to start something again,' Melissa said.

'I am *not* frightened, I just need to get some fresh air,' Alfie said. He told Leo what time he needed to be at his house and told him not to be late.

'Not a chance of that,' Leo said. 'I wouldn't miss this for the world.'

Careful to take a wide birth of Salter and his friends, Alfie walked away and exited the dinner hall.

Alfie managed to avoid Salter for the rest of the day. After the last lesson, when the bell sounded, Alfie walked part of the way home with Leo and Melissa. They talked excitedly about what would happen later. Leo was sure that Salter would poop his pants in fright and Melissa was certain he would be so scared he'd turn into a quivering mass of jelly. Alfie was just disappointed he wouldn't be there to see it.

'Why won't you be there to see it?' Melissa asked him.

'I've been grounded,' Alfie said. He knew Melissa would ask why, so he did some quick thinking. 'Me and Eddie were fooling around in his bedroom and I knocked a glass of water on his XBOX. It won't come on now.'

Struggling to keep a straight face, Leo took an interest in a bird that was flying overhead.

'Oh dear,' Melissa said to Alfie. 'Not sure if that can be mended using magic, but hey-ho, you never know. Anyway, back to what you were saying about missing out on this evening's antics. There is a way you can see it.'

'Yeah?' Alfie said, intrigued. 'How?'

'You'll find out later,' Melissa said, going her own way. 'Six forty-five, yeah?'

'Yes,' Alfie said. 'Don't be late!'

'I won't,' Melissa said.

She skipped and hummed a tune as she disappeared down the street.

'She goes the same way as me, so I'm going to catch her up,' Leo said, following after her. 'And yes, I know: six forty-five. I won't be late.' He smiled a big, toothy grin, waved, then took off after Melissa.

When Alfie arrived home, he got a nice surprise. Mrs Trotter told him that she and Mr Trotter had been talking last night. They had come to the conclusion that grounding Alfie for a month was a bit harsh, given that they'd confiscated his magical items. A period of two weeks was suggested by Mr Trotter and agreed upon by Mrs Trotter, much to Alfie's delight. Alfie asked if the period of punishment could begin tomorrow as there was somewhere he wanted to go this afternoon, but his parents' leniency wouldn't stretch that far.

At six forty, when Leo knocked on the door, Alfie greeted him and beckoned him inside.

'Uh-hum!' Mrs Trotter said, appearing in the hallway. 'Are we struggling with the meaning of the word "grounded" here, Alfie? I'm sorry, Leo, but he can't come out this evening, because of what happened yesterday.'

'We're going to my bedroom,' Alfie said. 'You told me I couldn't go out, but you didn't say anything about having friends around.'

He went to his bedroom with Leo, leaving a frustrated Mrs Trotter to brood in the hallway.

A few minutes later there was another knock at the door, then Mrs Trotter shouted upstairs, 'Alfie, two more of your friends are here!'

'Send them up!' Alfie replied.

As Charles and Melissa entered the bedroom, Mrs Trotter followed them in.

'So what's this all about, then?' she said, eyeing everyone quizzically. 'What are you lot up to? Not homework, I take it.'

Alfie said, 'Seeing as I'm going to be stuck in the house for a few weeks, I thought I'd ask a few friends around. Please tell me you're not going to embarrass me by telling them to leave, because that would be a poor show of hospitality on your part, mother.'

'I'm not asking anyone to leave,' Mrs Trotter said. 'I just want to know what you're up to.'

'We haven't decided yet,' Alfie said. 'But we'll let you know when we do.'

Mrs Trotter gave him an icy stare. 'Don't you be sarcastic with me, young mister. Especially after what you've done. I'm going to have a word with your father about this and we may have to reassess the terms of your grounding.' She left the room in a huff.

Alfie waited until he was certain she was out of earshot, then said, 'I should have thought this through a bit better. Come up with a believable excuse for you lot being here.'

'I don't think you did yourself any favours there,' Melissa said, looking around the bedroom. 'You certainly do like your Star Wars. And Avengers. And Lego. Yep, this is a true boy's room, all right.'

'What did you expect?' Leo said. 'Dolls houses and Barbie dolls and make-up sets?'

'So how come you're grounded?' Charles asked Alfie. 'What have you done?'

'He dropped a glass of water on his brother's XBOX.'

'Oops,' Charles said. 'Electronics and water don't mix well.'

'Never mind that,' Alfie said. 'Have you got the potion?'

Producing a small vial from inside his jacket, Charles said with a smile: 'We're good to go.'

'Great stuff,' Alfie said. 'Are you still up for this, Leo? You still game?'

'I'm still game,' Leo replied, beginning to look nervous. He asked Charles if he was one hundred percent – no, *two* hundred percent – certain he'd brewed the potion correctly and that the effects would wear off.

'I triple-checked the ingredients,' Charles said. 'And, even if I have got it wrong, the effects will begin to wear off after thirty minutes, give or take. You've got nothing to worry about. You have my word.'

'Okay,' Leo said, still looking nervous. 'After swallowing it, how long will it take to work?'

'About five minutes,' Charles said, 'so I'd hold off on swallowing it yet. Unless you want to parade through the streets, causing panic and mayhem.'

'He does that already,' Alfie said, giving Leo a smile.

'The words pot and kettle come to mind,' Leo replied, offering a smile back. He was wearing a hooded top under his jacket. Slipping a hand over his shoulder, he pulled the hood up, then pushed it back down. 'Thought it would be a good idea to wear this, just in case I need to hide my face when the time comes.'

Charles checked his watch. 'Right, I think we should go. Better that we get there early and wait around than risk missing him.'

'Just one thing to do before we leave,' Melissa said. Reaching into her pocket, she pulled out a small glass ball and handed it to Alfie. 'So you don't miss any of the action.'

'Thanks,' Alfie said, feeling the weight of it in his hand, admiring its crystalline structure. 'How does it work?'

From Melissa's other pocket, she produced an identical ball. 'What I see, you'll see. Just make sure you're holding it when the time comes, otherwise you'll miss everything.'

'See-Globes,' Charles said, impressed. 'They're quite rare. Where'd you get them?'

'They're my grandad's,' Melissa replied. 'I borrowed them. Hopefully he won't notice.'

'But how will I know when I need to hold it?' Alfie asked.

'The club kicks out at seven-thirty,' Charles said, 'so be ready from then. Should we come back here afterwards, or will it be too late?'

Alfie said, 'I don't want to give my mum anything else to moan about, so don't come back here.'

'Okay,' Leo said, patting himself down as if he might otherwise forget something, 'are we all set? Ready to go?'

'We're ready,' Melissa said.

'Ready and eager,' Charles said, producing his wand from inside his jacket, then stowing it away again.

As they were leaving, Melissa said to Alfie, 'Just so know, you won't be able to hear anything through the Globe.'

'I won't be able to hear anything!' Alfie said, aghast.

'It's called a See-Globe,' Melissa said. 'Not a See and Hear Globe. Please don't break it; I *really* don't want to have to explain that to my grandad.'

'I won't,' Alfie said.

No sooner had the front door clicked shut, Alfie heard footsteps on the stairs, so he hid the See-Globe under his pillow. Then Mrs Trotter entered the room, wanting to know why Alfie's friends had left so soon.

'I didn't invite them around,' he said. 'They were just passing, on their way to the park, and popped in to see me. They know I've been grounded, so I guess they felt a bit sorry for me. That was nice of them, wasn't it?'

Not looking convinced, Mrs Trotter said, 'Yes, very considerate.'

She told Alfie that she'd baked some cookies earlier. She said that he should come downstairs now because she was putting a bowl of them on the table. Eddie was due home soon from his football training and would make them disappear quickly, so best to get in early. Figuring he had enough time to scoff some yummy cookies, Alfie went downstairs and watched TV.

At seven twenty-five, he went back to his bedroom and closed the curtains. He sat on his bed. Retrieving the Globe from under the pillow, he cupped it in his right hand and stared down at it, waiting for something to happen. But nothing did. After a few more seconds passed, Alfie thought: *maybe I'm holding it wrong.* He was about to try grasping it in both hands when the Globe misted up inside. He wondered whether it was working properly. Then the mist began to clear, semi-darkness filling the void in its place. In the darkness, Alfie could make out the silhouetted figures of two people standing in a wooded area. The one on the left was tall and gangly, surely Charles. The one on the right was short and stocky, surely Leo. Or was it? Melissa held up what must have been a small torch, using it to illuminate the figure's appearance. And ... yes, it was definitely Leo. Yet, in a gruesome way, it wasn't. Through the crystalline structure of the See-Globe, a huge, hairy face stared back at Alfie. Baleful red eyes gleamed like jewels from beneath a jutting forehead. A cavernous smile revealed rows of razor-sharp teeth, glistening with saliva.

The potion had worked. Leo was now a werewolf.

Kicking his feet out in excitement, Alfie tried to figure out where his friends were. As Melissa turned to her left, Alfie could make out a sporadically lit pathway in the distance and figured this to be the one that led to the sports hall. Charles began moving in that direction and the other two followed, Leo pulling his hood up as he went. When they were near the pathway, Charles and Leo held back while Melissa stepped out to look towards the sports hall.

Kids were coming out, going in different directions. Most were heading for the car park. A few were walking along the path, towards Melissa. Alfie couldn't see Salter and thought that it would be just his luck for this to be the one night when his arch nemesis had decided not to attend training. A few minutes past as everyone dispersed, moved away. And then Alfie saw him, walking through the foyer with a bag slung over his shoulder. Exiting the building, he headed along the path, in

Melissa's direction, so she darted back into the trees. Charles said something to her and she must have said something back, because he nodded. He looked towards Leo, whose red eyes glowed from underneath his hoodie. And then Leo gave a thumbs up, which prompted Melissa to divert her attention back to the path.

Salter walked past. Moving from under a light, he produced a gaming device from his pocket and began playing on it. When he was a safe distance away, Leo pulled his hoodie down low over his face, then moved out onto the path and began following him. Melissa and Charles waited a few seconds, until Salter was a good distance ahead, then they started moving through the undergrowth, pushing tree branches out of the way as they went.

They're hanging back so Salter won't hear them stepping on twigs and stuff, Alfie thought. *That's smart.*

From Melissa's vantage point, Alfie could see that Leo was gaining ground on Salter, who was still fiddling with his gaming device, oblivious. All seemed to be going well, according to plan … until Charles tripped over something and went sprawling. Whilst Melissa was helping him up, she glanced towards the path and Alfie was able to see that Salter had stopped dead. He was looking in Charles and Melissa's direction, but then he noticed his pursuer. Because Leo still had his hood down over his face, Salter couldn't make out who was approaching him. It wasn't until Leo got quite close to Salter that he began to panic. His mouth dropped open in shock and he turned and ran off at a pace that Alfie didn't think he was capable of achieving.

By this time, Charles was back on his feet and crashing through the undergrowth. Past trees and bushes he went, drawing his wand, with Melissa right behind him. She kept glancing towards the path, but Salter was now out of view. She could still see Leo, though, giving chase, moving surprisingly fast as well, for a stocky kid. No doubt sensing that Salter was going to get away, Charles took lurching steps as he veered in the direction of the path. Emerging from the trees, with Melissa still right behind him, he took aim with his wand. But he couldn't cast his spell, because Leo was in the way.

Look behind you! Alfie thought. *Move to the side!*

Leo kept up the pursuit.

STOP AND *LOOK BEHIND YOU!* Aflie thought again, more forcefully. *MOVE TO THE SIDE!*

Then Leo *did* stop. He moved to the side.

With a clear line of sight, Charles raised his wand and cast his spell.

It was as if someone had pressed a pause button. One second Salter was bombing along, like he was trying for a world record in the hundred metre sprint. And then he stopped, in mid-stride. His left leg was stretched out at the back, reminding Alfie of an Olympic long jumper who was about to spring off. His right arm was outstretched, gaming device still in hand, reminding Alfie of a relay racer holding out a baton.

Melissa moved out onto the path, looking both ways. Alfie figured she was checking to see if anyone else was about. But there wasn't anybody else: it was just Salter and Charles and Melissa and … Leo the werewolf, who had now pulled his hood back. As long as Charles and Melissa stayed behind Salter, he wouldn't see them, thanks to Charles' statue spell.

Catching up with Salter, Leo positioned himself in front of him and smiled, showing off his long, pointy incisors. Leo's tongue lolled out and his eyes burned a fearsome red: issuing a warning. Then Leo began to speak and Alfie found himself wishing he could lip read. Alfie could only imagine the fear that must now be gripping Salter. *Bet you'll need a change of underwear when you get home*, he thought with glee. As Leo continued to talk to Salter, Melissa looked behind her to see if anyone else was around. Satisfied the coast was still clear, she turned her attention back to the action. Leo was now brandishing a clawed finger at Salter: the standard gesture of someone issuing a warning.

'Alfie, can you come down here for a second, please!' Mr Trotter called up the stairs.

Oh, no! Alfie thought. *Not now! Not when things a getting really interesting!*

'I'll be down in a minute!' he called back.

'I need you down here now!' Mr Trotter said. 'Don't make me ask again, matey. Not when you're already grounded.'

'Ahh, no,' Alfie muttered in a low voice. 'I *don't* believe it.'

He took one last look at the See-Globe – Leo was still brandishing his clawed finger, still issuing a warning – then he put it under his pillow and went to see what his father wanted. Alfie hoped this wouldn't take too long, so he didn't miss out on any of the action. Fortunately, it took less than two minutes. Unfortunately, this was about thirty seconds too long. Someone had moved one of Mr Trotter's golf trophies from above the fireplace and he wanted to know where it was. As it turned out, Mrs Trotter was the guilty party. She had moved all his trophies so she could do some dusting, then left one on the bookcase.

Back in his bedroom, Alfie eagerly snatched up the See-globe from under his pillow. The Globe had misted over, so Alfie cupped it in his hands again, expecting the connection to be re-established. But nothing happened – it remained misted. This got Alfie wondering: had something gone wrong, or had Melissa stopped broadcasting because Salter had been fully dealt with. Alfie knew he would have to wait until the morning to find out, but he still held the Globe for a few minutes in the hope he would see something more.

Finally giving up, he stowed the Globe beneath his bed, out of sight. And then he went downstairs to watch TV in the back room. He thought that an hour or so of watching Sylvester chase Tweety would take his mind off things, but he was wrong. As he delighted in the bird continuously getting one over on the cat, his mind was not so much on Salter as something more important. Alfie knew that dealing with Salter was a minor thing compared to other troubles that loomed on the horizon. Troubles that involved a powerful wand known as the Stormbringer and a powerful wizard named Renwald.

CHAPTER 10
(The Second Lesson)

On school days, Alfie rarely crawled out of bed before 7:30am, except on special occasions, such as his birthday. Today was most definitely not a special occasion. It was a cold Tuesday morning and he was comfy under his covers, lying on his side with his knees tucked up to his chest, snoring lightly. The knock on the front door didn't wake him. But the second knock, much louder, did. Opening his eyes to no more than slits, Alfie wondered who could be calling at such an early hour.

He heard Mrs Trotter answer the door, then say, 'Leo, what are you doing here at this time? Have you got bugs in your bed or something?'

The way Alfie sprang out of bed, anyone would have thought it was Christmas. He finished putting his uniform on just as Leo came into his room.

'You changed back, then,' Alfie said.

'I did. But not before I'd had a *lot* of fun.'

They both looked at each other, all smiles.

'So ...' Alfie said, 'are you going to fill me in, or what? I want to know what you said to Salter. I want to know *everything*.'

'Basically, in a nutshell, I told him that if he doesn't stop bullying kids at school, I'm going to come back and eat him. I told him that I know where he lives and that he looked like he'd be a tasty meal. I've never seen anyone look so scared and I *loved* every minute of it.'

'I bet you did. My dad called me downstairs, so I didn't see what happened at the end.'

'After I'd finished with the threats, Charles waited 'till I was clear of Salter, then he unfroze him. After that we just ran off through the trees, so you didn't miss anything.'

Leo scratched behind his neck. 'I had a shower when I got in, but I've still been itching ever since I changed back. My mum wanted to know why the plug hole was clogged up with thick brown hairs. And d'you know what, I'm sure I've got flees or something.'

'Don't worry about it,' Alfie said, 'we'll take you to the vets after school.'

That got both of them laughing.

At school, Alfie kept an eye out for Salter, but he didn't see him. He quizzed a geeky boy called Harold to see if Salter had attended registration. (Harold was another one of Salter's usual victims and unfortunate enough to be in the same form). He told Alfie that he'd overheard Bradley and Mason talking and they'd said that Salter's mum had rang in, stating he was sick. More smiles from Alfie. And, at dinner time, when he told Charles and Melissa, they were all smiles as well. When Alfie gave Melissa the See-Globe back, she looked it over, inspecting it.

'I haven't damaged it,' Alfie said. 'It's as it was when you gave it me.'

'Still need to check, just to be on the safe side,' she said. 'Just need to get them back in my grandad's cupboard without him noticing.'

Without Salter around, his friends weren't a problem. They gave Alfie dirty looks and Harrison even snarled at him as they passed in the corridor. But Alfie was sure that this type of behaviour would cease when Salter returned from his bout of "sickness". Salter was the chief of that little gang and what he said was gospel as far as they were concerned. Alfie was sure that they would be curious as to Salter's change of heart with regards to terrorizing other kids. But he didn't think Salter would tell them about what'd happened, because they would surely believe he was either joking or lost his mind.

So, all in all, Alfie had probably the best day at school that he'd ever had, thanks to magic and some help from his friends. He even passed his assessment test in maths, gaining an A-. This was pretty good for Alfie, who was normally a Bs and Cs, middle of the road kid. He made a mental note to tell his parents, because he knew this would go some way to making up for the broom-flying shenanigans.

Things were going so well, right up to the close of the day. Alfie was halfway home when he realised he'd left his pencil case in his desk. It was a Lego Batman one, which had cost him five pounds, so he didn't want to risk it being stolen. Fortunately it was still there and Alfie was able to breathe a sigh of relief.

Upon leaving, had Alfie taken a left down the stairs on the second floor corridor, instead of going straight ahead to descend the ones at the far end, he would not have had to deal with the quandary he was about to be presented with.

Passing one of the classrooms, he noticed Mr Langford seated at his desk, talking to himself. Or at least that was what it looked like at first. On closer inspection, as Alfie positioned himself to the side of the doorway, he saw that Mr Langford was in fact talking to a flat holographic sphere, which was floating in front of the desk. Or, to be more specific, he was talking to the person who was inside the sphere: a hooded figure with no discernible features.

'So can the Kingdoms of the North rely on the Shadow People for their allegiance, Dragan?' Mr Langford said to the figure. 'It is in your interests to join us. Renwald bears your kin no love, but we both know that he'll make promises of how you'll benefit under his reign – promises he *won't* keep.'

'Those promises have already been made,' Dragan replied in a voice that was a silky purr. 'My answer to you is the same as to him. We will take no part in any war to come.'

'You *will* take part in this war, one way or another. There is no species or race of people who won't get dragged into this. And you are south of the Canyon, so it will be your kind who will suffer first. Renwald has the wand. You know what that means. You know of the power he now commands.'

'I do. And I also know that our kind has never been conquered, not in the thousands of years we have lived in the Darklands. Many have tried, including those Northern Kings who you would align us with, and all have failed. Wand or no wand, Renwald will fair no better than anyone else, if the worst comes to the worst.'

'You underestimate the power of the Stormbringer.'

'And you underestimate the power of the Shadow People.'

'Renwald has already persuaded many to join his cause: the Forest Trolls ... the Marsh Ghouls ...'

'Dangerous as they all are, they do not number enough to mount a serious attack.'

'Others will join, too. I've heard from a reliable source that Renwald plans to meet with the Giants.'

'The answer is no. I have made up my mind and you will not make me change it.'

Mr Langford slumped forwards in his seat, rubbing his chin, deep in thought. He was no doubt wondering what he could say that would change Dragan's mind. Alfie didn't like his chances. The shadow man seemed adamant that he would play no part in any war, no matter what argument Mr Langford put forth.

A voice echoed along the corridor, making Alfie jump in surprise. 'Oi – what are you doing?' Mr Leech, the caretaker, said. 'Why are you loping around that door?'

Stepping away from the door in the bat of an eye, Alfie didn't hang about to offer an explanation. He darted down the corridor and down the steps. *He's got it*, Alfie thought as he exited the building. *Renwald has the Stormbringer*. He was tempted to go straight to Charles' house, so he could discuss this with him. He decided not to, however, because he knew he would be seeing him in a few hours anyway, at the academy. Plus there was the small matter of being grounded to consider. Mrs Trotter would notice if Alfie came home late from school and she'd want to know why.

Alfie was usually hungry when he arrived home from school. Not today. Mixed emotions were dampening his appetite. On one hand he was excited about attending his second magic lesson. On the other he was anxious about what the consequences would be of Renwald obtaining the Stormbringer.

Sitting at the table with the rest of his family, Alfie spooned risotto into his mouth, chewing unenthusiastically.

'You usually wolf that down,' Mrs Trotter noted, dabbing her lips with a napkin. 'Is everything okay, Alfie?'

'I'd have thought you'd be elated,' Eddie said, smiling.

Alfie had told him that the trick on Salter had been successful.

'Why should he be elated?' Mr Trotter said, eyeing his sons through narrowed eyes. 'Is there something me and your mother should know?'

'He got an A in his mid-term assessment,' Eddie said. 'And he's off to magic school with his magical father, so there's nothing to be miserable about.'

'It was an A minus,' Alfie said, correcting him.

'Whatever,' Eddie said.

'Hmm,' Mrs Trotter said in a doubtful tone.

Alfie forced himself to finish his meal, just to keep her happy.

Afterwards, when all the pots had been cleared away by Alfie and Eddie, Mr Trotter slipped his shoes on. He asked Alfie if he was ready to go and what he needed to take with him.

'I'm not sure,' Alfie replied, donning his black robes. 'Mr Pendred didn't say.'

'Right-o,' Mr Trotter said. 'We'll take everything apart from your broomstick, because I don't think you'll be needing that yet. And the less we see of *that* the better, given what's happened. People might wonder why you're wearing those robes, so take them off and slip them on when we get there.'

'For all anyone knows, I could be in fancy dress as a wizard. I don't think anybody will guess where I'm really going.'

'First the broom-flying antics and now this attitude towards how you dress when going to the academy. You're not getting it, are you, Alfie? Yes, people will probably think you're going to a fancy dress party, but why risk drawing attention to yourself when there's *no* need. Just put the robes on when you get there. Problem solved.'

As Mr Trotter reached for his jacket, Alfie noticed his hand was shaking. He noticed something else, as well: a thin sheen of sweat on his father's brow. Alfie felt guilty that he hadn't given any thought to how his father would feel going back to the academy after all this time.

Mr Trotter went upstairs, then returned with the cauldron, which had all the other items that were needed stowed inside. Removing the lid, Alfie placed his potions book and robes inside. He knew where his parents had hidden his magical items: under their bed. He'd sneaked into their room for a nosy before retiring to sleep last night. He just couldn't resist.

'Ready?' Mr Trotter asked, offering a nervous smile.

'Ready,' Alfie replied, offering a supportive one back.

'Right, we're off!' Mr Trotter said loudly, so that Mrs Trotter and Eddie would hear.

Mrs Trotter was first to react. She came through from the kitchen, glowing with excitement.

'Have you got everything?' she said, fussing over Alfie, brushing him down and giving him a quick once-over. 'And couldn't you find a better top than that to wear? What about the nice brown one I bought you a few weeks ago. I haven't seen you with it on yet. Why?'

Because I don't like it, Alfie thought. 'I'll wear it next time.'

Appearing from the living room, Eddie said, 'Have a blast, bro. Enjoy yourself.'

'I will,' Alfie assured him.

'Come on, squirt,' Mr Trotter said, putting an arm around him, 'let's get gone; we don't want to be late.'

'It's down here on the right,' Alfie said as they were nearing the academy.

'I know where it is,' Mr Trotter replied, dropping his Astra into second gear, then taking them through the gate.

As they proceeded along the driveway, he leaned forwards in his seat to get a better look at the academy. Silhouetted against the darkening skyline, it was every bit as imposing and impressive as Alfie remembered from his first visit. A light was on in Mr Pendred's tower study, but there was no face at the window.

'Hasn't changed in the slightest,' Mr Trotter said. 'Not a jot.'

'Since when?'

Mr Trotter gave Alfie a brief sideways glance, a searching look, then he averted his gaze back to the driveway.

After a brief silence, while he was backing his Astra into a space in the car park, he said, 'I'll confess that I've been past a few times over the years, just out of curiosity. To see if the entrance was still here. I always knew it would be, but ... you know how it is. Sometimes nostalgia takes over and you go off on a whim.'

'And you came here with Mum, too.' Alfie slapped a hand over his mouth. 'Oops,' he said. 'My big mouth strikes again.' He expected Mr Trotter to get angry, but he didn't; he just smiled and nodded slowly.

'You're about as good at keeping secrets as your mother,' Mr Trotter said. 'That was the only time I've actually been through the entrance in the last twenty-five or so years. As you know, it's not visible from the road, because it's set so far back. One time, when we were in the area and I mentioned that the academy was around here, she asked if she could see it. I said that we could drive past the gate and that was it. She seemed okay with that at first. But then, when we got here and I touched her so she could see the gate, she wanted to go inside. I said no and she seemed okay with that. But I know when your mother's not happy. She goes quiet and all you get out of her are snappy, one word responses. "Shall we go home now?" - "Yes." "Are you going shopping with your friends this weekend?" - "Yes." You know what she's like.'

Alfie did. He had been on the receiving end of those one word responses many times.

Mr Trotter continued: 'Not wanting to have the silent treatment for the next week or so, I turned the car around and gave her what she wanted, because I didn't want her to be unhappy. I wanted her to see the academy in all its glory, just so *I* see the look of awe on her face. She didn't give any thought as to how it would affect me, clapping eyes on this place again. I tried not to look concerned as we parked up, but either my face or the tone of my voice betrayed me. After about a minute of being parked up, sitting here, talking to each other, I thought she was going to suggest we walk around, or even go inside. She didn't, though. To my surprise, she asked if we should leave. A queue of kids and parents was forming by the front door, just like now. And then the door opened and Mr Pendred stepped out, looking almost the same as I remembered. I hadn't seen him in twenty years and he'd hardly changed at all. There was a few flecks of grey in that long, silky black hair of his and a few more lines around those wise old eyes, but there was no mistaking that it was him.'

'He's very distinctive looking,' Alfie said. 'Not someone you'd miss in a crowd. His hair is still long and silky, but it's totally grey now.'

'Time withers us all. Even a great wizard such as Mr Pendred.'

'So what happened when you saw him? Did you say hello?'

'Oh gosh, no. Soon as he laid eyes on me, that was it. I drove me and your mother out of the gate and never looked back.' Drumming his fingers nervously on the steering wheel, Mr Trotter cast a keen eye over the ever-growing queue. 'I do wonder, you know, whether I'll see anyone I recognise. Most of the kids I came here with will have had children of their own. Some will be magical and some won't. I'd imagine a parent or two might recognize me. I haven't changed that much since I studied here. I've still got all my own hair.' He ruffled his thick, brown mop to emphasize this point. Then he continued to drum

213

his fingers on the steering wheel, looking more and more nervous by the second.

Alfie put a reassuring hand on his father's knee. 'You don't have to go in with me; I'll be fine on my own, Dad.'

'Nonsense,' he replied without hesitation. 'I'm staying.'

'Really, I'll be okay. You can pick me up afterwards; it's not a problem.'

'I fled last time I was here and I'm not doing it again.' Mr Trotter got out of the car, then ducked back down and said, 'Are you coming, then, or what?'

Alfie didn't need a second prompt. Stepping out, he reached for the sky, stretching like he'd been on a long journey.

Mr Trotter retrieved the cauldron from the rear seat, then handed Alfie his robes. As Alfie slipped them on, Mr Trotter groaned because of the weight of the cauldron.

Alfie spotted Melissa and her granddad, who were near the front of the queue. Melissa spotted Alfie and gave him a wave. He returned the gesture with a smile.

'A new friend?' Mr Trotter asked him as they joined the end of the queue.

'Kind of,' Alfie replied. 'She's in my form at school, so I've known her for a while (just to say hello to and that).' He didn't want his father to think he was getting too pally with a "girl".

'But you've started talking to her more since you found out she's magical, like you, right?'

'Yes, that's right.' *Her and Charles,* Alfie thought.

'I guess that's one good thing about magic: how it can bring people together. It's things like that I should focus on, rather than anything negative, you know. I need to concentrate on the positives in life. Need to be a pint half full type of person, rather than a pint half empty ...'

Listening to Mr Trotter ramble on about pints being half full, Alfie looked along the line to see who'd returned for the second lesson. The twins, Marlon and Murray, each with a cauldron in hand, were at the front. They were waiting eagerly by the door with the adult who'd accompanied them last time (Alfie still couldn't tell which twin was which). Next to them, just in front of Melissa, was Amelia: the know-it-all girl with the superior Willow wand. She was talking to the little mousy girl (Leila? Was that her name?), who did not look impressed by what she was saying. Joining the queue behind Alfie was Troy, who'd ended up covered in soot during the first lesson after trying to create a fire by saying the words for the spell incorrectly. Another late-comer filed in behind him. James: the boy who was always blowing his nose. There were others that Alfie remembered, but he couldn't put names to their faces. No, that's not true; Alfie was quite sure that the nervous-looking chubby boy on the lawn was called John.

'I'd stay away from those,' Alfie said, noticing that he was straying a little too close to the slug-eating plants. 'Can't you read the sign?'

Mr Pendred had been good to his word and placed one in front of the Limus Carnivorous plants: **CAUTION – KEEP CLEAR (UNLESS YOU WANT TO LOSE YOUR FINGERS!)**

'I know exactly what they are and exactly what they can do,' John said, staring dreamily up at the gargoyles protruding from the building. 'I've read all about them in a book.'

'Ah, the slug eaters,' Mr Trotter said reflectively. 'Or finger eaters, as we used to call them. Mr Pendred has been growing those for years. I remember one boy foolishly losing a thumb because of a dare. *Very* messy business. And *very* painful, I'd imagine. Took him a week to regrow it using a special potion.'

Just then, the front door creaked open and Charles appeared, greeting everyone as he let them in. He didn't look happy. Alfie did not need two guesses as to why. Charles managed a smile when he saw Alfie and Mr Trotter.

'This must be your father,' Charles said. 'It's good to see you here.'

'It's good to be here,' Mr Trotter replied, shaking hands with him.

'This is Charles,' Alfie said, 'the boy who got me recruited at the academy.'

'So *you're* the one responsible for all the upheaval,' Mr Trotter said in a jovial tone.

Charles replied, 'Guilty as charged.'

There was no hanging about in the hallway this time, no messing about in front of the painting that showed different things to different people. Everyone filed straight into the classroom. Unlike the first lesson, most of the parents left their kids so they could pick them up later. A few parents stayed behind, though. Amelia's mother seated herself next to Mr Trotter at the back of the class, beneath the flickering glow of a candle-lit wall lantern. *Good luck with that one, Dad,* Alfie thought. He made his way to his desk, chuckling to himself.

'What's so funny?'

Alfie turned to see Melissa.

'Oh, hi,' he said. He nodded towards Mr Trotter. 'I don't think my dad will want to come again after an hour of being seated next to *that* woman.'

'Hey, you never know, they might get on really well. I'm glad you persuaded him to come, though; I can tell it means a lot to you.' She placed her cauldron by her desk. 'I hope we don't have to lug this thing here every time we do potions.'

'That will not be necessary,' Mr Pendred said, appearing at the front of the classroom as though he'd popped out of thin air. For all Alfie knew, he might well have. Mr Pendred addressed the class. 'Please feel free to leave any items you do not wish to take home with you inside your desks. They will be perfectly safe here at the academy, I can assure you.'

The Stormbringer wasn't safe here, Alfie thought.

'Where should we leave our cauldrons?' Troy asked.

'In your desks,' Mr Pendred said.

Amelia opened the lid on hers. 'There's barely room to fit any books in here, never mind a *cauldron.*'

Mr Pendred was pacing back and forth at the front of the classroom. He stopped and looked at Amelia, his steely grey eyes unblinking. 'If I say it will fit inside, then it will fit inside. I do not like having to repeat myself.'

216

Averting her gaze, Amelia looked like she was about to burst into tears.

Alfie opened his desk and peered inside. Amelia was right, as far as he could see. There was only enough room to fit small items. Shrugging, Alfie picked his cauldron up and went to place it inside. As he did, the bottom of the desk began to drop away. With a great deal of effort, he held the cauldron in place, then bent over to look at the underside of the desk. From this vantage point, the bottom did not appear to have moved at all. Not even an inch.

'Amazing,' Alfie said, straightening himself up. At first, he was surprised, but then not surprised in the slightest, after giving it some thought. 'I wonder how much stuff I could get in here.'

'Quite a lot, I'd imagine,' Melissa said.

'Everyone take a seat, please!' Mr Pendred said, his voice booming off the walls.

Alfie leaned towards Melissa and whispered, 'He doesn't seem to be in a very good mood.'

'And I think we know why,' she replied.

'*Quiet!*' Mr Pendred snapped, spinning around on one heel to face his students. He looked towards the back of the classroom, his attention drawn by something, or someone.

Following his gaze, Alfie realised that Mr Pendred was looking at Mr Trotter. *He recognises him*, Alfie thought. *Even after all these years, he* still *recognises my father.*

'Apologies,' Mr Pendred said, addressing the class. 'Please forgive my foul mood. I ... I have a nasty migraine coming on, so I'm finding it hard to concentrate.'

Alfie wasn't sure whether this was true or not. Taking into consideration what had happened since the first lesson, the onset of a migraine seemed plausible. Alfie couldn't help but think that the headmaster was lying, though. *Surely there's a potion for that sort of thing*, he thought. *Or some Aspirin would do the trick.*

As if reading his thoughts, Mr Pendred said, 'I'll take something for it in a bit ... Anyway, putting my grumpy demeanour aside, let's get on, shall we. True bravery can only ever come from within! But it doesn't hurt to have a little help now and again, which is why we're going to be brewing a bravery potion.'

Alfie could think of quite a few times when this one would have been useful (his many run-ins with Ryan Salter came to mind).

'Cauldrons ready on your desks and tuck your chairs away, because you'll need to be standing for this,' Mr Pendred said, addressing his students, who all did as they were requested. 'Charles, if you can do the handouts, please.'

Charles had already anticipated what he would say and was busy placing items on desks: a black pouch full of stuff for each student, plus a sheet of paper listing the quantities of the ingredients that needed to be added. He worked his way from the back of the classroom to the front.

'I cannot overstress how vital it is to measure out the correct amount of Worm Seeds,' Mr Pendred said. 'Better to have too little than too much. Too little and you won't be quite so brave. Too much and you'll want to conquer the world.'

'Sounds good to me,' one of the twins said.

'I'll have a double dose,' the other chirped in, giggling.

'That level of bravado has never worked out well for anyone,' Mr Pendred pointed out.

Alfie wondered whether he was thinking about Renwald when he said that.

Charles placed a pouch and sheet on Melissa's desk. Then he placed a pouch and sheet in front of Alfie.

'I need to speak to you after class,' he said in a low voice, focusing his attention on Charles and then Melissa. 'I need to speak to both of you.'

'I can guess why,' Melissa said.

Mr Pendred's voice boomed across the classroom, 'No talking, please! I will not have lessons disrupted by idle chit-chat!'

Charles gave Alfie a knowing look, then disappeared to the back of the room.

Seating himself behind his desk, Mr Pendred gestured everyone to commence. 'If you're not sure about anything, just ask. Either me or Charles will help. When you're finished, take a seat and wait. We'll test your concoctions at the end of the lesson.'

With that, all the students began reading from their sheets and adding ingredients to their cauldrons.

Alfie took four cloves of Bylazore Extract (whatever that was?). He measured some out accordingly.

'For your next lesson, I'll be quizzing you about these ingredients, so learning about them can be your homework,' Mr Pendred said. 'You'll find a glossary of terms at the back of the book, which will tell you everything you need to know.'

'But we get homework at school!' Amelia exclaimed.

'Yes,' Mr Pendred replied. 'And you'll get it here, too. You enjoy learning about magic, don't you?'

'Of course I do,' Amelia said. 'But ...'

'You'll enjoy sifting through that glossary I've just mentioned, then, won't you?' Mr Pendred said. He didn't wait for a reply.

Opening his desk drawer, he pulled out a book titled *Stargazing*. He began reading it as he reclined slightly back in his chair. Amelia watched him with a look of bewilderment on her face, then she went back to work, measuring out a green liquid, which Alfie noted was called Snapjack's Tears. He wondered what a Snapjack could be (it wasn't a creature he'd heard of). Perhaps it was one from Kordoba?

Melissa was first to finish. Satisfied she'd mixed her potion correctly, she seated herself. She gave Alfie a smug smile as she twirled her blonde curls with her fingers.

It's not about who finishes first, Alfie thought. *This isn't a race.*

Leila, the mousy girl who'd created a fire nearly as big as Alfie's in the first lesson, raised her hand. Charles was with her before Mr Pendred even noticed.

It was five minutes later when Alfie added his final ingredient: two pinches of salt. This was the only one on the list he was familiar with. Despite him thinking this wasn't a race, he was glad to note that he wasn't the last. James looked like he was struggling. As did Amelia, who Alfie was sure would have a meltdown if she was last to finish.

'How are we all getting along?' Mr Pendred said, placing his book aside, addressing the class. 'Are we winning?'

Several murmurs of 'Yes' and a few unsure grunts suggested that nobody was sure whether they were winning or not. Only Melissa seemed confident. Alfie hoped she'd made a mistake, just to teach her a lesson.

'I'm done,' James announced, seating himself.

The inevitable outburst came from Amelia, 'These instructions aren't clear,' she said, close to tears. 'It's says to add two pinches of salt, but what if I pinch more than someone else, or less? Everyone's fingers aren't the same size, after all. How daft! It's just *daft!*'

'Something's daft,' Troy said.

'Or someone,' one of the twins suggested.

This was greeted with laughter around the room.

'Don't laugh at me,' Amelia said, fixing all the offenders with a death stare. 'Don't you *DARE* laugh at me!'

Her mother noticed what was going on and was quick to come to her side.

'Who is laughing at *my* daughter!' she blustered, throwing accusatory looks here and there. 'I demand to know what's going on here!'

Sweeping down from the front of the room with his robes billowing out behind him, Mr Pendred was quick to deal with the situation. 'Anyone who ridicules another student in this class will be dealt with harshly. This is not the sort of behaviour I want at this academy and it will *not* be tolerated. Do you all understand?'

All the students stated loudly and clearly that they did, but not loudly and clearly enough for Mr Pendred. 'Do you *all* understand?' he repeated, with a lot more boom to his voice.

'YESSS!' they all said in unison, loud enough make Alfie wince.

Then, to Alfie's surprise, Mr Trotter became involved the situation.

Taking Mrs Loveday by the arm, he escorted her back towards her seat, telling her everything would be okay because Mr Pendred was dealing with things now. Alfie was sure that any second she would shrug him off and start making a fuss again. She didn't, though. She was flustered and clearly upset, but more than happy to let Mr Pendred tell off those that needed telling off now she was receiving attention from Mr Trotter.

Hmm, Alfie thought, watching them with interest. *Not what I expected.*

Meanwhile, Mr Pendred was talking to Amelia in a low voice and she was nodding, whilst wiping tears from her eyes. By the time he had finished, the tears had stopped and he even managed to get a smile from her.

'Charles,' Mr Pendred said, 'if you'd be so kind as to help Amelia add in her last few remaining ingredients while I continue with the class.'

Charles took over from Mr Pendred, who went back to the front of the classroom and addressed his students.

'Right,' he said, 'since we're all so confident, let's see what you can do. We need to find something that everyone's afraid of. What about spiders? That usually does the trick. So how are you with spiders?'

'They don't bother me,' Troy said.

'I hate them,' Melissa said.

'Depends on how big they are,' James said.

One of the twins pointed at the other. 'He pulled the legs off one once.'

'No I did not,' the one who'd been accused protested. 'You're such a liar!'

'Okay,' Mr Pendred said, appealing for calm. 'We'll go with arachnids. You'll find a small vial in your pouch. Fill it with your newly-mixed potion and swallow it down in one quick gulp.'

All the students did as instructed.

Finding the taste quite acidic, Alfie said, 'That wasn't very nice.'

'Most potions aren't,' Melissa said.

'If you want a tasty drink, then get yourself a can of coke,' Mr Pendred said. 'Are we done yet? All finished?' Everyone was, so he produced his wand from beneath his cloak. 'The potion is fast-acting, so let's have everyone to the front of the class, please. Form a line. Wands at the ready.'

Eager and confident, Troy was first to present himself. Everyone else filed in behind him. With Charles' help, Amelia had finished mixing her concoction, so she swallowed it (eh! That's gross!), then went to the back of the line.

'Feeling confident, are we?' Mr Pendred asked Troy.

'*Yes*,' he replied.

'Good,' Mr Pendred said. 'You'll be using a repelling spell. As with any spell, make sure you pronounce the words correctly: Parabit Nibilis. We'll practice first. All together now, lowering your wands so you don't repel someone into a wall by accident, pay particular emphasis to the S on the end. You need to draw it out – *sssss*: like a snake.'

'Parabit Nibilis!' all the students said in unison.

'Excellent!' Mr Pendred said. Then he conjured up a spider, which was no bigger than a pound coin.

Troy sniggered and so did some of the others.

'Not big enough for you, I take it?' Mr Pendred said. 'Fine – not a problem.' He enchanted the spider so it became the size of a tarantula. 'How's that? Still feeling brave, are we?'

'No,' one boy said.

'It won't hurt you,' Troy said. 'My dad told me they're more scared of us than we are of them.'

'Bigger, then,' Mr Pendred said. This time his enchantment bloated the spider to the size of a small dog.

'*AHHHH!*' Amelia yelled, backing away in horror.

And she wasn't the only one. James looked ready to turn tail and run for the door. The twins were taking turns pushing each other forwards as they tried to hide behind one another. Leila's mouth had dropped open and her eyes were as wide as an owl's. Even Troy was concerned. He edged away, making an attempt to look brave, but doing a poor job of it.

So much for the bravery potion being fast-acting, Alfie thought.

He looked towards his father, trying to gauge his reaction. If Mr Trotter was concerned, then it would be time to start worrying. But Mr Trotter wasn't concerned. Quite the opposite; he was now standing at the back of the class, looking on with interest. And Mrs Loveday was next to him, quite unafraid.

'There's nothing to be scared of,' Alfie said to Melissa. 'I don't think it can hurt you, because I don't think it's real.'

'It looks real enough to me,' she replied, not convinced.

And it did, too. It had eight eyes, each of them like small, shiny black pearls. Clear liquid was dripping from its fangs, pooling on the floor.

Anything with more than four legs had always given Alfie the creeps, so this episode wasn't helping with his phobia.

'*Eh* – it's moving!' Troy said. 'It's coming to get me!'

The spider's eight hairy legs began to skitter as it advanced towards him.

'Quick, use your spell,' Mr Pendred instructed. 'Repel the creature.'

Raising his wand, Troy said the magical words, 'Parabit Nibilis!', which stopped the spider dead in its tracks.

'That's it,' Mr Pendred said. 'Good. Now hold it there until the next in line can take over.'

Next in line was one of the twins. He stepped forwards and, as he cast his spell, Troy moved out of the way, then stood by the wall. The other twin took over from his brother and successfully repelled the spider. It was desperately trying to come forwards, its many legs slipping and sliding on the wooden floor as it tried to breach the invisible barrier. On it went, each student taking their turn, until Alfie found himself facing the spider.

'I must have mixed my potion wrong,' he said, 'because I *really* don't feel any braver.'

'Don't hesitate,' Mr Pendred said. 'Raise your wand. Cast the spell.'

The spider lunged forwards, baring its fangs.

Alfie heard gasps of terror, the scuttle of feet as those behind him backed away. Casting his spell, Alfie stopped the creature just in time. A split second later and it would have been too late. What then? *Would I have been its dinner?* Alfie thought. *Or am I right and it isn't real.* He figured he would find out soon enough.

Meanwhile, the spider was still trying to get at Alfie, who was close enough to see his reflection in its many eyes.

'Retracto Reversum,' Mr Pendred said, casting a spell to drag it backwards. He then cast another to keep it rooted to the spot. 'Alfie, you did well. Now stand with the others by the wall. How many are yet to have a go?' He did a head count. 'Okay, the three of you need to make sure you don't hesitate and then we can avoid anymore near misses like that. Leila, please resume.'

Alfie wanted this whole exercise to come to a close. He was the only one who hadn't managed to keep the spider a safe distance from him. He noted that Amelia was yet to have her go. Surely she would get it wrong. She'd have some sort of melt down, wouldn't she?

Leila didn't dither. She repelled the spider before it'd barely moved.

Second to last was a fat boy named Benjamin. Alfie had never heard him speak and he didn't speak this time, either. With a face as expressionless as stone, he stopped the creature with no effort at all.

This just left Amelia. Alfie found himself willing her to fail, then felt ashamed of himself for doing so. And he was surprised when she stepped forwards with no hesitation. Yes, she looked afraid – petrified, even – but that didn't stop her from completing the task. After she'd held the spider at bay for a good ten seconds, Mr Pendred called a halt to proceedings.

He made it vanish in a cloud of smoke, then said, 'Well done, everyone; you all performed exceptionally. You must have brewed your potions correctly. Could you feel the bravery coursing through you as you faced your fear?'

'Yes!' Amelia said, giving herself a small round of applause.

'I did, too!' one boy said.

Others agreed with them.

'I didn't,' Alfie said, surprising himself by speaking up. He noticed the funny looks he was getting, so he explained: 'I'm almost certain I brewed mine right and I didn't feel any braver. Not even a little bit. I don't think the spider was real, either.' He looked at Mr Pendred, who was nodding and smiling. 'The whole thing was fake and done just to prove that we could be brave without any potion. It was done so we could prove to ourselves that we have it in us and we don't need any help.'

Now it was Mr Pendred who gave a round of applause. 'Bravo! You're a very clever boy, Alfie Trotter. And everything he says is true: the creature wasn't real and neither was the potion; it was a harmless concoction that does nothing. But you all managed to do it, so the next time you face a terrifying situation, you'll remember this exercise. You'll think to yourself: if I can face-down a gigantic arachnid, I can face down anything.'

'I knew it was all fake,' James said. 'I just *knew* it.'

'Oh that'll be why your hand was shaking so much then,' one of the twins said.

James said, 'My hand was *not* shaking!'

'Yes it was,' Leila said.

'*Quiet!*' Mr Pendred said. On his desk was a golden watch on a chain. He used it to check the time, then told the students that there was just long enough in the lesson to practice a simple spell. 'If you can all line up again, please. This time you'll learn how to body lock someone, like they've been turned to ice, or stone. Your magical words are Fangrom Icedam. Draw the G and R out, like a dog growling: *grrrrrr*. And give the I in Icedam some gusto: *I*-cedam. And to unlock, it's Relatco Icedas (with even more gusto to the I). To begin with, I need a volunteer.' When one wasn't forthcoming, Mr Pendred selected Melissa.

'Why me?' she said, not happy at all.

'Why not?' Mr Pendred replied. 'Don't worry, you'll all take your turn. Someone has to be first.'

Still not happy, Melissa did as he asked and once again the students formed a line. When it was Alfie's turn to be body locked (by Amelia, no less), he found it to be even scarier than facing the spider. He'd never felt so helpless, so vulnerable. Not being able to move a muscle, not even his eyes, wasn't something he wanted to experience again (*Being frozen like that must have scared Salter almost as much as being threatened by a werewolf*, Alfie thought). It was a lot more fun casting the spell and this time Alfie didn't hesitate; he froze one of the twins into a motionless statue, then unfroze him with no problems.

By the time everyone had finished, it was nearly the end of the lesson. Mr Pendred showed his students another spell: one for cleaning up mess, which they used to clear out their cauldrons so they were smudge-free and shiny again. He congratulated his students on their potion-making and spell-casting abilities. Then he told them to pack their things away and that he looked forward to seeing them next week.

'Will we be needing our broomsticks?' Leila said hopefully.

'No, I'm afraid not,' Mr Pendred said. 'The only thing you'll need is your wand.'

Leila walked away, sulking.

Alfie left his cauldron inside his desk, so he wouldn't have to lug it home and bring it back for the next lesson (it still tickled him how he could get such a big thing into what should have been a small space). He decided to take his other items home, though. He wanted to have his books to hand, just in case there was something he needed to look up. As for his wand, he just wasn't comfortable leaving that behind, despite Mr Pendred's assurances that it would be safe.

Alfie told Melissa that he wanted to talk to her in the library, then he honed in on Charles, who was packing stuff away, into a cupboard.

'Can you meet me in the library in a bit?' Alfie said. 'It's very important.'

Charles didn't need two guesses as to why. 'I'll fill you in on what happened soon enough. But not here, not at the academy. You'll have to wait.'

'I already know what happened,' Alfie said.

His father was talking to Mr Pendred, so he moved closer to hear what they were saying.

'... and I'm very proud of Alfie for figuring out the spider and potions were fakes,' Mr Trotter said. 'I remember when you pulled the same trick on me and no one in our class figured out they weren't real.'

'To be fair, those that have figured it out have been few and far between,' Mr Pendred said. 'Alfie is a clever boy and he'll make an excellent wizard, in time. I see real talent and power in him.' He noticed Alfie and beckoned him over.

Alfie stood by his father, who put an arm around him.

'When Alfie introduced himself as a Trotter,' Mr Pendred said, 'I must admit, I did wonder. And now I see you pair together, you do look alike. You have your father's eyes, Alfie. Has anyone ever told you that?'

'A few times,' Alfie said. 'It took quite a bit of persuasion to get my dad here.'

'Well all that persuasion was worth it, though, wasn't it?' he said. 'And it is good to see you back here after all this time, David. You have always been welcome and always will be.'

'Thank you,' Mr Trotter said, gushing. 'That means a lot; it really does.'

Alfie asked Mr Trotter if it was okay if he browsed the library and Mr Trotter said he could have ten minutes. So Alfie left them talking and went to find Melissa. He found her in the history section, reading a book titled *The Great Wizards & Witches of Yesteryear*.

'I think I might borrow this one,' she said, turning a page. 'Looks like an interesting read.'

'Never mind that,' Alfie said, 'I've got some important news.' He made sure no one was in earshot, then told her about Mr Langford and his conversation with the shadow person.

'Crikey,' she said, taking a few seconds to digest what she'd just heard. She put the book aside. 'The Shadow People: I've heard about them. They'd make very powerful allies, so it's no wonder Renwald wants to get them on his side.'

'The one he was talking to was called Dragan. They were communicating through some sort of holographic disk.'

'You can conjure one of those up easily enough. I can show you how; it's not a difficult spell. So what happened at the end? Was it an absolute definite no from Dragan, or do you think he might change his mind.'

'I didn't hear what was said at the end, because Mr Leech chased me away. But that shadow guy didn't want any part of any war that might be coming.'

'Have you mentioned this to Charles?'

'Mentioned what to me?' Charles said, appearing at Alfie's side.

Alfie told him what he'd said to Melissa. But Charles wasn't surprised.

'Mr Pendred was almost certain that the Shadow People would refuse to help,' he said. The question had to be asked, though. Mr Langford has always proved himself to be an excellent diplomat in such situations, but ...' Charles shrugged. 'You can't win 'em all, as they say.'

'Other than that, what is Mr P. doing about the situation?' Melissa asked him. 'Will he be getting involved in the war – heaven forbid – or is he going to keep out of it for a while and see what happens.'

Charles said, 'He's only spoken to me briefly about it and I didn't want to quiz him for any more details . As you've probably noticed, he's been a bit on edge ever since the Stormbringer was taken. Not surprising, really, given what's happened. I don't think keeping out of it is an option for him. But what he's going to do about it ...' Charles offered another shrug, his boney shoulders moving up and down. 'Your guess is as good as mine.'

'Something's got to be done!' Alfie said. 'And fast. Mr Langford was convinced that when Renwald had conquered Kordoba, he'd then try and take over our world.'

'Keep your voice down,' Charles said. 'Remember that this is a library.'

They saw Amelia coming, so they fell silent. She gave them a funny look as she went past. Then she lingered around in the Potions Section at the end of the aisle.

Keeping his voice low, Charles said, 'You've got a mischievous look in your eyes, Alfie. What are planning on doing? Please tell me it's not what I think it is.'

Also keeping his voice low, Alfie said, 'Now I know you pair are going to say no and that I must be must be mad, but I'm sure we all agree that something has to be done. So ...' He inhaled, exhaled, then managed to get the words out. 'I think we need to go to Kordoba and see what's happening there.'

Charles and Melissa exchanged a look that communicated an easy to understand message: is he *bonkers!*

And then that's exactly what Melissa said, 'I've always thought you were bonkers, but now I *know* your are.'

'What good will going to Kordoba do?' Charles asked Alfie. 'As if we could change anything that's happening there. And how would you get there, anyway? You need an Emoruld and the only one I know of is in Mr Pendred's safe.'

Alfie didn't say anything; he just looked at them with raised eyebrows and a smile playing at the corners of his mouth.

'You wouldn't get past Doris,' Melissa said. 'She'd know what you were up to. She's telepathic, *remember?*'

'Keep the volume down,' Charles said. 'Anyone could be listening to us.'

Amelia had disappeared from the end of the aisle, but the twins were now coming towards them at the opposite end, giggling to themselves about something.

Alfie led Charles and Melissa to the far aisle, which was clear of students.

'Doris didn't dob me in last time,' Alfie said, 'so maybe she won't this time.'

'Oh I think she will,' Charles said. 'And if she doesn't, I will. Forget this, Alfie; you don't know what it's like there. I do. Tell me you're not going to try and steal that Emoruld. Tell me this is a joke – and a bad one at that.'

'It's no joke,' Alfie replied. 'If Mr P. isn't going to do something about this, then maybe we should.'

'Who said anything about Mr P. not doing anything,' Charles blustered. 'What is it with you and trouble? You seem magnetized towards trouble. Last warning. One more word about this and I'm straight off to rat on you, all right.'

'No you're not,' Alfie said.

'Want to bet?' Charles said.

'You pair, really,' Melissa chirped in. 'Calm down or you'll attract an audience.'

'I'd take a bet,' Alfie said to Charles. 'Any amount you like.'

'Right,' Charles said, storming off in a huff.

'I'll tell him about your trips to Kordoba,' Alfie said.

Charles stopped so suddenly it was as if someone had hit him with a freeze spell. Then he turned to face Alfie.

'You wouldn't,' Charles said.

'Only if you dob me in,' Alfie responded.

'You've been going to Kordoba,' Melissa said to Charles. 'Wow – didn't see that one coming.'

'There's a girl there that he's got the hots for,' Alfie said. 'Her name's Hulda.'

'Enough,' Charles said, fixing him with a steely gaze. 'I mean it, Alfie – *enough*.'

Melissa put a hand on Alfie's shoulder. 'He's right. Just forget this and concentrate on your studies.'

'You always say the right thing and act the goody two-shoes,' Alfie said to her, 'but my guess is that you're just as desperate to see this place as I am. Given half the opportunity, you'd go. Don't deny it.'

'The only place I'm going is *home*,' Melissa said, walking away.

Offering nothing more than a shake of his head, Charles followed behind her.

Alfie watched them as they headed for the door. He wanted to say something to make them stay, but no words would come out of his mouth.

And then a voice spoke up behind him: 'You've well and truly annoyed them.'

With a heavy feeling in his guts, Alfie turned to face Amelia.

'How long have you been standing there?' he asked her.

'Long enough,' she said.

'How much of that did you hear?'

'Enough.'

This was the first time Alfie had seen Amelia smile. It was a wicked thing to behold.

####

'Did you enjoy your lesson?' Mr Trotter asked Alfie as they drove home.

'Yeah. Of course. Why do you ask?'

'You look a bit down, son. Lost in your thoughts. Is everything okay?'

'Yeah, everything's just ... great. Couldn't be better. Apart from the fact that I'm grounded, of course. Things would be better if I wasn't going to be a prisoner in my own home for the next two weeks.'

Dropping his Astra into second gear and rounding a corner, Mr Trotter said, 'Sulking and whinging about it won't change anything. You know what your mum says. You – '

' – do the crime, you do the time,' Alfie said, finishing the sentence for him.

'Not that any of the punishments we give you seem to do any good. I do wonder about you sometimes, Alfie Trotter; I really do.'

'I don't think you're the only one,' Alfie muttered under his breath.

'Sorry? Didn't catch that.'

'Just whinging again.' *Diversion tactic time*, Alfie thought. 'Everything was all nice and cosy between you and Mr Pendred. He seemed genuinely pleased to see you, which I thought was nice. And then there was Mrs Loveday: Amelia's mum. I saw you chatting away with her at the back. I felt sorry for you, getting lumbered with her.'

'Sorry? Why?'

'She's not exactly a bundle of laughs. Although you made her smile plenty enough. *That* can't have been easy.'

Alfie gave his father a sly sideways glance, as if to say: what was that all about, then?'

Mr Trotter gave Alfie an accommodating smile. 'Gelda and I used to sit beside each other in class. I helped her out many times when mixing potions and casting spells, so that's why she was pleased to see me. She's changed quite a bit, but I still recognised her straight away. As for Mr Pendred, it *was* good to see him. I'm glad you and your mother persuaded me to come. Just wish I'd done it sooner. Exercised some demons, that has.'

'So ... does this mean you'll be doing magic again? You could resume your studies and we could learn together.'

'I'm a little long in the tooth to be enrolling at the academy again. Let's take things one step at a time, yes? I'll help you with your studies – brewing potions and casting spells – but, for now, I'm not sure I want to do anymore than dip my toe back into that magical pond, if you get my drift.'

Alfie did. 'Not a problem, Dad. One step at a time it is.'

When they got home, Mr Trotter ordered some takeaway food to be delivered. Mrs Trotter and Eddie shared a pepperoni pizza, whilst the other two plumped for a shish kebab each. Everyone enjoyed their food. Mr Trotter loved telling his wife about his visit to the academy and how proud he was of his son. Everything was fine, until a few hours later, when Mr Trotter began complaining about stomach cramps. A short while later he dashed to the toilet with a bad case of the runs. And then Alfie, who by this time was in his Pjs and ready for bed, began feeling ill, too. He banged on the bathroom door, telling Mr Trotter to hurry up.

'Just need ... another minute,' he said, groaning in discomfort.

'I don't think I can hold it that long!' Alfie cried.

'Oh my,' Mrs Trotter said, expressing the inevitable motherly concern. 'You pair are in a bad way.'

And, inevitably, Eddie was on hand to make fun of them. 'Oh dear,' he said, giggling, 'the magical pair have got a case of the magical poops. What's up, did you swallow a duff potion?'

Still groaning in the bathroom, Mr Trotter said, 'Alfie swallowed some potion, but I didn't, so it can only be the kebabs. That's the last time I *ever* order anything from that shop! Oh God, I feel awful – just *awful*.'

Alfie banged on the door again. 'Let me in, before it's too late!'

There was no reply. But the sound of loo-roll being pulled frantically from the dispenser suggested that Mr Trotter was getting a shufty on. When he finally did emerge, walking slightly bow-legged and looking pale, Alfie pushed past him, then locked himself in the bathroom for twenty minutes. Whilst he was in there, Eddie bugged him through the door with jokes: 'Hey, why did the boy take toilet paper to the party? Because he was a party pooper ... What do you give an elephant with diarrhoea? Lots of room ... Did you hear about the giant with diarrhoea? You didn't? It's all over town.'

On and on it went, with Alfie doing his best to ignore his brother.

Above Eddie's incessant barrage of jokes, Alfie could hear his mother and father discussing the situation in the kitchen.

'Are you *absolutely* sure it isn't a potion that's causing this, or something else you've done at that academy?' Mrs Trotter said. 'Has someone put a spell on you, perhaps? One that you're not aware of?'

'I know I'm out of touch with that sort of thing,' Mr Trotter replied, 'but I'm almost one hundred percent sure that can't be the case. Why on earth would anyone want to intentionally give us the trots? No, no. It has to be the kebabs ... Oh ... *oh*, I need to go to the toilet again!'

Alfie, who was still on the toilet, thought to himself: *it's going to be a long night.*

And it was. Mr Trotter was certain there was a potion to cure food poisoning, which Alfie confirmed by referencing his academy book. The problem was that they wouldn't be able to get the ingredients until ten AM in the morning, which was what time the Enchanted Cove opened. Fortunately, Mrs Trotter had a stash of various medicines in a cupboard in the kitchen. She sorted Alfie and Mr Trotter out with something that eased their discomforts. They both still felt awful though, so there was only one place for them to wallow after that. By eight forty-five PM, Mr Trotter was tucked up in bed (still moaning and groaning) and Alfie followed suit shortly afterwards (minus the moaning and groaning).

As he lay under the covers, shivering and yet sweating, he felt more annoyed than anything else. Normally he'd have welcomed any reason not to attend school – even a bout of illness – but he was desperate to speak to Charles, *desperate* to talk him around. Sleep did not come easy for Alfie. Three or four times in the night he woke, tossing and turning.

At some point he dreamt about a castle: one with big turrets and a huge wooden gate, which had been busted in. As Alfie walked through the gate, into a cobblestoned courtyard, he was horrified by what he saw. Dead bodies everywhere. Some were dressed in armour, whilst others – peasants, Alfie assumed – were wearing raggedy clothes. A man with a metal helmet on his head was lying prone across a large wooden cask. Alfie saw a sword on the cobbles near the man and went to take a closer look. Kneeling beside it, he caught a glimpse of his reflection from the blade and noticed that he was dressed in funny clothes (raggedy old ones, like the peasants). He examined an engraving on the handle of the sword, which was embossed with a blackened wolf's head. The tunic the man had on over his armour featured the same thing, set in a gold-woven square with a red background. In the distance, Alfie heard someone calling out, so he stood up and tried to figure out where the person could be. The voice had seemed distant and yet close. Alfie moved farther into the courtyard so he could get closer to the source. He heard the voice again and realised it was ...

'*Alfie!*'

.... his father.

Alfie woke with a start. Mr Trotter was calling up the stairs to him.

'*Alfie! Your friends are here!*'

My friends are here, he thought. *Which ones? And why?*

Despite still feeling dreadful, he bounced out of bed and bounded down to the front door to see who was there ...

Charles and Melissa.

Like Alfie, Mr Trotter was still in his pyjamas. And, like Alfie, Mr Trotter still looked quite unwell.

'It's very early,' Mr Trotter was saying to the visitors. 'A bit eager, aren't we?'

'We're always eager,' Charles replied. 'It's the only way to be, if you want get on in life.'

'Wise words,' Mr Trotter said. 'Now, if only my troublesome son would subscribe to that mentality.'

'Where's mum?' Alfie asked him.

'She had some errands to run before work, so she left early. I'll ring school in a bit to let them know you're not coming in.'

'Not coming in?' Melissa said. 'Why?'

'Food poisoning,' Alfie replied, rubbing his belly. 'Me and Dad had kebabs last night and now my innards feel like a washing machine on slow spin.'

'Ditto,' Mr Trotter said, sporting a pained expression.

'There's a potion for that,' Charles said. 'You can get everything you need at The Enchanted Cove.'

'We know,' Mr Trotter said. 'I'm going there in a bit to get the ingredients. Will be nice to see Mrs Tippings after all these years. Assuming she still runs the place, that is.'

'She does,' Melissa said.

'Right,' Mr Trotter said to Alfie, 'I suppose I better get your brother out of bed. Not the easiest task, which is why I usually leave it to your mother.'

Moving slowly and awkwardly, Mr Trotter made his way up the stairs.

Alfie looked at his friends, his expression conveying the question: how come you pair are here?

'We need to talk to you,' Melissa said.

'Preferably somewhere where we won't be overheard,' Charles added.

Alfie led them to his bedroom. After making sure the door was firmly shut, he seated himself on the edge of his bed so he could rest himself.

'You really don't look well,' Charles said.

'I *really* don't feel well,' Alfie replied. 'So what's up? Please don't tell me you haven't come here to have a go at me again and try to convince me how mad I am for wanting to visit Kordoba.'

'No,' Melissa said. 'We've come to tell you that we're coming with you.'

'Eh,' Alfie mumbled, shocked. He was sure his illness had somehow caused him to mishear what she'd said.

Charles quickly dispelled that theory. 'When I got home last night, I got thinking. Nothing we say or do is going to stop you from trying to get to Kordoba. Melissa knows you better than I do and in the few weeks I've been hanging around with you, it hasn't taken me long to figure out that you're the most stubborn person I've ever met.' Melissa nodded agreement. Alfie just carried on listening, hanging on every word. Charles continued: 'Yeah ... so ... obviously I can't tell Mr Pendred about what you're planning on doing, because that'd be like shooting myself in the foot. I figured if you can't beat 'em, you may as well join 'em. Plus, I was ... I was already planning on going back this week anyway.'

'You were?' Alfie said. 'So you gave me a hard time for suggesting we go, when you were going yourself. I mean, *really!*'

From on the landing, they heard Mr Trotter still trying to get Eddie out of bed. 'Come on, get yourself moving or you can walk to football at the weekend. I'm not joking. Don't make me have to come back up here when I'm feeling ill!' He stormed down the stairs, cursing to himself.

'Me going on my own is one thing,' Charles said to Alfie. 'Taking anyone else with me is a whole different matter. The more of us that crossover, the higher the likelihood that something will go wrong. I want to check that Hulda is okay. She can tells us what's happening there. I've told Melissa everything; she knows all about my trips to Kordoba, so it'll just be the three of us. No one else should be involved.'

'Ah,' Alfie said. 'That could be a bit difficult.'

'Why?' Melissa said. 'Who else knows?' She plumped for a guess. 'Leo.'

'I was hoping he could come, too,' Alfie said. Both Charles and Melissa opened their mouths to protest, but Alfie continued talking, not giving the chance to speak.'He's not going to be the problem, though. While we were discussing things in the library, Amelia overheard us. She knows everything.'

After a short moment of shocked silence, Charles spoke up. 'Oh great, we're for it now.'

'She'll *definitely* tell Mr Pendred,' Melissa added.

'No she won't,' Alfie said. 'Not if we bring her with us.'

Charles rolled his eyes. 'Is there anyone else who'd like to come? Perhaps we should put an advert in the local rag or something. Hey-ho, the more the merrier.'

Something occurred to Alfie. 'Didn't Hulda's father say that if he saw you again, you'd regret it.'

'He did,' Charles confirmed. 'But he's not going to see me, because I'm staying well clear. One of you will have to speak to Hulda. We need to set ourselves a time limit of thirty minutes in Kordoba, no more. Just to see what's going on.'

They heard movement, the sound of floorboards creaking.

'That's Eddie crawling out of his pit,' Alfie said. 'Keep your voices down.'

'We could invite him, too,' Charles suggested jokingly. 'He is your brother, after all.'

'Please,' Melissa said, appealing for him to calm down, 'this isn't helping.'

'She's right,' Alfie agreed. 'The sooner we accept that it's going to be five of us ...'

'*Five?*' Charles said, interrupting. 'Don't you mean four?'

'I really want Leo to come as well,' Alfie said. He was beginning to get used to Charles looking at him as though he'd lost his mind. 'He knows what we are and what we can do. He knows about the school. And he knows about Kordoba.'

'All thanks to you,' Charles said.

'Only because he's my best friend,' Alfie said. 'I haven't told anyone else – and I won't.'

'One more along for the ride won't make much difference,' Melissa said. 'We won't need to worry about Leo; it's Amelia that'll be the problem. The words spoilt brat don't even begin to cover it.'

'Fine,' Charles said, still not looking happy about the situation. 'Five it is then.'

'Great,' Alfie said, mustering the strength to stand up. 'So when are we doing this and how are we going to get past Doris. Charles, you've got permission to go into the safe and she's let you borrow the Emoruld quite a few times, so it shouldn't be a problem if you try and borrow it again.'

'Forget about Doris,' Charles said, reaching into his trouser pocket and producing an ... Emoruld. 'All that palaver won't be necessary.'

'You've already been into the safe,' Melissa said.

'No, I haven't,' Charles confessed. 'This little beauty is my father's.'

Alfie said, 'So you lied about the typewriter letting you pass?'

'Yep,' Charles said with a tinge of smugness. He held the Emoruld up, admiring it. 'This has been in my family for years. It was my great, great grandfather's, apparently. I'm not sure how he came by it, because every time I've asked my dad about it, he gets cagey.' He shrugged. 'Anyway, I don't suppose it matters much. The main thing is that we have it and we're going to use it to get through the trees. I've always gone on a Wednesday or Thursday, because I can get access to the grounds during lesson times. Mr P is busy teaching class, so he's too distracted to notice.'

'I take it your dad doesn't know that you keep borrowing your family heirloom,' Melissa said.

'No,' Charles said. 'He'd go nuts if he checked under the floorboards beneath his bed and noticed it wasn't there.'

'How did you know it was there?' Alfie asked.

'I found it about four years ago, when I was searching in my parents' bedroom. They'd sent me to my room, because I'd been naughty. I can't even remember what I'd done, but I do remember what they'd confiscated from me as part of my punishment. Pikachu: my favourite Pokemon teddy. Well, I wasn't having any of that. So while they were downstairs, I snuck into their bedroom to look for it, because that's where they always hide stuff they've taken from me. The first place I checked was under their bed. I moved some empty suitcases aside, a pile of old clothes, and that's when I noticed one of the floorboards was slightly raised. Intrigued, I lifted it up. And that's when I found the Emoruld. I didn't know what it was at first. Obviously I knew it was a jewel and most likely worth a few bob, judging by the look and size of it. But even though I was intrigued, I put it back. I wasn't too interested in finding a jewel – even one that'd been mysteriously hidden away – I wanted my Pikachu. It wasn't until I was enrolled at Pendred's a year later that I found out what it was. It took me a long time to pluck up the courage to use it (about five weeks ago, this was). And look at the trouble it has caused. The only positive thing that's come out of this is meeting Hulda.'

'You're even sneakier than I am,' Alfie said. 'But what about your Pikachu teddy? Did you get it back?'

'Never mind that,' Melissa said. 'All I want to know is when we're going? This evening or tomorrow?'

'I'm good for this evening,' Charles said, 'if everyone else is?'

Melissa nodded

Alfie went to nod too, but any excitement he was feeling soon drained away when he realized something. 'I'm grounded for the next two weeks, so this could be difficult for me.'

'I don't think we can wait that long,' Charles said. 'A lot can happen in two weeks and it could be too dangerous to go by then.'

'I'll get around this,' Alfie said. 'I'll find a way – some way – to be there tonight.'

'And what if you can't?' Melissa said.

'I *will*,' Alfie responded. 'I'm the most pigheaded person you've ever met, remember? Do you think I'll let a grounding stop me from coming with you lot? *Nothing* is going to stop me. No way.' He could feel his bowels moving again. Another trip to the toilet was going to be needed sooner rather than later. Feeling not much better than he did the night before, he sat back down heavily on his bed.

'Okay,' Charles said. 'I'll let Leo and Amelia know what's happening. If we all meet up on Rush Street Park, on the playground, then we can go from there.'

'What time?' Melissa asked.

Charles thought about this, then said, 'Quarter past six. The lesson will be underway by the time we reach the academy. We can just stroll through the gate and into the backyard. Easy as pie.'

'Have you found out what happened to Ullin and the others who were helping him transport the Stormbringer?' Alfie asked him. 'I'm guessing it's not good news, seeing as Renwald now has the wand.'

'Mr P filled me in after class yesterday,' Charles said solemnly. 'Ullin and two others were flying it back to Kordoba on their broomsticks when they were ambushed. Just after they'd passed through to the other side, this was. None of them survived, as far as we know.' He turned away from the others, unable to meet their gaze, his eyes glazing over with wetness as he fought back tears.

Putting an arm around him, Melissa said, 'It's not your fault. Nobody will ever blame you and you shouldn't blame yourself. You were put in an impossible position. I would have done the same and so would Alfie. Wouldn't you Alfie?'

'I would,' Alfie confirmed. 'Absolutely definitely. Family first – always.

'Still doesn't stop me from feeling guilty,' Charles said, shaking his head. 'If I hadn't gone to Kordoba, none of this would have happened. Renwald would be none the wiser as to where the Stormbringer was and three people wouldn't have lost their lives.'

'You said none of them survived, as far as you know,' Melissa said. 'You didn't say that they're definitely dead.'

Alfie stood up so abruptly that his friends stepped back, no doubt wondering what was wrong with him.

'Oh no,' Alfie said. 'I need the toilet again – I'll be back in a minute.'

Charles moved out of the way as Alfie swept past him and opened the door.

Then Alfie stopped dead in his tracks – because someone was blocking his way.

'Well, well, well,' Eddie said, leaning against the jamb. 'Planning a little adventure, are we?'

CHAPTER 11
(Into Kordoba ...)

After Charles and Melissa had gone to school, followed by Eddie about twenty minutes later, Mr Trotter was the next to leave the house.

'Okay,' he said, checking the time on his mobile phone, 'the shop should be open by the time I get there. Hopefully I'll make it there without pooping myself and hopefully Mrs Tippings won't keep me talking too long. From what I can remember, she's one for chopsing. Bit like your mother, really. I'd suggest you rest while I'm gone. Don't do anything strenuous. Not that that's likely, if you feel anywhere near as bad as I do. Right-e-o, see you in a bit.'

While Mr Trotter was gone, Alfie stretched out on the settee and watched TV. An episode of the Avengers cartoon was on BBC1. Normally this was the sort of program that would have had Alfie's eyes glued to the screen. Not today, not at this moment. Whilst half of his interest was directed towards the TV, the other half was trying to figure out how he could persuade his parents to let him out of the house this afternoon. The only thing he could think of was to tell them that he wanted to go to the academy library to exchange his books. And that's exactly what he said to his father, upon his return, forty minutes later.

'Do you know what,' Mr Trotter said, taking off his jacket and throwing it over the armchair, 'that shop has hardly changed since I was last there. And Mrs Tippings was every bit as helpful as I remembered. She gave me a couple of pre-made potions so we wouldn't have to faff about brewing some. How nice is that? I've swallowed mine and I'm already feeling better.'

'Did she remember you? From when you went in as a boy?'

'She told me I looked familiar, but she didn't recognise me as such. Not until I told her who I was.'

Mr Trotter handed Alfie his vial of potion. With some effort, Alfie pulled himself up to a sitting position, then downed the contents in one bitter go. '*Ooh,*' he said, 'that was disgusting.' Then, while Mr Trotter was kicking off his shoes, Alfie blurted the question out: 'Do you think I might be able to, erm ... go to the academy library tonight to ... exchange some books?'

Looking at Alfie, Mr Trotter took a few seconds to process this request. Then he said, 'To go to the academy and that's all, yes? To exchange your books and nothing else?'

Alfie didn't like lying to his father and there was at least a half-truth in this request. He *was* going to the academy, after all. Just not to exchange books.

'I'll be an hour and a half at the most,' Alfie said. 'And I won't go anywhere else before or after. I promise.' This was a promise he was sure he could keep.

'If it was to go out and play, the answer would be no. But I can't see any harm in you going to the academy to further your studies. Preventing you from doing that wouldn't solve anything.' Alfie could sense another "but" coming and then it did. 'But ... if I get even a whiff that you've betrayed our trust and you're out gallivanting ...'

'I'm not going to be galli ... whatever it was you just said. I'm swapping my books and coming home. And that's it.'

'Okay,' Mr Trotter responded, looking semi-satisfied. 'I can't see your mother having a problem with this, but I'll have to run it by her, just to be on the safe side.'

When Mr Trotter left the room, a big smile spread across Alfie's face.

Game on.

Ten minutes later, Alfie was well enough to have some breakfast (baked beans on toast) and thirty minutes later he was sprightly enough for adventure. Satisfied his son was back to his normal self, Mr Trotter disappeared off out to deal with a work-related matter. This left Alfie alone in the house. He felt too excited to watch TV any more, so he switched it off. He began pacing back and forth in the living room. And he was still restless when Mr Trotter returned home.

'Got ants in your pants?' Mr Trotter asked Alfie. 'If you're stuck for something to do, get your homework out and work on that.'

'I'm up to date with my homework.'

'Read a book, then: one of your academy ones. You may as well get the most out of them before you take them back.'

'I'm not in the mood for reading books, Dad.'

'Well you need to do something, because I'm not having you buzzing around this house all day. It's only eleven o'clock, so it's not too late for you to go to school, I suppose.'

Alfie didn't like the direction this conversation was taking, so he went to his bedroom and closed the door. Spotting his box of Lego in the corner, he dragged it to the centre of the room and sat, crossed-legged, next to it. *What can I build?* he thought, looking to while away some time. He remembered back to the strange dream he'd had – a dream that'd seemed so *real* – and he shuddered.

He knew what he should construct, so he set to work, feverishly clipping bricks together and putting them in place. An hour later, Mr Trotter came to check on Alfie and was eager to know what he was building.

'You'll have to wait and see.'

'Oh, okey-dokey, my cagey little friend,' Mr Trotter replied, leaving him to it.

By the time Eddie returned, at quarter to four, Alfie was doing the finishing touches.

'Weh-hey,' Eddie said, taking a gander. 'You must have been at that all day?'

'Not quite, but it has taken me a while.'

Alfie's knees popped as he stood up and admired the castle he'd built.

'Awesome,' Eddie said, admiring it as well. 'How did you get on with Dad? Did he give you permission to go out this evening?'

'Yep. Told him I wanted to go to the library to exchange my books and he was okay with that.'

'Good. I knew you'd come up with something.'

'Subject to Mum's approval.'

'It's in the bag,' Eddie said. 'She won't say no 'cause she'll know you've got your hopes up. Charles told me to tell you that Leo and Amelia are good for this evening. So how many are going, exactly?'

'Six, including you. I don't suppose there's any point in asking you not to come, is there?' Alfie felt compelled to ask this question, even though he knew what the answer would be.

'No way am I missing out on this,' Eddie said, 'so don't even think of trying to go without me. Mum and Dad will know about it before you've reached the end of the road, bro.'

'That's mean.'

Eddie shrugged. 'What can be bad about having your older brother along for the ride to watch your back?'

Good point. Alfie had to admit to himself – in part, at least - that he would feel safer with Eddie around.

'This is gonna be flippin' awesome!' Eddie said, ruffling Alfie's hair. 'I can't wait!'

'Me neither.'

Alfie could not, in his life, ever remember feeling so excited.

When Mrs Trotter returned from work, she okayed Alfie's trip to the academy. She gave him the same warning as Mr Trotter, wording it in a slightly different way and waving a cautionary finger in Alfie's face. 'If I have even the smallest suspicion that you've been out mucking around with your friends instead of going to that library, your feet won't touch the ground. Are you hearing me, mister?'

He was. Loud and clear.

And one more time: game *on*.

Eddie left the house at five past six, telling his parents he was nipping to a friend's house for a few hours. Shortly after that, Alfie put his books in his rucksack, strapped it to his back and went to leave.

'Oh,' Mr Trotter said, appearing in the hallway, 'are you leaving already? I was going to give you a lift.'

'It's okay, I'm going to walk. The fresh air will do me good after that bout of illness. Thanks for the offer, though.'

Alfie left before Mr Trotter could say anything else.

When Alfie got to the end of the street, Eddie was waiting for him on his BMX.

'So come on then, magic boy,' he said, brimming with eagerness. Hop on the back and I'll show just exactly how fast you can go down this hill.'

And he did. Seating himself behind his brother, Alfie held him tightly around the waist as they set off. Down the hill they went, with the air rushing past their faces.

'Woo-*hoooooo!*' Eddie yelled, getting up more and more speed. 'Is this fast enough for you?'

More than fast enough, Alfie thought. But he didn't want Eddie to know he was scared, so he said, 'Mum could cycle faster than this.'

Big mistake. Eddie went even faster, making Alfie's stomach lurch.

Alfie felt relieved when they reached the bottom and continued on their journey.

Arriving at the park, they sped across to the swings, where the others were waiting. Charles and Melissa were sitting next to each other, pushing themselves back and forth as they discussed something or other. Amelia was standing nearby with her arms

246

folded, looking impatient. Alfie noted she was wearing a small backpack and wondered what could be in it. He also wondered something else, as well ...

'Where's Leo?' he said, as Eddie stopped in front of Charles.

Charles nodded towards the field beyond and Alfie swivelled to see Leo ducking in and out of view as he cycled across the slopey terrain.

'There was no way he was ever going to miss out on this,' Melissa said.

'Me, *neither*,' Eddie said, grinning.

'And ... who are you, exactly?' Amelia said. 'I thought there was only supposed to be five of us.'

'There *was* supposed to be five,' Charles said. 'Now there's six. This is Alfie's big brother, Eddie.'

'I don't recognise you from school,' Eddie said to Amelia. 'You're not from Eldon Road, are you?'

'*No*,' Amelia said, as if perishing the thought. 'I go to Greystoke High.'

'Ah, a private school,' Eddie said. 'A posho, eh?'

Amelia looked ready to unload a verbal assault on Eddie, but Leo timed his arrival well, distracting everyone. He stopped next to Alfie and Charles, then gave everyone a nod of acknowledgement.

'How did you get out of your grounding?' Leo asked Alfie. 'You did get out of it, didn't you? Do your mum and dad know you're out of the house?'

Eddie explained how his brother had got around this problem. 'Hence the bag of books on his back.'

'Cool,' Leo said. 'I knew you'd find a way.'

Charles and Melissa had left their bikes leaning against a wooden bench.

'Okay,' Charles said, kicking off from his swing, strolling towards the bench and mounting his bike, 'if we leave now, we should arrive at the right time.'

He reached inside his jacket, pulled out his wand, then stowed it away again. 'Any of you bring yours?'

'Of course,' Amelia said, hooking a thumb over her shoulder to indicate hers was in her bag.

'I couldn't risk trying to get mine, with it being confiscated,' Alfie said. 'I'd get in too much trouble if one of my parents noticed it was gone.'

'I've got mine,' Melissa said.

'Don't look so down,' Eddie said to Alfie. 'You're not the only one without a wand.'

The only magical one, Alfie thought glumly.

'Wish I had a wand,' Leo said dreamily.

Melissa mounted her bike , leaving only Amelia without a ride.

'I can give you a croggy,' Eddie said, tapping his handlebars. 'My brother can ride with Leo.'

'I think I'd rather crawl,' she replied, giving him a contemptuous glare.

'*Woooo!*' Eddie said, feigning insult, then repeating what she'd said, parrot fashion: 'I think I'd rather *crawwwl!*'

'Use my bike,' Melissa said, cycling up to her. 'I'll croggy with Leo.'

Amelia seemed happy with this arrangement.

Once they were all underway, Leo spoke over his shoulder to Melissa, who was holding him tightly around the waist. 'So what lie did you tell your parents about where you'll be this afternoon?'

'The same one as your brother. Told them I was going to the academy library to browse.'

'Told my mum and dad I was hanging out at Alfie's for a bit,' Leo said.

Eddie called ahead to Amelia: 'And what about you, little miss sweetness and light?' he asked her. 'I can't imagine you'd have been comfortable lying to your parents.'

'You're right,' she replied, putting her nose in the air and cycling ahead. 'I wasn't comfortable with it.'

'Leave her alone,' Melissa said to Eddie. 'I know she's a snob, but she's really not that bad, once you get talking to her.'

'We'll see,' Eddie said, smiling.

A short while later, when they were a few streets away from the academy, Charles mounted the pavement and stopped next to a substation. The others pulled up around him, forming a circle.

'We'll leave our bikes behind here,' he said.

'They could get nicked,' Leo said.

'That's unlikely,' Charles replied, producing a long chain lock from his jacket pocket. 'If we secure them all together, they'll be fine. It's either that or we leave them at the academy. If we do that, we'll be advertising we're on the grounds; it's just safer all around if we leave them here.'

Leo couldn't argue with this logic, so he just went along with what Charles was suggesting.

Once all the bikes were secured together, everyone began walking.

Amelia forged ahead, stomping purposefully. Her bag was still strapped to her back.

Following behind her, Eddie said, 'So what's in that rucksack? We're not going for a picnic, you know.' When she didn't reply, just kept stomping, he directed the question towards Alfie: 'What do you think's in that bag?'

Alfie shrugged. 'I have no idea ... Books, maybe. She might have used the same excuse as me and told her parents that she's going to the library.'

They rounded the corner onto Mysterium Road and Leo burst into a sudden spring of excitement.

'I can't believe we're going to another world!' he said, shaking Alfie's arm. 'I still can't believe it!'

'Let's try not to advertise it, shall we,' Charles said. 'Keep your voice down.'

'There's some creepy houses on this street,' Eddie remarked.

'You wait 'till you clap eyes on the academy,' Melissa said. 'It's quite something.'

Outside the gate, Charles brought everyone to a halt. 'Okay, we need to make sure everyone can see the entrance and get inside.'

'What entrance?' Leo said, looking around.

'Yeah, what entrance?' Eddie said.

'Remember what I told you about the place being hidden,' Alfie said to Leo. 'Only magical people can see the academy, or ...'

'Ordinary people who've been touched by someone magical,' Amelia said, finishing his sentence.

Eddie held his hand out to her. 'I'm game if you are.'

'No thank you,' she said, disgusted at the prospect.

Melissa took Eddie's hand and he gave her a wink. Then she took Leo's.

Five seconds later, Leo said, 'I'm not seeing this entrance.'

'Me, neither,' Eddie said. 'There's a hedge on the left, at the front of number thirty-two and some bushes on the right, outside thirty-four, which look like they're in need of a good trim. Perhaps this magical touch thing isn't working ... ah, whoa ... hey, that's weird.' He took a half-step backwards, his eyes widening. 'Okay, okay, I think I'm starting to see it!'

Alfie felt Leo's grip begin to tighten.

'I'm seeing it too!' Leo exclaimed.

Alfie counted to ten, then said, 'Are we good to go now? Are you pair ... fully adjusted yet?'

'Yeah,' Eddie replied, not taking his eyes off the gate, which he was clearly now seeing. 'I'm ... adjusted. Fully a-djusted.'

'What about you?' Charles asked Leo. 'Are you ready?'

He nodded. 'Ready,' he said, awestruck. 'Yes, I'm ready.'

They let go of each other's hands and walked through the entrance, up the driveway.

'That's the *weirdest* experience I've ever had,' Eddie said. 'One second there was nothing there, then – bam – it just popped out of thin air and expanded into my view.'

'Same here,' Leo said. 'Weird but cool experience.'

'We should keep the noise to a minimum from here,' Charles said. 'They should all be in class now, but let's not take any unnecessary risks.'

When the academy came into view, however, looming large and impressive, its towers silhouetted against the darkening skyline, Eddie couldn't resist opening his mouth again. 'Oh, man, I would *love* to look around that place.'

'There are ghosts,' Melissa pointed out.

Eddie gave her a questioning sideways glance: yeah, right.

'No,' Alfie said, 'she's not lying; there really *are* ghosts. I haven't seen one yet, but I've had a few eerie moments when I've been sure someone was watching me.'

'Someone probably was watching you,' Leo put in, 'but I'll bet it wasn't a spook.'

'There *are* ghosts!' Amelia blurted. 'My mum told me that when she was studying here, one stuck its tongue out at her while she was on the back lawn. A bald man dressed in long black robes with a big scar down the side of his face.'

'That was Eldiris Laybould,' Charles said. 'He used to tend the grounds here. No more talking now. Not another word until we're clear of the academy on the other side. 'All it takes is for Mr P to look out of that classroom window at this moment and we'll all be for it. He'll recognise someone who's not supposed be here in a heartbeat. Okay, fast as you can, you lot.' He broke into a jog.

Everyone followed him and they disappeared around the side of the building. They moved across the courtyard, then through the arches, into the lawn area.

'Come on, slowpokes,' Charles said, surging ahead. 'Keep up.'

Alfie's backpack full of books bobbed up and down behind him as he trailed at the rear of the group. Leo looked over his shoulder and smiled at Alfie, which encouraged Alfie into a burst of acceleration. Coming alongside him, Alfie retuned the smile, then showed him his heels. Across the grass they all went, grinning at each other and taking turns to overtake one another. Even Amelia managed a smile as she scurried along in her pink plimsolls. They passed beyond the lawn, which gave way to the scrubland area full of low-lying knotted bushes and tangles of weeds. Eddie attempted to jump over one of the bushes and clipped the top with his foot. He fell forwards and looked like he was about to go down, but he managed to right himself and kept moving. As they neared the woods, Charles raised a hand, bringing everyone to a halt.

He reached into his pocket and produced the Emoruld. 'Okay, we'll all need to hold hands so we can all pass through.'

Eddie held his hand out to Amelia and received the same cold, hard stare as before.

And, as before, Melissa stepped in and did the honours. She offered her hand to Eddie, who gave her a smile this time instead of a wink. From there, Eddie then linked with Alfie, who linked with Leo, who then linked with Charles. Spreading out, they faced the woods and began walking.

Passing through the trees, they were forced to move in single file, with Charles taking the lead. Twigs and fallen leaves scrunched underfoot as Alfie followed on behind Leo. It was darker here under the canopy of branches overhead, which rustled lazily in the breeze. Alfie realized it would be full dark by the time he and his friends passed back through the woods on their return journey. He didn't like the idea of that. It was creepy enough as it was, with the long shadows cast down by the branches in the fading light. An owl hooted and Eddie hooted a reply.

'Do we have to walk far?' Leo said.

'Not too far,' Charles responded.

'How long will it take?' Amelia asked.

'Not long,' Charles responded. 'Five minutes and we'll pass through to the other side. We're staying for no more than half an hour, remember. I'll set the alarm on my watch when we've crossed over.'

'Do you know what, I can't recall ever feeling so scared and excited at the same time like this,' Melissa said. 'My heart's pounding.'

'Your heart's pounding because you're holding hands with me,' Eddie said with a sly grin. 'I have that effect on girls.'

'Not me,' Melissa said.

'Or me,' Amelia put in.

Alfie noted how slick Leo's palm felt with sweat.

'Nervous?' Alfie said. 'It's not too late to turn back. You can guard the bikes until we get back, if you want?'

'No chance,' Leo said, shaking his head at Alfie as he glanced back at him. 'This is one adventure I'm not missing out on.'

On and on they pressed, further into the trees, still holding hands.

On and on towards adventure ...

Author note:

Dear Reader, I hope you had as much fun reading this book as I did writing it. For updates on further books in this series, please check out my Facebook page (just search for my name). I was originally going to include some illustrations in this book, but the story ended up being too long. I will post them up on Facebook, though, so you check them out. I will probably do the same with book 2, which I envisage being even longer than this one. If you enjoyed reading this story, please let me know, because I'd love to hear from you.

Warm regards,

Paul Johnson-Jovanovic